CARLA—

THANKS 4
MAKING ME
IS NOTAB PUB...
THIS BOOK. IF
ANY COMPLAINTS YOUR
TELL THEM IT'S DICK

WINK

The Confession of a Serial

Monogamist

Rusty Lane

Copyright © 2012 Rusty Lane

All rights reserved.

ISBN-13: 978-1481071574
ISBN-10: 1481071572

For A. R., who taught me more than I will ever know

Acknowledgements

Many thanks to my critique partners Cindy, Juanita, Teresa, Glenn, Elea and Daniel for their support and gentle advice. And to my advance-copy reader, Carla, who loves a good beach book.

Special thanks to my partner, Sarah, for understanding why I wanted to tell this story.

Copyediting and cover design by Audrey Mackaman.

Table of Contents

Prelude to a Dance	11
Two Stooges and a Dwarf	17
Artemisia	33
Deception	49
Desolation	65
Turning the Table	79
Teddies	93
Love Hurts	113
Continental Divide	129
Breast Reduction	145
Falling	163
Smile, and I'll Send You a Wink	177
Rebekah	195
Mount Beth	213
Girl on a Swing	227
Lacrosse, Anyone?	239
Intermezzo	255
Closure	271
Contrition	285
Confession	301

10 ~ Rusty Lane

Prelude to a Dance

What do you expect, I wonder? Will this be a love story, full of endings and beginnings? Or will it be a tale of loss with little redemption? Or maybe it will be more contemporary than that, more here and now, in your face, unguarded.

Whatever it will become was as unclear to me in the beginning as it is to you now. All you have at this point is a title, albeit a long one, a title that promises more than I may want to deliver. But deliver I shall, if for no other reason than I need to get it off my chest. That's the nature of confessions, isn't it? They offer a way out, or at least a way to tell your side of the story.

I worry what you will think of me after you hear what I have to say. Perhaps you will judge harshly, perhaps you will simply find me pathetic. I'll have to live with that, I suppose, but regardless of what you may decide, I have come to know myself, and I have come to like myself, as well. I have loved and been loved. I am satisfied.

Our story begins a few months ago, we two, Andrew and me. You will quickly learn he has a nickname, Deke, though I seldom call him that. It will take longer to realize that I will not be seen for a while, except I just told you, and at this point you are inclined to believe what I say. You may change your mind, though, and if you do, I will not fault you.

I'll give fair warning that I plan to tell the story the way I want to, or, perhaps, need to. I will play my part, and you will play yours, and at some point I hope you will see things from my point of view. Until then, you will undoubtedly see them from Andrew's, and I'll admit he's a much more sympathetic character than I am. But, who knows, maybe I'll grow on you.

~ ~ ~

Right now, a short time after his wife left him, Andrew is looking through the window of his upscale condominium at boats out for an evening sail on Lake Union, a small body of water within Seattle city limits. According to Andrew, it acts as a go-between connecting freshwater Lake Washington to saltwater Puget Sound. Lake Union is slightly brackish, he says.

"What are you looking at?" I call out from the adjoining bathroom.

He turns, staring across the room through the open door. "You," he says, and walks toward me.

It is the fall of 2007, September 30th to be exact. The war in Iraq and the upcoming presidential campaign dominate the news, but Andrew and I hardly notice. It might be fair to say we are self-absorbed. The reasons for this are not entirely clear. I think I understand what has happened to Andrew, and if so, I know why he finds himself in this unusual relationship with me. I amuse him and perplex him, and he seems prepared to ride it out to see what happens. I worry, though, that I may end up hurting him.

C'est la vie, I suppose, or maybe, caveat emptor. He's a big boy; he can decide for himself.

But what possible reason is there for me to be here

at all? Fun and games? Yes, but not only those. Love or money? Hmmm. I suppose you may say it's money, always a motivating factor. And it's true Andrew has enough to attract a bevy of young women. But I haven't decided yet whether I'm actually all that into him.

But maybe I am. And I'm not that much younger than Andrew anyway, thirteen years, more or less. And really, does age matter in a contemporary love story? Hollywood doesn't think so, that's for certain. They delight in placing nubile actresses in the arms of powerful-but-shopworn actors.

But that's enough about age for now. Let's talk looks and character. You might envision Andrew as an amalgam. He has the boyish-but-mature charm of Tom Hanks in Sleepless in Seattle, but he's blond and blue-eyed, though just as clueless as the character Tom played, Sam Baldwin. Nor does he have a son, but having one someday may fill a need he isn't even aware of yet.

Then there's the sexual side of Andrew. That calls for a bit of the rogue, but playful: Don Juan meets the boy next door. Not the sort you parade around to impress your friends, but the sort who spends the night getting down with you. That's the way I see Andrew. I think Andrew is a thoughtful-if-unsophisticated lover. But he happily follows directions, if you get my drift.

What about me? Well, I'm a bit like Natalie Portman. She played Alice, the stripper in Closer. Like Natalie, I have dark brown hair and full lips. I'm a few inches shorter, though. If I'm not careful with what I wear, I end up looking stumpy. Or so my sister tells me. But I've turned quite a few heads in my time, and my face is every bit as sweet as Natalie's, just more cute than it is beautiful. I have a crooked smile. But I will claim the same aggressive sexiness and deep-brown bedroom eyes.

It's my eyes that Andrew is now looking into as they glance back at him from the bathroom mirror. I'm in the midst of preparing for my Saturday night assignation. I have so far put on nothing but a strapless Victoria's Secret push-up bra and a rather plain-looking pair of bikini panties. They don't match, so you can assume I have no intention of bedding my date.

My face is another matter. The dusky eye shadow edged in black eyeliner and rouged cheeks suggest a dark venue, perhaps a romantic restaurant with candles to accent my fine features, or a dimly lit blues club. You haven't seen my dress yet so you can't tell. But maybe I'm not as sophisticated as I'm pretending to be; maybe I've just put on too much makeup. But, no, I understand exactly what I'm doing, shooting for that slightly slutty look young guys like.

In any event, Andrew is watching. I smile mischievously at him and my eyes glow. Is it anticipation of my date, or is the look just for Andrew? He doesn't know. He smiles back then makes a face. I giggle, and the eyebrow pencil I've been manipulating takes off on its own, turning my makeup artistry clownish.

"Out! Out!" I yell at him and slam the bathroom door in his face, but relent and reopen it. "I'm almost done. You can give me your opinion then."

Andrew leaves me be and goes to the kitchen to grab a beer. In a few minutes, I come out of the bedroom wearing a skin-tight, carmine tube dress so short my ass is barely covered. That draws a whistle from Andrew. The cut of the dress, I know, in combination with my narrow hips, makes my legs look longer than they really are. The overall effect would rate a nine on his oft-quoted peter meter. I'm quite confident of Andrew's reaction and turn slowly to tease and allow a close inspection.

"Soooo, how do I look?"

"Edible. Absolutely edible."

I reward him with another mischievous smile then pick my coat off the chair where I've left it and walk through the front door and across the hallway to press the down button. Andrew leans against the doorjamb watching me. As the elevator door glides open and I enter, I turn to say, part question, part statement, "You'll wait up?"

"You know I will."

Our eyes lock for a moment. The door glides shut and I am gone.

16 ~ Rusty Lane

Two Stooges and a Dwarf

As I sit relaxing on deck, I hear a commotion up at the gate. It's locked as always to keep out the riffraff like my three buddies clamoring for entry. My neighbor, Chuck something-or-other, onboard his sloop in the finger opposite, looks up from polishing his stainless steel brightwork to see what the hubbub is all about then glances over at me.

"They yours?" he asks in a tone halfway between annoyance and amusement.

"Afraid so," I say. "Think I should let them in?"

He hesitates, unsure if I'm serious or joking, then, having decided I'm using him as my foil, he shoots back, "Suit yourself." Again, he can't quite keep the annoyance out of his voice.

He knows perfectly well, of course, that these are my friends. He's met them before. They call him Captain Crunch behind his back but Commodore to his face, and even though they always greet him with jovial, hail-fellow-well-met fervor, he correctly senses that they think he's affected and somewhat ridiculous. This is how I see him too, but in my many years of sailing—Chuck calls it yachting—I have run across a substantial number of boat owners who take their leisure sport far too seriously. But then they probably think I don't take it seriously enough. I've often been treated as the poor rich kid with the boat he never earned. In fact, I bought my sloop with my own hard-earned money and, face it, at forty-five I'm long past the kid stage. I can hear Doc laughing his ass off at my claim to ownership. He'd say, "You mean you bought it with Carole's money." While this is not strictly true, it's true enough; throughout our long marriage, Carole has been the moving force behind our financial success. I smile to myself wryly as this thought flits across my consciousness. Then I sigh, give Commodore Chuck a flip salute, and head up the dock toward my noisy, wayward chums.

I suppose I should call them my mates. That's what Carole calls them, her Aussie slang bleeding through. She has spent the better part of twenty-five years here on American soil and has become adept at turning on and off the down-under accent to suit her purpose. I have to admit it worked on me. She had me at G'day. Well, that and her string-bikinied golden tan. The money came later.

While sauntering up the dock I realize money was the problem. Not too little, too much. It became Carole's *raison d'etre*. And it gave her the freedom to "move on" as the contemporary parlance has it. Having come to this realization right now, I say to myself, "No shit, Sherlock. Took you long enough." Then my mind wanders off into what I have come to think of as the danger zone. But I'm quickly brought out of my reverie by supplicating calls from the head of the dock. "Deke, oh Deke, please let us in."

As I approach the gate, I wonder when it will be replaced with the high-tech glass and keycard setup already installed on most of the others. Good luck being heard through one of those, I think. They can holler until the gulls come home.

The antiquated construction of the old gate, a cyclone fence topped with barbed wire, allows Larry and Curly to kick off their flip-flops and monkey-climb halfway up the gate with their fingers and toes pushed through the wire. Then they hoot like howlers. My guess is they've begun the traditional Saturday late-afternoon beer drinking a bit early. Climbing the chain link has to hurt, but maybe they've had enough anesthetic not to notice. Meanwhile, Doc goes down on both knees, and in mendicant subservience begs, "Will the kind Master allow entrance to these poor, lowly petitioners?"

They are here to cheer me up, I know, so I have to play along. I swing the gate open wide, bow slightly from the waist, and intone condescendingly, "You may pass." Larry and Curly provide another crescendo of hoots then scramble down off the wire and into their discarded flip flops again, both of them taking one of his own and one of the others. They hold up the mismatched sets for me to notice. Doc waits his turn then rises slowly off his arthritic knees. He feigns more pain than I know he feels, so I add, "Step quickly now."

"But, Master, I am old and crippled."

"In a pig's eye, you are." I know he has just come from a late morning tennis match.

Doc does suffer from early-onset arthritis, but he pops Advil by the handful so he can continue his passion for whacking a yellow sphere back and forth across a low net. He belongs to a pricey Seattle tennis club, I forget which one, and is fairly high up in the rankings for an old fart. Actually, he's only forty-two, but since the club's top players are ten to fifteen years younger, old fart he is. His day job matches his moniker. Doc is a doctor of some repute, a cosmetic surgeon whose oft-repeated claim to fame, "I've lifted both the breasts and spirits of a multitude of Seattle matrons," says as much about his character as it does about his skill. Doc calls them his girls. "They come to me as women, and I send them away as teenagers," he brags. Doc quotes Bob Seeger's *Night Moves* lyrical description of a teenage girl's breasts when referring to the magical aftermath of his clients' procedures. He's got the photos to prove it, too, and since we've all seen them, I have to allow that while Doc is short on ethics, he's top notch in skill.

Doc is single right now. Larry and Curly—Carole's dismissive names for them that Doc and I have adopted as endearments of a sort—are single as well, Curly because he calls himself "Bachelor-for-life, heavy on the living part," and Larry because he and his wife, Gretchen, or Gretch as he calls her, have an open marriage, which seems to mean they don't ever wear wedding bands and they sleep with whomever they want. Doc has been married, then subsequently and inevitably divorced four times, and he's working on number five right now. Or she's working on him. He seems to be taking this relationship more slowly and less seriously and is still dating other women, so perhaps he's not ready to commit right now, even as temporary as such commitment will become. As for his collection of exes, The Former Wives Club, Doc seems not to care at all about providing their support. He insists it's the cost of quality in his choices, and I have to agree his choices are always gorgeous. Having met each and spent time getting to know her, I can also say every one has been charming and intelligent. When I ask, "Why?" after each departs, Doc just shrugs it off with a smile and a quip, "I'll find another. Variety is the spice of life."

There is a term for what Doc is. Carole uses it disparagingly to describe his inability to stick to one woman, each separation followed quickly by the next entanglement. Doc is a serial monogamist. And while I have never liked the tone she uses, I can't deny the accuracy of Carole's summary judgment.

That's Doc in a nutshell. He meets a woman. She falls in love with him and he falls in love with her. I can see that the emotions on both sides are real. Doc can be very charming. He is also a bundle of energy, self-confidence, and ready humor. The combination of these personality traits along with his obvious financial well-being and chiseled good looks makes him irresistible to women. I imagine each prospective partner thinks she's hit the jackpot. And when Doc is falling, I truly believe he is not being superficial. But Doc knows his record and he knows there is always a shelf life to his feelings. So it matches the serial monogamist definition; each relationship is entered into with a "how long will this one last" frame of mind.

Doc does know himself, but at some level he also believes the next woman will be different. Maybe she can hold his interest. Curiously, they leave him, not the other way around, but Doc admits they have good reason. Not that he ever cheats on them once committed, but as his interest wanes, his eyes wander and his thoughts follow suit. So, in a sense, he leaves them first. And we can always see it coming. In the first place, Doc begins hanging out with us more often, and in the second, his stories change from the endearing to the caustically humorous. Or maybe caustically is the wrong word. Doc is never mean-spirited. But his current love is always the butt of his story and often suffers the revelation of the sort of intimate details that really ought to remain intimate.

Nevertheless, we all laugh uproariously at his descriptions and denigrations of sexual techniques or bodily anomalies or pet phrases designed to excite that no longer do, and funniest of all, his amazing mimicry of his current partner's exclamations and exhalations amidst the throes of sexual climax. These last are incredibly funny; they are also incredibly embarrassing after the attendant alcoholic buzz wears off and we see her again. Awkward doesn't even cover it. Half the time I can't meet her gaze without hearing Doc's mimicked cries of passion.

For all the eventual pain and anger at the end of each relationship, though, Doc remains steadfast in defending each woman he parts company with, whether he marries her or not. This last point is important to understand. He only marries some of them, a fairly small portion of the total he dates and sleeps with. Some last a few months, some a year or more, and all the marriages have lasted at least three years, with just over five years the record. That was Jeri, wife three. It's also important to understand that he treats them like queens right up until the last days, and even afterwards, if you can excuse his ribald stories.

Doc rejects Carole's designation of serial monogamist, though he doesn't criticize her for saying it. He freely admits most people will see it that way, but he refuses to agree. "I always love each of them, and I always think the next will be the last. Maybe I'm just a hopeless romantic."

It's sad but true that more marriages than ever split up within three years. Serial monogamists can stay with partners for that length of time or even longer, making it a source of frustration to be labeled with this title.

At the end, Doc always says how much he loved the one he has just left and that he has done his best to care for her and make her feel loved each day. "Love just doesn't last forever." Once, I thought he was wrong about this, as I looked out at his successive relationships from within the warm, mutually supportive confines of my own marriage. Now I'm not so sure.

~ ~ ~

As Doc and I stroll along leisurely, Curly and Larry have bounded ahead. I see them stop opposite Chuck's ketch, lock heels and give him a crisp salute. "Ahoy, Captain," they say in unison.

Chuck has been buttoning up his boat. He steps off now, re-clips the lifeline, and turns toward the two of them, who are still holding their joint salute. Larry, on Curly's right, is saluting correctly with his right hand. Curly uses his left. Standing side-by-side in their white tennis garb, they resemble an albatross preparing for takeoff.

"When did I get demoted?" Chuck asks.

Again I hear that tone. Larry and Curly turn toward each other, looking quizzical. They shrug, don't get the joke. With neither nautical nor military background, it's unlikely they'd know that a Navy commodore is a one-star admiral. But they're quick to respond.

"Keel haul'im, Commodore."

"Forty lashes, not one lash less."

"You'd like that, wouldn't you?" Doc says. He never lets a straight line go unanswered.

In a vain attempt to assuage Chuck's dignity, I add my two cents, "She's looking good, Chuck. Shipshape. Nice job. I should be working on mine right now."

Chuck nods in agreement, turns, and begins to walk up the dock. But he simply can't resist a backward glance at my boat, which really needs a good cleaning and polishing. "She could use some elbow grease," he says. "Why not put your crew to work for a change?"

My crew, as he calls them, bursts out laughing. Chuck continues up the dock shaking his head. Larry calls after him, "We'll call the boat cleaners first thing Monday morning, Captain. Never fear."

~ ~ ~

I suppose I should try to explain Larry and Curly. In the first place, even though I'll continue to refer to them by Carole's pet names, Larry is actually Charlie and Curly is actually Sam. So when I talk about Chuck, Larry-Charlie always says, "I'm Chuck. He's Captain Crunch." And when Doc mentions his former wife, Sam, short for Samantha, Curly says, "I'm Sam, and I have never slept with you. At least not that I remember."

And it must be said that Larry and Curly live up to their names. I can no longer remember if they behaved like two of the Three Stooges after Carole dubbed them or before. But in either event, they have embraced their monikers with comic passion. Curly even shaved his head. Of course, that probably had more to do with the contemporary trend for balding middle-aged men than any acceptance of Carole's assertion. Nevertheless, Curly Sam looks the part, albeit in much better shape than the original Curly.

Larry the Chuckster also fits his role. He has naturally curly, reddish-brown, thinning hair that recedes away, leaving a broad sloping forehead. For a while he tried a comb-over, but the resultant matt lifted off in even the lightest breeze and made him look ridiculous, something a trial attorney cannot afford. It didn't help with his Saturday night conquests either.

Anyway, it's Larry and Curly now. They understand Carole's disdain and treat it lightly. Curly will say to Larry, "It's no wonder Carole thinks you're scum. You sleep with half the women in Seattle but never with your own wife."

"That is just so untrue," Larry will respond. "I haven't slept with a quarter of them yet and I come home every night to sleep with my wife. Oh, wait, you mean have sex with her. I would never do that. Have you seen the size of that woman's ass? I might get lost and never be heard from again."

Then Curly will come back, "Hah! Liar! I happen to know you don't sleep with your wife. You have separate bedrooms. Doc was with her just the other night."

Well, that's a sample of their repertoire. I met the two of them three years ago. They are Doc's sidekicks, wingmen, or whatever term you'd like to apply to the roles they play in the weekly bar hopping, bacchanalian adventures of what they call the SSFC, Saturday Sport Fucking Club, which is an honest and self-descriptive term for a truly puerile and personally repulsive pursuit.

Carole is aware of their exploits and is suitably disgusted. While I have shared her opinion of Larry and Curly, I have come to enjoy their company, at least in small doses. And, as you'd expect, their stories exceed their actual successes. After all, women can see a player coming a mile away. My guess is if they play along, it becomes difficult to determine just who is playing whom. Of course, some might balk at sex with Larry if they knew he was married, but Doc insists that Gretchen really doesn't care so neither should they. I suppose he has a point, but since I'm not built that way and have no way to truly understand open marriage, I have trouble accepting the underlying dishonesty.

Who, then, is Curly? While I'm the one who typically gets the gibes about being a kept man—again not really true but there is truth in it—Curly is the one operating on someone else's money. He's a trust fund baby. The details are unknown to the rest of us, though we do know that the trustee, in his infinite wisdom, has refused to transfer large sums at Curly's request. To say this irks Curly is putting it mildly. But he would just blow it all, and since he is never short of funds or generosity, we all presume he doth protest too much. Doc estimates Curly's annual allowance in the multiples of six digits, though how he knows this is anyone's guess. Unlike Doc, Curly has no interest in forming any sort of lasting relationship. Only occasionally does he actually date a woman. Hooking up is more his speed, though Doc claims there are occasional repeat performances and weekend-long interludes in an otherwise solitary life.

Larry is a criminal lawyer and a good one, if Doc is to be believed. I know it's hard to imagine, juxtaposed with his childishness. I have come to think of his juvenile behavior as necessary release after a week of backroom dealing and courtroom intrigue. Gretchen is a lawyer as well. She specializes in divorce cases. Perhaps she thinks an open marriage that lasts is better than the string of short alliances pursued by Doc. I have never met her nor seen a photo, but Doc whistles when her name is mentioned. Clearly, he thinks Gretch is hot.

~ ~ ~

"That Chuck is quite the tight-ass," Curly says in a voice loud enough to carry down to the gate where Chuck is now exiting.

"I am not either," purrs Larry (aka Charlie). "I'm as loose as they come. You ought to try me sometime."

Then the two of them continue their badinage while I stare without purpose across the marina. In peripheral vision, I can see Doc studying me. I know he's honestly concerned. Carole left me three weeks ago and I'm just as stunned now as I was the day I got her note.

Curly's reaction had been quick and retaliatory. "About time. Boy, is this gonna cost that bitch. Don't take any crap. You get half of everything and a fat paycheck every month for the rest of your life."

Larry had asked if I'd like Gretch to represent me. "She's the best," he said, an uncharacteristic compliment. "She'll negotiate a big settlement and make the other side think they got a great deal."

Doc's reaction had been guarded. "Any chance she'll be back?" he asked. "Maybe this is just about sex. After all, you guys have been married, what, twenty years?"

"Twenty-three. We married right out of college.

Lots of love. No money. Couldn't have been happier." I had paused and looked down at my feet then lifted my eyes to meet Doc's. "She says she's been seeing this guy for four years, Doc. Where the fuck was I?"

Doc just looked at me sadly for a minute then answered, "Not paying attention."

I guess I deserved that. And I know he meant it to be supportive, but all I really wanted at that moment were comments like Larry's and Curly's. I wanted Doc to tell me I couldn't possibly have seen it coming. I wanted him to call Carole a heartless bitch. I wanted to hear how lucky I was to be rid of her. But he was right. I had not been paying attention.

Instead, after Carole and I had both decided to part company as business partners, I marched my way through six different, and indifferently committed to, jobs.

Why did I stop working with her? I think the success got to me. That, and the long hours. Carole just could not relax and let someone else do part of the work. She had to be at the office seven days a week. But she wasn't like that from the beginning. Or was she? I guess now that I think about it, she was always driven to succeed, while I was never driven to do much more than live day to day.

We met in Seattle where we were both enrolled in business classes at the University of Washington. After we graduated in 1985, we each found jobs in the burgeoning real estate market. We worked for small outfits, she in West Seattle and me in Bellevue on the other side of Lake Washington. If you know anything about these side-by-side cities, you know that Bellevue and its neighboring bedroom communities promptly took off, expanding exponentially. For the first few years, I worked half of Carole's hours and sold twice as many homes. This was mostly dumb luck on my part. I chose what I thought would be the lower pressure territory. And it was lower pressure; it just paid better.

After five years of working her ass off every day, and after studying at night in order for her broker's license, Carole finally caught up to me in annual income. A year later, she passed me out and never looked back. In 1992, she rented office space in Issaquah, just east of Bellevue, having decided this would be where the new action was, and took on her first employee. That would be me.

We struggled a bit at the outset, but by the millennium we had expanded into several more office suites and had forty agents working for us. The money was rolling in. We bought a newly remodeled 3,000-square-foot condominium with to-die-for views overlooking Lake Union, and I bought a forty-foot Valiant cutter and rented a slip at Shilshole Marina.

Carole was annoyed by my boat purchase, which she complained was a waste of money, since we didn't have time to use it. She came onboard seldom in the ensuing years and that was only to treat the high-roller clients she sometimes picked up. But she was even more annoyed by my lack of commitment. I had begun to work less and hang out on my boat more.

The beginning of the end was spring of 2003. I can see that now. Carole had decided to take on a commercial real estate partner. His name was Tony. He had a broker's license and his own company. It was smaller, but he had pursued and won some impressive deals.

We argued about it, with Carole pointing out how much more money we would have once the two companies were merged, and me complaining that we already had more money than we could ever spend but not enough time to spend it. The conversation became heated, and at some point I walked out. That night I slept on the boat. The next day, I called Carole and told her I was quitting my job. She countered that I hadn't been working hard enough for her to care one way or the other and hung up on me.

A week later, we made up. For one thing, it was April and living aboard was less than inviting. My boat didn't have a heating system. The other thing was that I really missed Carole. Even at the worst of times in our marriage, the sex had been great and our companionship warm and mutual. She happily welcomed me back and we had a short respite from what became an oft-repeated argument that summer. I resumed my desk in the office but also resumed my desultory approach to selling.

By fall, Carole decided something had to give. Since I had refused to agree to the merger, she could not move forward. We were equal partners on paper, even if she did most of the work running the business. She asked me to reconsider the new partner. I had met Slick Tony a few times and didn't like him, though I recognized he was successful at what he did. Mainly I objected to what I saw as Carole's obsession with growing her business. "Why not sell out to old Tony and sail off into the sunset with our reward?" I suggested, knowing full well what her reaction would be. Carole did not disappoint. She exploded at me about "her company" that she had built from the ground up and would never sell. I held up my hands in defeat and said I'd sign whatever she wanted me to but I thought it might be best for our marriage if I didn't work there anymore.

Now I can see the mistake this was. Yes, we continued together as husband and wife, and we still thought of each other as companions. But I drifted from job to job and increasingly spent nights on my boat, while Carole invested herself in the hard work of merging two enterprises and turning it into a minor-league player in the King County real estate market. We saw little of each other, and even when we did, Carole was too tired to enjoy the time we spent together.

Inevitably, I suppose, Carole turned to Tony. She saw him as the person who understood and shared her passion for what now was "their" company. It must have only been a few months until they began an affair.

Four years later, I understand why it happened. And I understand why Carole decided to leave, once Tony convinced his wife to agree to what must have been an expensive divorce. But I cannot for the life of me understand why I never saw it coming.

Artemisia

As we lounge in the cockpit, drinking our beers and watching the sun set behind the Olympic Mountains to the northwest, Doc launches a concerted effort to get me to join the SSFC tonight. I know he means well, and he may be right when he says what I need is a "romantic diversion," but I'm nowhere near ready for it. Curly disagrees with both of us.

"Wrong, Doc. What he needs is a piece of ass. The younger the sweeter."

"No," says Larry. "Something more experienced and kinky would be just the thing to rock the Deacon. Something we might find at Teddies."

Larry's tone worries me, but I've been to Teddy's. It's a neighborhood sports bar. "You mean the tavern off Roosevelt? Pool tables, pinball, darts, jukebox?"

"Not Teddy's. Teddies, as in lingerie. A cozy spot off the beaten path. Expensive drinks and cheap women," Doc answers with a lurid smile. "I'm not sure the Deacon is ready for Teddies quite yet, Larry. How about something a bit tamer?"

"How about Ray's Boathouse?" I ask. "The Deacon is ready for dinner, not dates."

"Dates?" Curly says. "As in meeting some perspective available woman for the purpose of getting to know if you will be a good match?" His snort dismisses my antiquated term.

I wave off his comment, but Larry can't resist needling him. "That's pro-spective, not per-spective, you moron. And if any of the bimbos you hook up with were per-ceptive, they'd run the other way."

"You've got some nerve. What kind of moron lets his wife sleep with half the Seattle Seahawks and laughs about it?"

As Curly and Larry settle in for a round or two of verbal sparring, I tune them out and watch the sun die fiery behind the Olympic Mountains. The last thing I hear is Larry defending Gretch in his own inimitable way. He insists she would never fuck a football player. "Too beefy for her tastes. Now, the Supersonics are another matter. She likes 'em lean and mean. Too bad they're off to Kansas or Oklahoma or some such desolate, god-forsaken place in the middle of nowhere. She can't have made it a quarter of the way through the roster yet."

I catch Doc eyeing me again wistfully. "Okay," he says, "Ray's it is. My men and I need to fuel up for our night on the town, and nothing really gets going before 10:00 p.m. anyway. Your treat though."

Larry and Curly groan at my selection of what they refer to as a snooty yuppie bar, never mind that they both qualify as yuppies, albeit yuppies with a penchant for self-degradation. While they clamber out of the cockpit onto the dock, I slip the hatch boards back in the companionway, slide the cover shut, and lock it. Then the four of us wander up to the parking lot. Doc suggests driving to "save his weary old arthritic legs," but since it's only a few blocks down to Ray's, we boo him until he caves.

It's 8:30 p.m. when we walk through the front door and climb upstairs to the "less snooty" section, composed of Ray's extended bar and outside deck seating. The upstairs has a limited menu, but you can pretty much get anything you want. They'll let you order off the downstairs menu if it's not too busy. As the hostess shows us to a table, I catch Larry and Curly scanning the bar for prospects.

"Give it a rest, will you?" I demand. "Save your energy for later or Doc will be the only one who scores. He's faster on his feet than he looks."

"Just checkin' the menu for an appetizer," Larry answers. "Anyway, Doc's not really all that fast."

The bar area is crowded, so the hostess seats us out on the deck where it's beginning to cool down. Even in mid-July, as soon as the sun loses its punch and the breeze picks up across the fifty-five-degree Puget Sound water, the temperature starts to drop. I'm wearing jeans and brought a lightweight jacket, as did Doc and Larry. Curly is wearing shorts and a polo shirt. Earlier, he had on a white tank top, what he calls a "beater," but changed at his car when I pointed out he'd never get into Ray's dressed this way. He made a few disparaging remarks but changed with little persuasion.

Once seated and done ordering, steaks for Larry and Curly, salmon for Doc and me, we relax and enjoy the gathering darkness. This is nautical twilight, the last faint sunrays skimming the horizon. The city lights, a few miles east of where we sit, set up a glow that occludes all but the brightest stars.

I look out across the sound, watching the late day container vessels and freighters move past on their way into the Port of Seattle. Several pleasure boats make the turn into Shilshole, or head for the locks and entrance to Lake Union, or continue south to Elliot Bay. I think about how tuned into the Sound I am, the ebb and flow of tides, the rising and tapering of wind, and the salt air shift from sweet tang to dense pungency. How crucial to my mood they are, the same ebb and flow in my thoughts. Then I turn slightly, and again in peripheral vision, catch Doc watching me. Trying to figure out if I'm going to implode, but it brings a faint smile to my lips to see him worry.

By 10:30 p.m., we finish our dinners, Curly has made three unsuccessful attempts at acquiring phone numbers from passing waitresses and has gone inside to warm up and cruise the bar. Larry, after hanging with Doc and me for a while, has left to join him. I look back through the intervening glass and see the two of them chatting up a likely pair of blondes half their age. The girls seem content to lead them on, and for all I know Doc and I will be leaving alone, though I doubt it.

After a few minutes, Doc shifts in his chair and asks, "You gonna be okay, Deke?"

I smile at his use of the silly nickname Curly has pinned me with. When Carole left so abruptly, I called Doc to ask if he knew. He assured me my call was the first he'd heard about it, but something in his voice told me otherwise. Nevertheless, that night he'd assembled the gang and we'd all gone out drinking. To give Larry and Curly credit, they stuck with me and left off from prowling the bars for fresh meat. Their eyes drifted but they stayed seated.

At some point later that night, Curly had looked across the table at me and sang the last line of the chorus from an old Steely Dan song, "Deacon Blues." I don't think Curly got the meaning in the song right, but he seemed certain I was both downhearted and too uptight to hit on any of the women strewn around the bars we frequented that night. Deacon Blues sounded like a perfect description of the "sad sack of shit" he said he was looking at.

For the record, my name is Andrew, and it is not, nor has it ever been, Andy. Deacon, and the shorter, Deke, are the only nicknames I've ever had. And whether Curly understood the song or not, its significance was clear to me. There are plenty of names for life's winners, and I might have counted myself among their number not so long ago. But today, having lost Carole, I feel like a loser in a wider sense. So Deacon Blues it is.

To be honest, though, I find I like it. I'm not sure why. Maybe Shakespeare is right; there's something in a name. And it seems sweet and endearing to me to have friends who like me well enough to make one up then stick to it. This is a thing Carole would not understand. She'd say it's a dumb guy thing. But she'd be wrong. It's a human thing. That would be something about which she knows nothing. If this sounds bitter, that's because it is.

Back to Doc's question: am I going to be okay? Too soon to tell, maybe. I vacillate between the empty feeling in my gut and accompanying loneliness, and the three T's: tumult, terror and titillation. Tumult of emotions over Carole, from anger to intense disappointment. Terror that, despite what I see in the mirror, I may be too old, too paunchy, or too un-hip for today's dating scene. But titillation as well, anticipatory to the "sex with strange women" my buddies tell me lays ahead.

I answer Doc in the affirmative. "Sure, why wouldn't I be?"

Doc just shakes his head and frowns, irritated by my flippant response. Then he gets up and leaves me sitting by myself. I watch through the window as he joins Larry and Curly, and without them even realizing he is doing it, steals both girls away.

Picture this. As we all watch, Doc reaches for his wallet. He fans it open nonchalantly, flashing a whole lot of green, then extracts two business cards and hands them to the girls. Each reads the card she's been handed as he talks to them. Their eyes rise from the cards and rivet Doc with full attention. I cannot hear what he says, but his hand gestures are clear. He's telling them what he could do to give them the breasts of goddesses. The girls both have decent figures but tending to the pudginess common today in the twenty-something crowd. They are wearing low-rider jeans and shorty tank tops exposing a midriff roll of flesh that Curly calls a "muffin top." Above the matched rolls are equally matched large breasts, which bulge from the tank tops in what, unfettered, must be pendulous excess. Doc is just about eye-level with the four of them. He's only five-foot-six, and the girls tower over him in their four-inch stilettos. As Larry and Curly look on in awe, Doc reaches up to cup the breasts of the blonde on his left while looking directly into the eyes of the blonde on his right. He lifts them and squeezes them together slightly in demonstration of what he might achieve if only given the chance. Then, believe it or not, he reverses the process, fondling the breasts of the blonde on the right, while the blonde on the left looks on appreciatively.

This is the Doc we all know and love, the one who gets away with anything. The Doc who left me sitting by myself is the other Doc. I've said that Larry and Curly live up to their names in more ways than one. Doc is another matter. Like Snow White's Doc, he's short, barrel-chested and good-natured. He's also temperamental and somewhat unpredictable. Occasionally he scares people. He's good at hiding this if he wants to, but there's always something else going on just below skin deep. If he catches me wrong sometimes, though, I know Doc has a soft spot for me, even if I don't know why.

But, really, does anyone know why someone else loves you? I don't, that's certain. I could have said why I thought Carole did a month ago, but I have no answer today. Maybe my sense of intuition has been shaken. Or maybe I'm not as intuitive as I imagine.

~ ~ ~

Next morning, the phone wakes me. I let the machine pick up, but I've left the speaker on, so I hear Doc's not-so-dulcet tones entreating in a whine. "Deacon, Deacon, time to get out of bed. The sun is high in the sky…"

He keeps up the drivel until I relent and answer, "Okay, okay, I'm up already. What time is it?"

"Past time to be out and about, of course. I have someone I want you to meet."

Great, I think. Doc wants to play matchmaker. I'm really not ready to face that yet, but I'm not awake enough to come up with a more effective put off than, "It's Sunday, Doc. Can't this wait?"

"Nope. I'm the doctor and what I say goes. Meet us at the boat at 1:00 p.m. You're taking us all sailing. It's 11:30 now, by the way, so you better go hop in the shower."

"Okay, fine. Who's 'us all'?"

"Diana, Connie, and me. You get Diana; I'm not done with Connie yet."

"I'm not done with Carole yet," I answer with a deep sigh.

There's a short pause then Doc says softly, "I know, Deke, but maybe it's time you were."

~ ~ ~

When I arrive at Shilshole, they are waiting for me at the gate. I've met Connie before. She's a short, sweet, blonde bombshell who looks many years younger than Doc and who is clearly head-over-heels in love with him. You can hardly pry them apart. I have no idea what Doc tells her when he goes out barhopping with the SSFC. And I don't want to know either. Maybe Connie is equal to the challenge and willing to put up with what she must believe is an interim period of less-than-fully-committed behavior.

Diana is nothing like Connie. In the first place, she's closer to my age, faint facial lines giving her away. She's also nearly as tall as I am, about 5'-10". She has shoulder-length, straight brown hair, intense golden-brown eyes, and a curvy but athletic figure. She's wearing scuffed boat shoes, khaki shorts and a tight, low-cut, navy blue tank top. The effect is casual but seductive. I'm going to have trouble keeping my eyes where they belong.

She holds out her hand and I shake it. She fixes me

with a look that would melt butter and softly purrs, "Pleased to meet you finally. I've heard so much and it all seems to be true."

I mutter something inane like, "Don't believe anything Doc tells you," but manage a sincere smile and turn away to open the gate.

Doc and Connie lead the way down to the boat while Diana and I follow a few paces behind.

"Am I your first date?" Diana asks. "I mean since your breakup?" I don't answer right away, so she adds, "You're mine."

I'm surprised by Diana's forthright statement. I presumed Doc would fix me up with one of his castoffs, not someone he knew was going through a divorce as I am.

"You're separated?" I ask, glancing at her left hand. Unlike me, no wedding band.

"Yes, for a long time, I'm afraid. I just haven't been able to face the whole dating-and-mating scene. Doc convinced me that since you were recently separated, you would make a safe date. And, of course, we have chaperones," Diana adds, motioning with both arms toward our leaders ahead.

There's something vaguely odd about Diana and this situation. Her words and tone are shy, but her look has a feline ferociousness that belies them. Maybe it's just her eyes. Doc knows how to pick'em, I think, that's for sure. And as this thought passes through my head, I realize Diana has referred to Doc by his nickname, not Harold, as Connie calls him. How long have they known each other? Has she met Larry and Curly? Maybe she is one of Doc's castoffs after all. Not really important, I decide. We're just going sailing.

When we reach the boat, Connie requires Doc's help, and even then nearly falls headfirst when *Repose* heels slightly from their combined weight. Diana unhooks the lifeline and refastens it out of the way then steps up onto the combing and down into the cockpit smartly. She has sea legs.

"You're a sailor," I say.

"Guilty," she returns, smiling sheepishly, and she nearly gets away with it, but I catch the look in her eyes. It's saying something else. I just don't know what that is.

~ ~ ~

We spend the afternoon tacking back and forth across the Sound in a fresh fifteen-knot breeze. I turn over the helm to Diana, who clearly knows her away around a sailboat. She needs no instruction whatsoever and instinctively steers a straight course. I never catch her watching the telltales, but she keeps us sailing near hull speed anyway, probably by feel. She may be more experienced than I am.

"Where did you learn to sail?" I ask at some point.

"Right here. Grew up in Port Orchard, sailing dinghies in the harbor."

"This isn't a dinghy," I comment, meaning there's a world of difference in what it takes to manage a forty-foot cutter.

"No, it certainly isn't. I take it as a compliment that you've handed her over to me. My husband had an old Sparkman & Stevens sloop we spent many years cruising up-coast on. And I still have sailing friends, so I get plenty of practice."

I watch Diana's eyes as the wind blows strands of

her hair across her face while she keeps her gaze trained on the horizon. Her look is sheer delight. Then she glances over at me, catching herself, and changes it back to the penetrating one she has fixed me with all day. It seems studied and deliberate. I think I prefer the unguarded look she had a moment ago.

By the time we get back to the dock, it's 6:00 p.m. Connie has been queasy and Doc makes their excuses, thanking both Diana and me for a delightful sail, then the two of them depart, leaving us to close up the boat. I put the hatch boards in while Diana fishes a hose out of my dock locker and gets ready to wash the excess salt off *Repose*.

"Do you want to scrub down the decks?" she asks.

"No, that's okay," I answer, accompanied by a don't-bother wave of my hand. "A quick rinse will do just fine."

Diana looks at me with mild disapproval at the way I treat *Repose*. Earlier I had caught her inspecting the water spots and incipient rust stains on my stainless steel fittings. She probably would agree with Capt. Crunch that I'm not a proper boat owner. But her frown quickly shifts back to a smile.

"Aye, aye, skipper," she says, playing her part again, and starts running water over the hull and decks.

When we're finished and walking back up the dock, she asks, "Since you treated me to a great sail, how about I treat you to dinner at Ray's?"

"Okay, you're on," I say, and, having made up my mind earlier to see how this whole thing plays out, I return the exact look she has trained on me all day. She glances away first, eyes shifting to her feet, but the smile is bemused and anything but shy. This is going to be interesting.

~ ~ ~

Dinner goes fine. Lots of small talk. I ask if she's met Sam and Charlie. She says, "You mean Curly and Larry?" This response answers my earlier question, but her friends-of-friends explanation seems too facile. I'm pretty sure now Diana is one of the regulars the guys meet at Teddies. I think about asking her if she's ever been there but decide against it. If this is what I think it is, why not just go along for the ride. The truth is Diana is a knockout and I have no reason on earth to turn down a night with her if that's what's in store. What I can't figure out is how she's going to shift from the shy it's-just-a-sailing-date woman she's purported herself to be, to the your-place-or-mine huntress I'm expecting.

The answer comes later, after a quiet meal and a slow stroll back to the marina and across the parking lot. Diana searches through her purse for keys. Not there. "Must be locked in the back of my car," she says in disgust.

We try the doors and they are indeed locked. She tells me she had the rear door open when she beeped the locks shut, and in the rush to decide between her light jacket and heavier coat must have dropped them. Her house keys, of course, are on the same ring. And her roommate won't be back until tomorrow. Naturally, I offer up the spare bedroom at my condo. So far I'm enjoying the performance and wonder how the next step will be made.

I get Diana settled into the guest room then she shoos me out after asking if I have a spare robe. "I'd like to get comfortable. Why don't you do the same?"

I offer Carole's, still where it was left a month ago, hanging next to its mate in the bathroom. Diana wrinkles up her nose and takes mine instead. Then I ask if she'd like anything to drink. I don't want her to have to work too hard at this supposed seduction.

A glass of wine would be nice. White or red? White, I think. And we find ourselves on the sofa in matching robes, looking out at the city lights.

We sit quietly, sipping our wine for a while, then she asks, "How long has it been?"

"Carole walked out three weeks ago," I say, unguarded.

"That's not what I mean," she replies, and when I look into her eyes I know what she's asking.

I look away and answer honestly, "Three weeks," then add, "And you?"

I forget this is a game, though now it doesn't seem like one. I'm expecting an answer like "It's been months" or "Last winter" but what she says is, "Yesterday."

I turn my head quickly and there's the self-possessed, ferocious look again.

"Who are you?" I ask.

"Does it really matter right now?"

I shake my head ruefully but smile. "No," is all I say.

Diana rises, removes her robe, and lets it drop where she has been sitting. Underneath is lace and silk. Where did that come from? Then, holding my eyes with hers, she lifts one thin shoulder strap followed by the other, and lets it fall from her body. We hold this pose for a long moment then she extends her hand to me, I take it, and we walk into my bedroom.

One to a side, we pull back the duvet until it drops off the end. The low headboard is centered under a window looking out on the water. City lights flood the pale sheets. I remove my robe and boxers and Diana motions for me to lie down on my back. She straddles my hips and leans down for a searching kiss. I trace her body into memory, moving my hands from along either side of her long neck, down soft flanks, angling out to wide hips, and back up to fondle her breasts. I can feel the faint scars under each that suggest Doc's work. The look and feel of them is completely natural.

She rises again and looks into my eyes. "Not too bad, huh?" she says, then smiles ear to ear as she watches me take her in, breasts to belly. The pale light illuminates every curve.

I smile up at her and answer, "You are beautiful."

"I have a big ass," she offers in mild contradiction then wiggles it delightedly.

Her movement elicits a groaned response, "You have a wonderful ass and that feels great."

She smiles and reaches behind for me. "Yes, I can tell it does." She takes me inside her and moves her hips back and forth for a minute then lifts off again.

"Me first," she says and shifts forward slowly until her knees are planted on the pillow at either side of my head. She puts her hands on the windowsill and lowers herself until my lips just brush her labia and my hands cradle her buttocks. Then she closes her eyes and begins a gentle back-and-forth rocking motion. I try using my tongue, but she says, "Not yet. Just lips."

We move this way, speeding up then slowing for a while, Diana postponing her release time after time until she can no longer stand it, and whispers, "Now,

now…"

At the last moment she lets go a low, gurgling noise deep in her throat, I watch her abdominal muscles contract forcefully, and my face washes in honeyed salt. She continues in a slowly descending pace then collapses, moving back down from her kneeling position to lie on my chest.

After a few minutes, she lifts her head and begins to kiss me, sharing her own taste. Then she mounts, taking me deep inside her, and once more begins the slow back-and-forth motion. This time she keeps her eyes open and watches me, looking and listening for the signs of my own pleasure and gauging when to slow down and when to speed up. Words drift through my mind: she's good at this. Then the thought of her wide experience disappears in a flood of sensation.

Afterward, we lie entwined, neither wanting to move. Eventually, we fall asleep. When I wake later, she is taking me in her mouth. I groan but do nothing to interrupt her, and once awake, move my hips in concert. This time it's my turn to be first.

~ ~ ~

When I roll over the next morning, Diana is gone. A note left behind on the nightstand explains she had her keys after all and has caught a cab back to the marina. She thanks me for last night and hopes to see me again sometime, though not soon.

"It's my rule," she writes. "No attachments. Hope you'll understand."

"Who was that masked woman," I say to myself, smiling, then in mock imitation of Curly, answer, "I not know, Kemo Sabe, but she had some bodacious titties."

Deception

It's 7:00 a.m. when I get out of bed. I wander around our condo for a while, looking out the windows and thinking about last night. I wonder if I should give Doc a call and thank him for the blowjob. Now that's what I call a buddy. Shit, I hope it wasn't paid for. No, Doc wouldn't stoop that low. I'm pretty sure Diana wouldn't either. Setup she was, paid hooker she wasn't.

So how do I feel this morning? Sated, that's certain. Wanting more? Well, not at the moment. I think I'd like to get to know the real Diana. Hell, of course I would; she's a gorgeous, intelligent woman who clearly loves sailing.

Still, she says no attachments, and I like the idea of being attached. Or do I? I have to admit I'm confused right now. And the stupid truth is I love Carole and have been miserable since she left. Until last night. At this very minute, I'd rather see Diana walk through my front door, so I guess I'm contradicting myself.

"Screw it," I say to no one present. "I need a cup of coffee."

I stumble into the kitchen, still half-asleep, to brew myself a double espresso. The coffee machine Carole bought looks like it should have a barista running it. It's a study in excess, but I have to admit it makes a great cup of coffee. Carole takes hers straight, but I like sugar and lots of cream. I walk out to the balcony in my boxers, not caring about the neighbors above me.

As I sit sipping my coffee, I think about what's next. I keep calling this place our condo, but it's my condo now, I suppose, since Carole has moved out most of her clothes and emptied the medicine cabinet on her side of the double vanity. That's how I found out she was gone. Took me an hour to notice the note stuck to the Subzero refrigerator door with one of her company logo magnets. It wasn't long:

Andrew;
This isn't working. I have to leave. I'll keep paying the mortgage until we sort it all out. You can pay the marina charges. I've already forwarded my mail. I've hired a lawyer and he'll be in touch shortly. The boat and the condo are yours. The company is mine. We can work out a fair settlement, I'm sure. I've moved in with Tony. I kept thinking you'd notice all the nights I never came home, but I guess it didn't matter to you anymore. Jesus, it's been almost four years, long past time for me to start over. Good luck, Carole.

The note is still stuck to the fridge. I see it again as I open the door to grab the half-and-half. I pour a little into my second cup and head back out onto the balcony, taking my cell phone to call my only speed dial number. Carole's disembodied voice answers and says to leave a message. It's not much, but it's the only time I get to hear her talk to me now. The lawyer has told her no direct communication. His letter, which I've refused to answer so far, is stuck to the fridge door along with her note. It's not all that long either.

Outlined in typical legalese is a settlement leaving me my boat, my car, my personal belongings, and the condo. Carole will quitclaim her half ownership in the property to me and I will assume full responsibility for the mortgage. I will quitclaim my part-ownership in our joint company to her in exchange for $1 million US dollars, a nice round number.

I pause to wonder again what other dollars might be meant if the lawyer failed to stipulate US dollars. Canadian maybe, or Australian? The law is a weird, otherworldly abomination. Larry would disagree, I'm sure. Or maybe not. He may be right, though; I could use Gretch's counsel. But I'm not ready to respond to the note. I'm waiting until I stop feeling sorry for myself and start feeling angry.

The settlement offer may sound fair on its face, but even I know it's just a trial balloon. After all, I'm a salesman. Nobody makes his best offer first. Doing the math, I estimate my boat to be worth about $150k and the condo about $1.5M. The mortgage is someplace around $500k. Since the Lawyer's estimate is $1.5M in total for my quarter of the company plus Carole's half of the condo, Carole seems to be giving me her share in the boat for free. Sounds generous, but it isn't.

The value of the company—let's call it Carole's Folly since I can't bring myself to say the actual inane company name—is hard to pin down. The offices are partly owned and partly leased. I have no idea what the terms are, since I was never involved. That was Carole's department. But my quarter has to be worth a lot more than the lawyer's estimate of $1M, since even though we each have small retirement accounts of roughly equal size, most of our profits have been put back into the company and its real estate holdings.

In all, it's a lot to think about, and my brain hasn't been up to the challenge lately. When I concentrate on what is fair and equitable, I have to admit the company is really Carole's. She built it while I watched. And face it, even though I worked too, it was Carole who grew Folly to its current size. So even if a million is a low-ball number, it's probably as much as I really need. I sure as hell don't need or even want this high-priced view condo. I could sell it, buy something smaller, and live off the delta and never work again. Or I could buy a larger boat and live on it. I suppose I should counter her offer anyway, if only for the sake of proper form. She'd never respect me otherwise. I'm just not sure I can do what Curly wants. He says go for blood. The problem is I still love Carole and I don't really care about the money.

I watch the early boats out on Lake Union. Mostly it's fishermen at this hour, plus a few larger pleasure craft heading for the locks. I can also see some kayaks plying the shore and one small sailing dinghy drifting lazily out in the middle. I decide to make another cup of coffee but first pull on yesterday's clothes and go down to the lobby to check the mail I haven't bothered with for a couple of weeks now, and to pick up my *Seattle Times*.

As I ride the elevator back up, I skim through my mail. Mostly junk and a few bills, but there's a letter from Carole's lawyer as well. I tuck it into my hip pocket while I make my third cup then head back outside. I set the letter down and drink my coffee slowly. I should be nervous but I'm not. I actually care very little about what it may say. Maybe it's a complaint that he hasn't heard from me. Maybe it's a threat to take me to court. Maybe it's a better offer. Who knows? Who cares?

When I finally tire of playing guessing games, I open the letter to find a restated offer. His client, he says, would like to complete the process quickly and is willing to increase her offer for my share in Folly from $1.0M to $1.5M in exchange for signing the enclosed agreement and returning it by July 20th. That's three days ago. Oh well, I suppose I can still get the deal if I want it.

What's the rush, I wonder? Probably isn't one. Just an acceptance on their part that the company is worth more than they said, I guess. In fact, it's probably worth more than they're representing now, but I really don't care. Maybe I'll give them a call later and accept. Carole just wants this done with, and I suppose I do too. No sense beating a dead horse.

I've just about decided to make one more cup of coffee then go to the Blue Star for breakfast when my intercom chimes. I go back inside and push the talk button. "You rang," I say in my deepest Lurch *basso profundo*.

"Alms for the poor, alms for the poor," comes back in Doc's little old lady voice. I buzz him in.

As he walks through the door, Doc looks at me sheepishly, not knowing whether or not I'm pissed at him. Since he's here early, it's obvious he knows Diana is already gone. I'm sure it was part of the agreement.

"You just missed her," I say, keeping my expression expressionless.

Doc's face registers surprise, but he recovers quickly and throws his hands in the air.

"*Mea culpa, mea maxima culpa.* It was all Curly's idea. Larry and I just went along even though we thought it was a mistake." Then he drops his hands and looks at me evenly. "Was it a mistake?"

I can't hold it in anymore and break out laughing. "Jesus, Doc, I hate to admit Curly is ever right but I might have needed that. Please tell me this was not a pro."

Doc has been laughing with me but stops now and asks, "Pro?" The confusion on his face quickly drains though, first changing to amusement then to feigned annoyance. In the most disgusted tone he can muster, Doc retorts, "Pay for sex? Me? Not for you or for anybody, and certainly not for myself. By the way, how was it?"

That starts me laughing again, but as I watch his face I realize this is a semi-serious question. He really wants to know. What the hell. Why should I care?

"Best I've had in three weeks."

He pauses long enough to consider whether I'm seriously referring to Carole then sees in my smile that I'm not. "Soooo, how was it? I want the blow by blow."

I wince at his bad pun but give him a detailed description, including an attempt to mimic Diana's orgasmic vocalization.

Doc listens in rapt attention then sighs. "Damn, I knew she'd be good."

Now it's my turn to be surprised. "Are you trying to tell me you haven't slept with Diana?"

"Yup," he says, then after a pause to find the right words, continues, "None of us has been treated to one of Diana's one-night-stands. In fact, she doesn't do one-night-stands, as far as we know. Couple of hours, tops."

We exchange looks, gauging each other's honesty then Doc asks, "She really spent the night?"

I frown. I'm not sure she spent the whole night, and I'm not sure why Doc is so surprised. I decide to answer with precision. "She rolled out before sunrise but she was definitely there at 4:00 a.m. when I got up to take a leak."

"Humph," Doc says as he stares at me befuddled.

I end the standoff with a question I know he can answer, "Coffee?"

~ ~ ~

As we wait in my kitchen for the espresso maker to heat up, I hand Doc the letter from Carole's lawyer and he reads dutifully. I watch the expression on his face for clues.

"What do you think?" I ask as he slowly tucks the letter back into its envelope and we take our cups of coffee out to the balcony.

"Not much. It's got to be worth more than they're saying."

"I'm sure it is, but Carole did all the work, so I don't feel she owes me half."

"Why not? That's the law in Washington, community property. You get half of everything. You could even argue for support payments if you wanted."

"I know. That's what Curly says too. And Larry just tells me to talk to Gretch."

Doc flashes his eyes up from the page to read my face then offers, "Probably good advice."

"I guess. But I don't want to fight. I mean, just

because I *can* ask for a bigger settlement, doesn't mean I *should*."

"How ethical of you," Doc replies, and I can tell from his tone what he thinks of my position on this. "Look," he continues, "this is up to you but I think you should have all the facts before you make any decision. What if we're not talking about the difference between $1 million and $1.5 million? What if we're talking about the difference between $1 million and $10 million? You really have no idea what the company is worth, do you?"

"Not a clue."

"Okay then, what if they're hiding something? Has it occurred to you the push to get this signed might be for some reason you don't know anything about?"

"I don't know, Doc. Carole's very honest. I don't think she'd do that."

"Oh, really? She's been carrying on an affair for four years and you think that's been honest?"

I look at Doc sadly and nod my head in agreement with him.

"And what about her lawyer? Think a lawyer might lie to you or 'withhold information?' Doc asks, bracketing the "withhold information" with a four-finger gesture.

"Okay, okay. I give in. What do you suggest?"

"I suggest we have a beer."

"What the hell. Why not?" I answer, and walk to the fridge. Doc doesn't like my heavier ales, so I get us a couple of Coronas and cut two lime wedges.

We sit in silence for a while, watching the parade of boats. The queue for Hiram Chittenden isn't backed up into the lake the way it was yesterday morning, but there are still plenty of boats heading that direction. The locks hold a lot of small craft in each cycle, but on summer weekends there's always a wait. That's why I use Shilshole marina. It's on the Sound. The argument I've heard for mooring this side of the locks is the fresh water. No barnacles and less bottom growth. The regular switch from fresh to salt and back again helps keep the hulls clear, but I'm happy to pay each year to have the bottom cleaned and painted, and the convenience of being five minutes from beginning a sail is too much to trade.

I glance over at Doc, who is quietly ruminating, drinking his beer, and staring off into space. "Any ideas?" I ask, after a minute.

Doc tilts his head back and closes his eyes then answers, "Yeah. Get out of Dodge for a while and let us boys do some research. Got someplace quiet and remote you can head for in *Repose*?"

"Sure. When do you want me back?"

"Let's say a week or so for now. Larry may have a better idea. Hand me your cell phone."

"Why?" I ask, expecting some convoluted answer.

"Because I need to make a call and mine is in the car?" he answers in a stupid-question tone, and he spreads his hands palms up in a gesture meant to say, "Why the fuck else?"

~ ~ ~

An hour later, Larry calls from the lobby and Doc buzzes him in. He hands me a cell phone as he walks through the door and I hand him a Corona. Doc summarizes the letter and our conversation, and Larry asks a few questions, the answers to which he mostly knows but needs to verify. He pauses to think for a few minutes then begins. "Okay, here's the drill. I want you out of communication with anybody but me for a couple of weeks. That cell phone has only one number it will call. Another phone like it." He pulls the companion from his jacket pocket. "Just push the talk button."

It looks like a regular cell phone to me. I shake my head and frown. "Why?" I ask and mean several things. Why do you want me to call only you? Why does a cell phone that only calls one number even exist? And, why do you have such a phone?

"I represent many men and some women who cannot talk on the phone ever and expect their conversations to be private. This ensures privacy. It is registered to someone who doesn't exist. I use a pair once then destroy them and obtain another."

I feel as if I'd just walked onto the set of Mission Impossible or maybe The Sopranos. "Is this really necessary?"

Larry shrugs. "Probably not. But you never know. I asked Gretch about Carole's lawyer, and she whistled. He's quite expensive. So I'll reverse your question. Why is a top-end lawyer really necessary in a straightforward fifty-fifty divorce? I don't know the answer, but I'm very curious."

I stare at him blankly and find nothing to say, so he prompts me.

"Doc says you don't know what the company is worth. That right?"

"Yeah—"

Larry cuts me off with the next question, "But you know the gross sales numbers, yes?"

"Ballpark? $100 million last year."

"What about the commercial side?"

"No idea. Carole just said Tony was holding up his end of the bargain."

"I'll just bet he was."

I give him a weary, defeated look. There's nothing I can say in my defense.

"Sorry," he offers. "Not fair to kick you when you're down."

I nod then look from Larry to Doc and back as if to ask, "Anything else?"

"All right then, we're finished here. You go pack your shit and head for the marina. I want you someplace else tonight. Don't tell me or Doc or Curly or anyone else where you'll be. What we don't know, we can't be asked to divulge. I probably won't call you unless I have another question or find something out, but if that phone rings, it's me. If it makes a buzzing sound, it's a wrong number so don't answer."

With that, Larry and Doc get up and depart, taking my cell phone with them along with the explanation that Doc will leave it on and say, if called, he was staying at my place while I was off sailing and I must have forgotten to take it along.

As we walk to the door, Larry asks nonchalantly but with a smile like the Cheshire Cat, "By the way, how was last night?"

I begin to answer in detail, but over his shoulder I catch Doc's odd expression and microscopic headshake. I quickly look down to hide my reaction. Why? I wonder. I look back up and shrug. "Very nice," I answer. "Think I'll keep the details to myself. I'll admit I needed it though."

Larry bows silently, accepting my thanks for his part in all this. "Tell Curly for me too when you see him," I add.

Larry grins and says he'll be sure to do that.

~ ~ ~

It's 2:00 p.m. before I'm ready to cast off. My old three-cylinder Yanmar coughs and belches thick diesel smoke, which drifts off northwest, away from Chuck's boat, thank goodness. It needs to warm up for a while before I can cast off. I look over and see Chuck has been polishing again. The dirty rags are folded in a neat pile atop his dock locker waiting to go home to be laundered. Mine, I know, are in the aft lazarette, dried, knotted, and caked with old polish. In uncharacteristic indolence, Chuck is now sitting in his cockpit with Mrs. Crunch, sharing a bottle of white wine. I pause to wonder if he ever actually sails, then walk over to say I'm off for a nice long cruise.

"Where are you headed?" he asks, and it seems he's genuinely interested. I begin to answer then remember Larry's advice to tell no one.

"North," I say. "Not sure yet. Just wanted to get away for a bit." Then, thinking I can plant a seed of misdirection, add, "Maybe Victoria."

Chuck nods. "Hope you get favorable winds."

I thank him, wave to his wife, and head back to my boat. Why am I playing Larry's silly game? Lawyers really do have a warped view of life.

The engine exhaust has dropped off considerably, but a thin gray pall of diesel smoke hangs in the air off the stern. I center the throttle/shift lever and the engine RPMs drop to 700, my idle speed. I listen for a minute to make sure it sounds smooth then hop off and gauge the wind. I'm stern into the dock so the southeasterly breeze is on the bow and pushing *Repose* away from the port side boat in our double slip. I let go the stern and spring lines and drop them into the cockpit. *Repose* remains steady in her position resting against her starboard fenders. I flip the bow line off its cleat, push off from the finger, and run back to hop into the cockpit, engage the gears, and give it a quick burst of throttle. *Repose* responds, and even though she drifts a bit to starboard, she clears the piling with room to spare.

As soon as I pass the Shilshole entrance and get into deep enough water, I spin the wheel and head back into the wind to ease the process of setting sails. I loosen the roller-furling control lines from their cleat, take a couple of turns around the main winch with the jib sheet, and pull out the headsail. It's a 150 genoa and will probably provide all the power I need in the fifteen-knot wind that's up right now. The headsail luffs and stutters in the stiff breeze so I fall off the wind, letting the sail fill and turning until I'm heading nearly due north. Then I crank the self-tailing winch, taking up slack in the jib sheet. The headsail steadies out and I can feel the power generated pulling me forward.

I shift the engine control to center, leave it idling in neutral, and check my speed through the water. I'm making just over six knots, heeled over at twelve degrees. That's plenty of speed, so I decide to leave the mainsail furled for now. I pull out the diesel cutoff, and the engine sputters to silence. All that's left is the sound of wind flowing over the curve of the genoa and the waves washing against the starboard side. I close my eyes and breathe in the salt air. This is my medium. I have known it since I was a child. I grew up on the east coast but came west when my father was transferred. I have never lived more than a bike ride away from the sea. I have probably breathed in more salt than most mid-westerners have eaten.

Pulled forward by the wind is not the mistake it seems. A sail is like the wing of an aircraft. It is shaped so the wind passing over it travels faster on the bowed side than it does on the flat side. This creates lift, which, through the vacuum that forms above a wing or in front of a bellied-out sail, makes the aircraft rise, or pulls the vessel forward on its course.

As I cruise along, I tick off the points I leave behind: Richmond Beach and Edmonds on the starboard side, Port Madison and Kingston far off to port. As I pass by Edmonds, I play tag with the two ferries, one passing forward of me and one to stern. The passengers wave a vigorous greeting.

Once past Edmonds, I turn to the northeast and set a waypoint into my NAV computer that will leave me a hundred yards offshore of the Clinton ferry dock on Whidbey Island. The computer uses GPS readings to keep me on course and adjust for current and the sideways drift from being pushed by the wind. As I pass by Possession Point on the far south end of Whidbey, I can see the bell buoy swaying side-to-side in the three-foot chop. Two huge bull sea lions on the rocking buoy sun themselves and bark at me when I glide by too closely.

As I approach the ferry terminal, I check my watch. It's nearly 6:00 p.m. I know the Clinton-Mukilteo schedule is every half hour on the hour and half-hour. I don't want to cross paths with the ferry, so I let out the jib sheet until my speed drops to four knots.

Promptly at 6:00 p.m., the ferry pulls away from the dock with its load of cars returning to the mainland. It is stuffed to the gunnels as usual, and the small outside deck is overflowing with riders enjoying the warm evening. By the time I come abreast the ferry dock, the departing boat is halfway across and its sister is approaching, but I'll be well past before it gets here. I sail close to the dock at six knots, having tightened the jib sheet again. Ferry dolphins and disappearing ducks part in front of me as I go by. Ferry dolphin is the local name for the double crested cormorant. They hang around on the pilings at ferry terminals then dive as the ferry pulls away, confusing the small fish with the powerful prop wash it leaves in its wake. The other sea birds, which I have dubbed disappearing ducks for their habit of diving so abruptly it seems as if they have vanished, are in reality classified as diving ducks. The most numerous are surf scoters, but I often see common and Barrow's goldeneyes, buffleheads, common and hooded mergansers, and horned grebes. Occasionally I see common and pacific loons, and though they are divers too, they are not ducks.

I continue on, turning due north again to pass by Langley. I'd like to stop at the decrepit marina there and walk up to town to pick up some groceries, but decide to follow Larry's advice slavishly and anchor offshore somewhere farther north. I check my charts and decide on Holmes Harbor for its proximity and good protection from southerly winds.

Rounding the point and passing Baby Island at the north end of the harbor about 8:00 p.m., *Repose* begins to beat into the wind, which has dropped to ten knots according to my instruments. I start the engine, shift to forward, and throttle up until I'm making six knots through the water. I set the autopilot to follow this course then release the jib sheet and start pulling in the roller-furler control line. Holding a bit of tension on the jib sheet allows me to furl the headsail neatly.

It takes another hour to get to the shallow, quiet end of the harbor. I check my NAV computer for the tides. High tide is at midnight, about plus ten feet. Right now it's plus seven. Overnight it will ebb to zero feet, so I need to allow for the drop and the five feet of keel under me. Don't want to wake up grounded. I drop anchor over near the southeast corner in twenty feet of water and set the anchor as firmly as I can in the silty bottom. It will hold well enough in the light breeze overnight, and there is no current here to worry about.

Desolation

A waxing moon floods the cockpit as I sit eating a dinner of canned chili and drinking a cold Alaskan Amber. Full moon is a week away. I think about the things I should be thankful for. First on the list is the presence of mind I had to turn on the boat fridge so my beer would be cold tonight; the rest of my thoughts center on my friends.

It hits me suddenly how lucky I am to have them. They've got my back in this divorce. They've been doing their best to keep me on an even keel and out of the grip of the depression I feel nibbling away at the edges of my consciousness. And now they're making sure Carole and her lawyer aren't pulling a fast one on me.

Would she really do that? I honestly can't imagine it. This is the woman I have loved as long as I can remember. How could she set all those years aside and think only of money?

I imagine that sounds naïve. Happens every day, Slick, anyone would tell me. But she was my best friend for more than twenty years. At least, I thought so. And now it all seems like a sham. No, worse, it seems like a betrayal. And it is, I guess. Carole did move right in with her lover of the past four years. And, I swear to God, I don't understand it. How could she make love to both of us at the same time? And I don't mean just going through the motions either. Carole had been more attentive and a better lover the past several months than she was when we were working together but arguing all the time. I honestly thought she had finally accepted me for who I am. And I thought she had decided to love that person and stop fighting to make me into a male version of herself. So, if all that's wrong, what has the good sex been about?

Okay, now I am depressed. I can't imagine starting over, dating again. Shit, will I become one of those men and women my age who come home from work and surf the internet-dating websites every night, sending out emails and waiting to see if anyone answers? The idea scares the hell out of me. But it scares me more to think I'll end up like Curly, prowling bars for one-night-stands and having monthly checkups for STDs. Maybe I'll become a hermit monk.

But really, does anyone know why a woman, or a man for that matter, sleeps with more than one lover at a time? We have rules about that sort of thing, so the transgressor must have a reason for not following them, yes?

What does Carole tell herself? Maybe she feels remorse for her affair with Tony and has been providing me with what I must admit may be mercy-fucks. If so, does she do that for my sake, or does she do it to assuage her own guilt?

Or maybe she has loved both of us enough to be unable to make a choice until now. Is that possible?

I'd like to think Folly is the root of Carole's motivation, not love. I want it to be all about the money. This is, of course, naïve. Money is just the measuring stick. Power is the real prize. Is that what drove Carole from my bed to his, from the self-proclaimed loser to the self-made man? Do I suppose she will realize her mistake and ask me for forgiveness and another chance? Frankly, I can't see it happening.

~ ~ ~

Holmes Harbor is quiet tonight. Perhaps it's quiet every night. There are other boats but they're all moored. I seem to be the only occupied vessel. A few cars pass on the road along the shore and I can hear others nearby, but besides these small sounds of civilization, I am alone.

The wind has dropped to a soft breath and the sky has filled with stars. Should be a good sleeping night, just a little rock and roll to lull me.

I'm about to go below and hop in my sleeping bag when Larry's cell phone rings. I grab it and push the talk button. Larry starts speaking before I say a word.

"Hope you're out floating around someplace remote," he says, then quickly adds, "Don't say where."

"Not a soul around for miles."

"Perfect. Thought I'd give you a jingle with an update. Want some good news?"

"Sure." Though I fear Larry's idea of good news and mine might be light-years apart.

"Oh, before I forget, what did you tell Brian?"

"Just told him I'd be gone for a week or so. He said no problem. This time of year we don't have much going on. I have one couple looking for a bargain in a Catalina 34 or 36. They've seen a few but haven't made any offers. Other than that, it's been quiet. If this were boat show season, it would be different. We need all hands then. Why do you ask?"

"Just want to make sure no one knows where you are right now, that's all."

"You're the boss. So, what's the good news?"

"I've got Curly out digging up the company dirt and he hasn't reported back yet, but I have the current partnership papers. I had Gretch threaten a subpoena, and Carole's lawyer sent them over right away. You owe her a retainer, by the way. Gretch doesn't do anything for free. Well, maybe a blow job if she's in the mood, but that's another story."

I laugh out loud in spite of myself. Larry says he's happy to amuse me then continues his report.

"The good news is you don't own one quarter of the company, you own one third."

Larry waits for the impact to settle in. "How?" is all the answer I can manage.

"Well, that's not entirely clear. As you might expect, Carole's lawyer only supplied the minimum documents necessary to comply with Gretch's request. But I'm guessing Carole drove a hard bargain when they talked merger. Or maybe there was some sort of real estate holdings buy-in she didn't tell you about. We'll get to the bottom of it. So, any questions?"

I think for a minute then ask, "What does Curly have to do with this?"

"You're kidding, right?"

"No."

"Where do you think Curly's money comes from? His family has been involved in commercial real estate in Seattle forever. Made a ton of money. Not always on the up and up either. Curly has connections even I don't want to know about. I've got him looking into Tony's past, present, and future. Might take a while, but he'll come through for us, rest assured."

"Is all this digging really necessary? Why not just get her lawyer to estimate my third and let it go at that?"

"Two reasons. First, they gave up this information too easily. They made us threaten a subpoena, but that's all they did. And they did it quickly. I would have drug it out. There's some timing issue involved. No idea what, but my guess is the longer we play this fish, the more nervous they'll become. I'm now thinking you'll need to be incommunicado for at least a month."

I sigh loud enough for Larry to pause. "Brian is not going to like that. But maybe a sailing vacation will be good for me. Wish I'd brought more clothes though. What's the other reason?"

"It's something Curly said. I told you he hasn't reported back yet, but he did call me after a quick pass through his contacts. I could tell he was nerved up."

Then Larry puts on his best Curly voice: "Ever see a shadow, but you don't know where the light's comin' from so you can't figure out what's makin' it? That's what we got here, a big fuckin' shadow."

~ ~ ~

The morning dawns bright and still, not a ripple in the harbor. A few gulls have circled my boat, sensing food and the possibility of a handout. Overnight, one of them has visited the cockpit and left his calling card. I flip the switch on my saltwater wash-down pump and sluice away the glaucous mess. It disappears down the scuppers in the cockpit deck and leaves a milky tinge in the water aft.

I put the teapot on to boil water for making coffee and check my NAV computer to decide whether Deception Pass at slack tide or passing through the Swinomish Channel will be the better course. My goal is to be someplace in the San Juan Islands tonight.

My NAV computer indicates the current through Deception Pass will be ebbing at 2.1 knots at 6:00 p.m. If I time it right, I can ride out with the ebb tide then turn north just in time to catch the beginning of flood and get a nice push toward Thatcher Pass at the entrance to the San Juans. I should make Spencer Spit Marine Park just inside Frost Island and catch a mooring buoy before dark. Canned dinner again I'm afraid. I'll pick up supplies tomorrow.

I've got about thirty miles to put behind me to get to the pass, so that's only five hours of motoring. I think I can get some sailing in if the winds come up later this morning. If I get to the pass early, I can pick up a mooring buoy behind Hope Island and wait until the current slows.

~ ~ ~

As I cruise north at low RPMs, I think back to my night with Diana. I understand she was doing Doc a favor, and while I'm not at all pleased at being used, I can't really complain either.

"No attachments," she said. Maybe that's what I need for now. I'm certainly in no position to make any sort of commitment, long-term or otherwise. Still, I can't see myself following Larry and Curly's lead. No barhopping, I decide. Not sure where that leaves me. Nowhere, I guess. Maybe internet dating is really all that's left if the bar scene doesn't appeal. But those women are looking for committed relationships, not an occasional date, aren't they?

My quandary goes by with the hours and I arrive at Deception Pass well in advance of slack tide. It's still ebbing strongly at nearly four knots. Too dangerous to plow through, so I wait it out at Hope Island, then an hour before slack, I head into the pass at 2400 RPM. The bridge towers 180 feet above me as I run beneath. The whirlpools in the narrows turn *Repose* this way and that, but she responds well to the helm and clears the pass at 6:30 p.m. As I round Rosario Head, I set a course for Thatcher, eight miles away.

Just before Thatcher Pass I decide to check for an open mooring buoy on the west side of James Island. It's a protected anchorage and it's typically full by this time in the evening, but today there's an open spot at the dock. I luck out and get to it just ahead of another boat with the same idea. First come, first served here. I tie up and walk down the dock to register. Since I have this year's Marine Parks sticker, there's no extra charge. After I sign the log, I go for a stroll around the island paths then return to *Repose* and talk to my neighbors for a while. They are just back from their first trip up the BC coast and speak enthusiastically about Desolation Sound. I've been there before and we exchange notes. I tell them about a cool freshwater skinny-dipping lake accessed from Grace Harbor, and they seem sorry to have missed it, but they intend to go back next year so they'll check it out then.

Onboard again, I settle in with a beer to watch the sunset. My plan tomorrow is to head for Roche Harbor to top off my diesel and water tanks and pick up supplies. It will take about four hours to motor there, an hour or two to get refueled and provisioned, and another hour or so of cruising to tomorrow's anchorage in Stuart Island Marine Park. That's where I'll hang out for a while until I hear back from Larry. I know I'll be within cell phone range there, but if I cross into Canada, I'm not so sure. Besides, I don't know if he wants me that far away.

~ ~ ~

The next day I motor in about 3:00 p.m., drop anchor in my favorite gunkhole tucked up against Satellite Island inside Prevost Harbor, bait and toss a crab trap off my bow, and inflate my kayak. Then I go for a paddle around the harbor. I count an even dozen boats on this side of Stuart and, after hiking over the top, find another six afloat in Reid Harbor. A bit crowded, but nothing compared to Sucia Island, where you might find dozens of boats on any fine summer weekend.

When I've had enough exercise, I head back to *Repose* and check my crab trap. I find a collection of four Dungeness and two red rock crabs, along with a sunflower starfish the size of full-wheel hubcap. They go up to three feet in diameter and twenty-four arms, but this one has only eighteen. It's brilliant orange, slimy, and truly gross. I toss back the rock crabs and sun star then check the Dungeness for size and sex. Can't keep females and one of the males is only five inches across the carapace, so those go back in the water. The other male is a good seven inches and will make a tasty dinner. Just need a little melted butter and a couple of bottles of pale ale.

After dinner, I turn on my FM radio and tune in the BBC. I like getting my news from a non-US perspective. Victoria is just a handful of miles away, so the signal comes in clear. Later, I put on some music and watch the sun go down. I sit thinking about the future and find I'm really not ready for it. I long for the past, or what I thought was the past, the life I had with Carole. Over the last three days I've done a lot of reminiscing, and what I've learned is I'm still in love with her. I keep trying not to be, trying to get angry enough to go for the gold, but can't bring myself to do it. I honestly don't care about the money.

What happened? Is it just about the business? I suppose Carole began, at some point, to see me as a traitor, since Folly was anything but folly to her. While I did nothing to undermine her efforts, I also did nothing to support them. Does she see this as betrayal? Why couldn't we each just let the other be, instead of what we each wanted the other to be? Too many questions without answers, but I find that asking them is beginning to resolve into something like understanding and even a touch of acceptance, and acceptance is where I need to get. I know I have to let her go, but that's much easier to tell myself than it is to accomplish.

Accomplish. To succeed or not to succeed. Also, to come to the end. But does that ever happen? Do we ever succeed in ending a relationship? I'm inclined to think not, but I'm doing my best, I believe, and perhaps I will reach some sort of internal equanimity after all.

~ ~ ~

A cool, dewy night settles around me while I sit remembering fonder times with Carole. The harbor is limned dimly by the faint glow from pale-yellow masthead lamps and by the reds and greens of running lights on returning dinghies, and I'm immersed in the sounds of rigging tinkling and ripples slapping gently on my hull in the near-calm water. Along the far shore, campfires burn and shadowy figures move, muffled voices reaching out toward me but never quite arriving. I have been casting back in memory to resurrect a time when Carole and I were happy together, a time before the fall, seeking to put a date on it and a face. As I do, I realize the seeds of our destruction were there from the beginning, my laissez-faire approach to life juxtaposed with Carole's intensity and drive. But I remember the camaraderie as well. I have lost my best friend and I know it.

I sigh deeply then rise to go below to read for a while. As I pick up Larry's phone, it rings. Startled, I nearly drop it overboard. I answer on the third ring, "It's your nickel."

"Hey, you still surrounded by *terra incognito*?"

"What? No, 'hello, Deke'?" I leave a few moments of silence then continue, "Just a few other boats. I'm keeping to myself, though not on purpose."

"Good, good, but not necessary anymore. In fact, we want you to be traceable."

I'm sure Larry can hear my weary tone as I ask, "Okay, why?"

"Well, that will take a while to explain. You anywhere near Canada?"

"It's 1.8 miles from where I stand, but I'm not planning on changing citizenship."

He laughs, makes a bad joke about our neighbors to the north, then continues, "Head across the border tomorrow and clear through customs. Keep your clearance number. That will provide us with a record if we need to prove later we couldn't get in touch."

"That actually makes sense for a change. But why now?"

"Gretch. She has a good relationship with judges and particularly with the Seattle judge handling your divorce case. The judge trusts what Gretch tells him. She has no problem with shading the truth or omitting facts, but she has no intention of lying. Doubt she'd do it even to keep me out of jail, and there have been a few close calls. I have no such compunction, and my reputation with judges went out the window years ago."

"All right. The Gulf Islands are just across the border or I can continue up the Strait of Georgia. Where should I go?"

"Doesn't matter. Just don't tell me where you'll be. Farther north sounds good, though, so when we finally *find you*, it will take you a while to return. Can you go someplace it will take a week or so to get back from?"

"Sure. That will give me a nice long cruise. Don't think your phone will work though."

"Actually, it would, but you can deep six it tomorrow. Literally. We won't be talking again. I want you to call Gretch's office on your satellite rig once you get where you're going but not sooner than two weeks from today."

"I suppose you have a reason for the delay, yes?"

"Absolutely. Here's the update. Still no definitive word from Curly, but he's getting closer. He says he now knows what he's looking for, just not how much. But he's not giving any hints, and Gretch needs you to buy her some time until Curly has the goods. Make sense so far?"

"Sure."

"Okay, next item. The timing thing is becoming a bigger point of contention. Carole's lawyer has been pushing Gretch to produce her client, and Gretch has been pushing him to provide all the documentation on the company assets. Yesterday, he did just that. Gretch figured on several boxes of files in no particular order, but what she got instead was a well-organized set of detailed records and a thorough summary. The good news is the settlement went up as well. They've added $1 million to their previous offer."

"What could possibly be the bad news?" I ask, interrupting him.

"They're still hiding something. And it's probably something big."

"How many times do I have to say I don't care about the money? What difference does it make?"

"Look, you don't know what difference it makes. Why not find out first? And Carole has been hiding all this from you. Doesn't that piss you off?"

"I suppose, but she's protecting her baby. This stupid company is her child. And I'm the absent father. In a way, I left her first. And she knows I don't care about it, so she's angry and she's protective. I really can't blame her."

"Okay, okay, I get it, but I'm not your lawyer, just your friend. Do this to humor me, all right? Take the next two weeks to think it through. Then call Gretch. Her plan is to catch a seaplane up to wherever you are and agree on a counteroffer. If you want to accept what's already been offered, you can do that. But talk to Gretch first, face to face. No point in hiring a lawyer if you won't listen to her advice."

I can hear the exasperation in Larry's voice and have to admit I'm being pigheaded about this, so I acquiesce. "Look, I'm sorry. I know you're all trying to help. I'll do what you say. I'll think about it and I'll wait to talk to Gretch first. Thanks."

"No charge, Deke. Call Gretch in two weeks. And relax, for Christ's sakes. Enjoy the cruise."

Turning the Table

Up early next morning to greet the dawn with a cup of coffee. I wipe down the cockpit, which has become heavily dew-laden overnight, and wait for the sun to climb higher. The harbor is quiet, though a few of the campers on shore are already up and getting cook-fires going. Mist still clings to the water but has lifted up to cover the island in a close-fitting shroud. It will take the sun a while to burn this off. Having checked my NAV computer last night, I know I need to make Gabriola Passage before 4:00 p.m. in order to catch slack tide. Otherwise I'll have to wait overnight in Pirate's Cove or blast through the passage as it ebbs at upwards of four knots. I'm looking forward to a good restaurant meal in Silva Bay on the far side of the passage so decide to get moving.

By 7:30 a.m. I'm underway, crossing the four miles or so of open water to the Canadian customs dock in Bedwell Harbor on South Pender Island. I pull up to the dock and tie off quickly. At the head of the ramp I find the customs office closed and a sign telling me to pick up one of the phones attached to the outside wall. A customs agent answers, gives me a clearance number then asks whether I have any booze, drugs, or guns. Why would anyone say yes? I tell her I just have a six-pack of beer.

"That's fine. Any fruit or vegetables?"

I think for a minute. "Just about everything is in cans. I do have some peaches and plums, though."

"You have to dispose of those in the dust bins there."

"You're kidding," I say then realize customs agents do not kid about anything so continue, "Okay, but why?"

"It's the pits," I hear her respond and realize she does have a sense of humor. "You can keep the fruit part, but the pits have to be properly disposed of."

"Thanks, will do." I dutifully cut up fruit for breakfast then toss the pits in the receptacles provided.

I shove off again and head back the way I came at first then turn east to round South Pender Island and head northwest up Plumper Sound. By 10:00 a.m. I'm passing through Navy Channel between North Pender and Mayne Islands. As I enter the narrowed channel, I see my speed pick up by a half knot. I'm getting a little ride on the current. Then off to starboard I see a small pod of black and white Dall's porpoises break off from feeding and angle toward me. They cross the distance between us in seconds and pick up my bow wave. I set the autopilot and walk forward to watch. There are four, no, five pushing through the water and leaping clear now and then. One hangs right on the bow, and I can tell he is surfing, expending only enough energy to stay within two feet. *Repose* is a carnival ride for porpoises. They stay with me until I clear the channel then break off again and return to feeding. I wave goodbye.

Motoring northwest in the Trincomali Channel, I pass Prevost and Saltspring Islands to port and Galiano Island to starboard. Two hours later it's Wallace, the

Secretaries, and Reid to port and Valdes to starboard. Then I enter Pylades Channel and pass by Ruxton and the De Courcy Group to port and make my approach to Gabriola Passage. Unfortunately, I'm a bit early, maybe ninety minutes before slack, so I float around waiting for the current to ease. At 2:30 p.m. I power through the passage, picking up three knots of push from the flood current. It's a bit squirrelly at the narrows and *Repose* heels over hard once, but I make it through just fine and head for Silva Bay and a fine dinner of locally caught king salmon.

I wake next morning to strong winds and rain. I flip on my VHF radio and tune in the weather channel. There are small craft warnings up for the Strait of Georgia and winds are expected to rise to gale force later, so I decide to stay another day right where I am. I have no interest in slogging across the strait in seven-foot seas. I read most of the day then, once the rain tapers off, go out for dinner and polish off a bottle of red wine with my steak.

By the time I head back to *Repose,* the rain has picked up again and I get soaked through. I'm pissed off, maudlin, and a little depressed. Probably just the wine and weather but that realization does nothing to improve my mood. As I sit staring at the bulkhead and feeling sorry for myself, I decide to call Carole. At least I can listen to her sweet voice on the answering machine. I flip the switch for my satellite phone and wait until it establishes its link then dial her number. Carole picks up on the third ring.

"Where are you?" she asks.

Speaking in person shakes me and it takes some time to respond. A few answers like, "What the fuck do you care," "None of your fucking business," and "What, no: hi Andrew, it's been a long time," flow through my mind, and before I answer, she continues.

"Look, I'm sorry. I should have called you sooner. I…I just thought you wouldn't want to talk to me."

I still don't say anything, but this time it's on purpose. I want to see what she'll try next.

"Andrew, say something. Are you okay?" she says softly with just a hint of endearing Aussie twang.

"I'm all right. A little drunk, maybe. And a little lonely." I pause and silence fills the space between us. "Are you okay?" I ask, and really mean it. Carole's soft voice has taken me back years to a happier place.

"I'm just fine, Andrew. I'm sorry for you and I'm sorry for the timing, but I need to get on with my life. You need to get on with yours too."

I can hear the steely edge creep back into her voice and the Aussie lilt disappear. I remain silent. I want to hear that softer, long-ago voice again and she does not disappoint.

"I guess we need to talk this out, don't we?" she asks, and, as I close my eyes, the young blonde Aussie girl comes back to me. I can see her sweet smile and her sunlit golden hair tossed by summer breeze throwing loose strands across her cheeks. The effect is overwhelming. I feel the tears fill my eyes and cascade over. I want to hold her.

"I just want you back," I say, and as soon as the words leave my mouth, I reach out my hands to take them away. I have broken the spell.

"That's not going to happen."

Into the long silence that follows I answer, "I know." It is the last thing I say to her as I break the connection. I sit staring at the handset for a long time before I rise to replace it and turn off the phone.

~ ~ ~

By noon the next day the rain is long gone and the wind has softened a bit. The forecast is for fair weather and moderate seas, and I'm tired of sitting still so I head out of the bay. There's a southwesterly blow still gusting at over twenty-five knots on occasion, so I decide to pull out the mainsail to the first reef point and run it and the smaller staysail for the twenty-four mile crossing to Smuggler Cove Marine Park.

The seas are running five to six feet with wind-blown salt spray, and by the time I reach the Merry Island Light on the east side of the strait and start the engine, *Repose* is coated with salt. I release the halyard for the self-furling mainsail, maintaining a bit of tension, and switch on the electric furler. The mainsail winds into the boom. The wind prevents it from winding smoothly, but I can fix that on the next calm day. The same proves true for the furling staysail. I think what Capt. Crunch's reaction would be and can only imagine his disdain. It brings a smile to my face.

I enter the narrow opening to Smugglers Cove and wend my way back to anchor in ten feet of water. Inside the cove the wind is nearly calm, and by evening it drops to a whisper and the sun appears just long enough for a kiss goodbye before it sets for the night. It's canned chili for dinner again and a few bottles of Sierra Nevada to wash it down. I'm not much of a cook. Before dinner I hose down the decks and cockpit and even give *Repose* a thorough brushing to scrub away the salt rime. One last sluice with fresh water and she's as good as new, or good enough anyway.

Maybe that's my problem, I think. I'm always looking for good enough. I'm sure Carole would agree. Or maybe she'd think I wasn't even up to that standard. What a pitiful performance last night. I should never have called her. I doubt she knows I was calling from *Repose*, though I'm not at all sure what sort of caller ID would register at her end of the connection. What did I expect from her anyway? Contrition? Change of heart? Understanding? No, none of those. I just wanted to hear her voice.

I guess it's really over; there is no Carole and Andrew anymore. And there never was a Carole and Deke. Maybe that's the way I should think about it. I need to leave Andrew and Carole to a past that once existed but now is gone. I have to concentrate on Deke, the slightly clueless, singles scene neophyte. He's already had one great night with a huntress, and if he let's go a bit, he'll probably learn to like himself. Nice theory. One thing is certain; I don't have anything to lose in trying.

I had a rough crossing today and have a long day tomorrow, so I go below early. I want to be tucked into Prideaux Haven in Desolation Sound tomorrow night. That's as far as I'm going. From there, I can explore the small bays and islets and enjoy the peace and quiet. But before I turn in, Larry's phone rings. I forgot to throw it overboard. I stand looking at it and wondering if I should answer. Bet Carole has told her lawyer we spoke and that's set up a firestorm.

"Don't be pissed at me," I say as I pick up.

"I'm not. But you are a moron. Fortunately, you're a lucky moron."

"I know it was stupid. I just needed to hear her voice. I never expected Carole to answer the phone."

"Like I said, you're a moron. You triggered an avalanche. Gretch had to dance fast in court. You really owe her. But the real news is Tony reacted too. He made some calls and that got back to Curly's contacts. Are you sitting down? Tony's been stalling payments of about $10 million in accumulated commissions from brokering a series of major commercial real estate purchases for a big Southern California private equity consortium. They're selling out down south while the prices are sky-high and investing in the Seattle market. Seems they think the LA real estate bubble is about to burst and Seattle is recession-proof."

There is silence on my end. Ten million?

"So, what do you think about your precious Carole now?"

I remain silent. What do I think? This is deception to a degree I would have never thought possible. Whether or not I deserve part of Tony's commission is beside the point. The two of them have been carefully plotting to make sure I don't get it. Then it dawns on me. Carole doesn't love me. She couldn't and do this. What I still feel is not what she feels. Larry's right; I really am a moron.

"That sneaky bitch," I say to myself but out loud.

"That's the spirit, Deke. Want to get even?"

"And then some," I answer and mean every word. "Should I start back tomorrow?"

"Nope. Gretch wants them to think they're going to get away with it. Give her office a call tomorrow and tell her where you are. She'll catch a plane the next day."

"Got it. I'll be—"

"Stop, don't tell me. Tell Gretch tomorrow. And, by the way, toss the phone overboard this time. Can you be somewhere tomorrow night Gretch can fly to?"

"Sure. I've seen float planes land nearby before. I can pick her up in my kayak."

I hear Larry start laughing on the other end. "Boy, would I love to be there to see it. So long, Deacon Blues."

~ ~ ~

I weigh anchor at 6:00 a.m. and head north, tossing Larry's phone overboard in the 300-meter trench off Texada Island. I have sixty miles to put behind me before I sleep tonight; that's ten hours of motoring since there's no wind expected today. I enter waypoints into my NAV computer at the turns all the way to Scobell Island, which guards the entrance to Prideaux Haven. The autopilot will take me there without any further effort on my part unless I cross paths with another boat. Once I engage the autopilot, I descend the companionway stairs, power up the satellite phone, and call Gretch's office. I leave my precise location for tonight with her assistant and give her my phone number, asking her to relay the expected arrival time for Gretch's flight.

As I head up the Malaspina Strait between the mainland and Texada, I go over my conversation with Larry again. Am I really finished with Carole now? Yes, I think I am. When I started this cruise, I recognized the irony of my journey through Deception Pass on the way to Desolation Sound. I thought the deception to be as minor as the deception for which the

Pass is named, a simple wrong turn that led Captain Vancouver nowhere he wanted to go. And I expected to find the same sort of desolation he found farther north, but I thought it might be the kind of absence of life that would help me to start over.

But now the presaged desolation has evaporated, replaced by a deeper understanding of how little I have come to mean to Carole. Once, it was otherwise, but time and circumstance have eroded away whatever love we shared. I sense in myself a milder regret at the loss, and I find I am really not angry with her, just sad. Nevertheless, all vestiges of sympathetic feeling for Carole and Folly have been forever banished. I will demand my full, legal share, my pound of flesh.

~ ~ ~

At 4:00 p.m. I drop my speed to three knots as I turn into the narrow fairway between Scobell and Eveleigh Islands. There are rock ledges reaching out from each shore. I'm careful to watch my depth gauge. Once inside and back in deeper water, I turn to port. There's a two-boat gunkhole I prefer nestled between Copplestone and the larger of the William Islands. I find only one boat there so I proceed to drop anchor on the north side, set it in deep, and watch to see if I have enough swinging room. My neighbor, a forty-five-foot Bayliner, is hogging the center, hoping, I suppose, to have the gunkhole to himself, so I inflate my kayak again and run a shore tie to Big William Island, wrap it around the trunk of a large madrone, then lead it back to *Repose*. I haul in enough line to keep me clear of the Bayliner and well inside of it. I will have an unobstructed view of the Paige Islets and the distant craggy peaks that encompass Desolation Sound like an embrace.

I've just settled in with a beer when my phone rings. Gretch's assistant tells me to meet the plane just outside Prideaux Haven tomorrow at 1:00 p.m. I tell her there's a small islet out there where I can wait. Have the pilot look for me.

Next morning, I paddle out the half mile, pull my kayak up on the beach, and wait in the warm sun for Gretch to arrive. Just before 1:00 p.m. I hear the Beaver approaching. The engine roar is distinctive. The pilot makes a slow circle and lands into the gentle breeze that's blowing. He sees me and taxis over to lie 100 feet offshore of the islet. As I approach the starboard side of the plane, a woman clambers out of the cockpit. She's the only passenger. When I get within thirty feet, I stop paddling. The woman I'm looking at is Diana. She holds my gaze for a moment then shrugs her shoulders and waves for me to come alongside. She drops her duffle into the kayak amidships, gives me an unreadable look, then skillfully shifts off the pontoon and into the forward kayak seat. She takes the extra paddle, and we return to *Repose* in silence.

I maneuver alongside the boat so the swim ladder is within Diana's reach, and she climbs aboard. Then I pass up her duffle and follow, tying the kayak to the stern rail once I'm back in the cockpit.

"Gretch," Diana says, extending her hand.

"Think I like you better as a lover than a lawyer," I reply but shake her proffered hand. I consider asking for some explanation but find I don't need one. It's entirely obvious what's happened. Gretch/Diana was just caught up in it. Not really her fault; a small failure in judgment, perhaps, but nothing more. I imagine this is all Doc's doing, and, as I peel back the layers, I realize he has orchestrated several things into one. First, he got me laid. No complaint there. Second, he set up Larry in the awkward position of having to know one of Gretch's lovers. Third, he set up Gretch to sleep with someone who could report back intimate details, which I have unwittingly done. Fourth, he has maneuvered Gretch into the untenable position of representing her lover in court. And fifth, he has set up this reunion of sorts, far from the madding crowd, in hopes something interesting will come of it.

As I ponder all this, Gretch watches me.

"I know this is uncomfortable for you. Are you as uncomfortable as I am?"

"I don't know. Just how uncomfortable are you?" I answer with the same deadpan expression I have carried for the past half-hour.

"You're not, are you?" She stands, head tilted to one side, considering what I may or may not be thinking. "You don't seem angry or even all that surprised. Where are you right now?"

Without hesitation, I cross the two steps separating us and take her in my arms. Our eyes meet in one last fleeting question then lips close together, first passionately then softening, melting together. When I pull away, her eyes are still closed. "Does that answer your question?" My deadpan expression is back in place.

Gretch gives me a weary look and shakes her head. "What have we done? I am so sorry this happened."

"It's not your fault. This is Doc's doing, and you know it, don't you?"

She nods and stares at her feet. When she looks back up, I'm smiling. It's a sad, defeated smile, but it's a smile nonetheless, a smile that tells her this will be all right, that we can play our multiple roles, and maybe, just maybe, we can be friends.

Gretch rises and comes over to settle onto my lap. We hold each other like this and rock with the boat, eyes on the distant horizon.

After a few minutes, I suggest a cold beer and Gretch eagerly agrees. Nothing like booze to make the world seem less troublesome. We sit opposite each other in the cockpit, and at some point she asks, "Do you still want me to represent you?"

"Sure. No point changing horses midstream. Besides, it would spoil Doc's fun."

Gretch shoots me an appraising look and, having decided I'm not joking, continues, "You're serious, aren't you? You'd give that diabolical dwarf the satisfaction he certainly doesn't deserve?"

"Well, it seems to me we might turn the tables on him. Just in good, clean fun, of course. What do you think? All's fair in love and war?"

Diana reaches across to shake my hand, and now it is she who is wearing the diabolical smile. The hunter and the prey have just switched places.

~ ~ ~

After a makeshift dinner of chicken-and-vegetable curry made by Gretch from my meager supplies (I had omitted telling the customs agent about the potatoes and onions), we discuss the settlement. Gretch explains her plan to confront Carole's lawyer with Curly's now-documented information. She tells me what she thinks

I'd get if we fight, and I decide to settle for two thirds so a fight won't be necessary. She'll ask for my boat, the condo with no mortgage, and $5 million dollars, take it or leave it. Carole's lawyer will know she could ask for more. He'll take the deal.

Then we get to the important discussion. What do we do about Doc? It's tricky because neither of us wants to hurt Larry, though we both agree he went along with the ruse so he's not really an innocent. We'd like to think Doc will end up chastened but we both know better. Still, it's worth a shot. I suggest we let Larry in on the plot and see what he says, but Gretch says it won't work. "You'd think a criminal lawyer could keep a straight face. But he'll blow it."

The obvious ploy would be to pretend Doc's meddling has thrown us together romantically, turning a one-night-stand into a long-term affair, but we don't think Doc will buy it. Then I remember his face when I told him Diana had spent most of the night with me. I relay this information to Gretch and her eyes light up.

"That's right, I never do."

"Just what Doc told me. So, what made you change your mind?"

Gretch pauses for a moment then begins slowly, "Well, I'm not sure really. It felt good for a change. I guess I was punishing Larry for his part in it. And I guess I thought you deserved more since we were deceiving you."

Then she stops again and seems to be considering whether or not to continue.

"I guess I did it for myself too. I have always slept alone. But I think I like the feeling of pretending to be in a real relationship."

I'm not sure what to say to her convoluted phrasing and decide to set aside further questions. Maybe Doc will buy this story after all. I ask Gretch what she thinks, and I'm rewarded with the same lascivious look she used a week ago. Then, unable to sustain it, she breaks up in laughter, reaches her hand across again, and we shake on it.

The next few hours are spent reviewing possibilities, scenarios, and potential pitfalls. Gretch has a first-class intellect and can see several moves ahead like a champion chess player. It's very late when we call it a night. An almost-full moon has risen and shines brightly through the companionway, washing the cabin in a pale glow, and limning the forward v-berth through the open hatch above. There is one awkward moment when I walk forward then turn to see Gretch hesitating. She knows there is a second stateroom aft. I smile and motion for her to follow, and she does, an incongruously shy expression on her face. We climb in together and kiss goodnight. Then she turns over and presses into me to spoon. The sensation is both endearing and delicious.

Teddies

The alarm rings at 9:00 a.m. I surface groggily to mash the snooze button. I've been back three days and still haven't adjusted to sleeping in a bed that doesn't rock and roll. I shift onto my stomach and clamp the pillow over my head to delete the sun pouring through the window. Saturday. The day of reckoning I'm not at all prepared for. First there's the afternoon sail with Gretch. Then there's the evening debauch at Teddies with the boys. The former confuses me with its implications, the latter outright scares me to death. But the truth is I have no one to blame but myself. It was my offer a week ago that set up the date today with Gretch, though it's Gretch who has called it "a date." And it was my spineless caving in to Doc's cajoling that led me to agree to attend Teddies second-Saturday-of-the-month festivities tonight.

I did manage to plant some seeds in Doc's fertile mind regarding Gretch and me. I chuckle remembering his reaction when he dropped by unexpected the day after I got back. First, I told him Gretch and I were going off sailing together on Saturday. That registered surprise. Then I told him we had shared a v-berth in the great Canadian wilds, emphasis on the wild part. The emotions playing across his face were priceless. I could almost see his thoughts, "What the fuck have I started?"

But I clinched it with my sincere, "Thanks, Doc. I owe you," without ever letting facial cues hint at my underlying amusement. It was easier than I thought. I kept Doc's deceptions central and responded in kind. I suppose I'm testing his divided allegiance between Larry and me, and maybe I'm taking advantage of his unquestioning trust, but what the hell, he deserves it.

What I think about Gretch is more complicated. When I asked if she wanted to go for a sail when I made it back to Seattle, she replied, "Just a sail?"

I immediately answered, "Just a sail," and threw my arms up in the air to indicate hands-off. Then she registered an impish grin, and said, "It's a date."

But as I continue to read her expression now, I can see more there. More what, though? Is Gretch looking for something from me? And if so, is it what I really want? Or is she gauging me to make sure a sail with her is all I'm after? My stomach is knotted in anticipation. Okay, one thing at a time. Shower then breakfast at the Blue Star then off for a friendly day sail, nothing more. I'll worry about Teddies later.

~ ~ ~

I arrive at Shilshole to find Gretch already waiting at the boat. It's likely some guy has let her through the gate. I doubt any could resist those eyes when she turns them on. Works every time for me. The way Gretch is lounging speaks of ownership, the I-belong-here overshadowing a sheepish expression.

"Making yourself at home, I see. Who let you in?"

Gretch points over at Capt. Crunch then mimes a winsome beseeching posture that makes her look like a little girl begging for a cookie. Some women can get away with murder. Chuck smiles, shrugs his shoulders, and points out the obvious, "Figured you wouldn't complain."

I climb into the cockpit and Gretch rises to kiss me, as much for Chuck's benefit as mine, I think. The kiss is long and searching, not passionate but possessive, the way a long-time lover kisses. When Gretch pulls back, her smile is gone. "So much for just a sail," she says sadly. Then, reading the confusion on my face, adds, "We need to talk, but right now I just want to go sailing."

As we motor away from Shilshole, Gretch is at the wheel. The wind is fairly steady out of the southwest at seventeen knots. I raise the main, tighten it a bit, adjust the boom vang and topping lift to about where I think they should be, then prepare to pull out the staysail. With this much wind, it's all we'll need. But Gretch is having none of this easy day sail idea.

"Pull out the genoa, all the way. Let's see if we can bury the rail."

Repose has a full keel and doesn't heel over readily. I'm not sure it's even possible. But if that's what the skipper wants, that's what she'll get. I pull out both the genoa and the staysail then take a firm seat, my back to the breeze, while Gretch turns the wheel to fall off the wind and *Repose* heels hard to starboard, about eighteen degrees. The rail, as I expected, refuses to dip below the waterline but Gretch is standing, left foot on the deck, right foot on the starboard combing and grinning from ear to ear. Her hair flies wildly.

We cross the Sound at seven–and-a-half knots then prepare to come about. I slacken the staysail a little so it will travel from one side to the other without any aid then remove the genoa sheet from the self-tailing portion of the starboard primary winch. When she sees I'm ready, Gretch spins the wheel, and *Repose* drives through the turn. She spins the wheel back at exactly the right moment. The sails snap firmly across from starboard to port as I release the starboard sheet, and having taken three turns around the portside winch, I pull it in hand-over-hand then crank it the rest of the way. Our speed never drops below seven knots.

"Nicely done, skipper," I say. Gretch's smile says she agrees.

We spend the next two hours beating into the wind, tacking back and forth, and occasionally manage to bury the bow into the wind-driven three-foot chop. Each time we do, a wall of water cascades over the deck and into the cockpit, soaking us both through and through. We make Blake Island Marine Park in the early afternoon. We drop the sails and pick up a mooring buoy to rest and share the picnic lunch Gretch has brought along. But first we go below to put on dry clothes. To my surprise, Gretch goes forward to change, closing the cabin door behind her for privacy.

Back in the cockpit, we eat a leisurely lunch and bask in the sun. I keep expecting Gretch to pick up our earlier conversation, but she waits until we've finished eating.

"Okay, here's the deal," she begins. "You and I could be occasional lovers, or we could be close friends...or I could get a divorce and marry you."

I'm stunned into silence by her terse summation.

"Just kidding about getting married. Fact is I like my life the way it is. You, on the other hand, have no idea what your new life will be. Not yet anyway."

Gretch pauses and searches my face for some reaction, but I'm not ready to respond so she continues, "Listen, Andrew, you are exactly what most women want: a great-looking, sensitive guy who likes strong-willed women. I'll admit to finding this seductive as well. I could let myself fall for you, but that would only make three people miserable. And I need more freedom than you could ever allow. You're a one-woman man."

Gretch stops there and lets this sink in. I go back over what she's said and can't find a flaw in her logic. Finally, I ask, "Strong-willed?"

"Yep. You want equal or better. I know your type. You're not the kind of guy who wants a submissive woman either in the living room or the bedroom. You love that I can sail *Repose* every bit as well as you can. You love that I seduced you instead of the other way around. And you love that it was even better for you because you knew the whole thing was a setup."

I smile ruefully and nod. She's right. Everything Gretch has offered sounds just right. I still don't have anything to say so she continues, "Okay, here's something you won't like, but I need to say it anyway. For you, I'm a brunette version of Carole. A replacement. I'm just as driven and career-oriented as she is and just as interested in exercising power in a male-dominated profession. Face it, Andrew, I'm your rebound fuck."

"That's not fair," I answer immediately. "And it's not true either. I didn't choose you. You chose me, sort of. I just went along for the ride. Are you as driven as Carole? Sure, or probably anyway. Am I attracted to your self-assurance? I never thought of it that way but I guess I am. I definitely like the bedroom aggressiveness. Don't all guys?"

"Oh, no. A little goes a long way. Most guys like sexy, playful aggressiveness. But the emphasis is on the play part. You like it too. Actual aggressiveness is another thing. Most guys will not submit. You love it. I think that's what I'll miss most."

"So, it's over? Just like that?"

"Look, Andrew, you need to go off with the boys and get it out of your system before you try to find another relationship. Carole will not go away as easily as the legal case. That's a whole different sort of settlement. I know. I've seen it hundreds of times. Most of my clients are women, but the truth is for all the hype about men from Mars and women from Venus, we are all from the same planet. The experts always say it takes time to get over a loss. In my opinion, that's a crock of shit. It does take time, but you don't get over someone you've truly loved, you get beyond. There's a difference and that difference is not just a small matter of semantics. It's a matter of how you look back. Do the memories just piss you off and make them easier to dismiss, or do they continue to cling to you, the bad fading and the good seeming larger than they ever were. The former describes Curly. The latter applies to you. I'm afraid it's going to take a long time, Andrew. Let it."

By this time I've hung my head and am staring at the teak deck, which could use some oil. I let a minute pass then ask, "And us?"

Gretch reaches across the cockpit and lifts my chin. She fixes me with a firm older-sisterly look and answers, "I said you were a one-woman man. And that's what you should be, but I am not a one-man woman. I never will be. I would love to be your occasional fuck-buddy, if it wasn't for the obvious fact my husband is one of your best friends. And even if we ignored that and you were happy for a while, it wouldn't last. You'd be stuck in neutral, unable to go forward. So that only leaves sailing buddy as a possibility, but I'm not sure we can be just friends. Not now anyway, not unless and until you can get beyond Carole. You know this is true. You just don't want it to be true."

As Gretch's words settle in, I relax. All the pent up tension drains away. I know she is right. I know I have a long road ahead of me, and though I'm not ready to face it yet, I have to. Holding on to her is what I long to do, not because it's what I really want, but because it's the safe, secure thing, Larry be damned. But it is true I need a woman friend, not someone to sleep with, someone to talk to.

"All right," I say, finally. "But I'm going to need help getting beyond Carole, and I need you to be my friend. I don't want to give that up." Then I smile and say, "Besides, we still have a dangerous dwarf to deal with. And, if I remember correctly, we already shook on it."

She nods and grins. Then, after considering for a moment, says, "Okay, it's a deal."

~ ~ ~

As we sail away from Blake Island, the wind drops to ten knots but remains southwesterly. I pull in the staysail and prepare to go wing-on-wing. The genoa is already on the starboard side, so I move the traveler all the way to port and tighten up the mainsheet and Gretch turns the wheel until the wind is directly behind us. Then she turns a few degrees more to starboard until the genoa begins to luff and the main jibes to port. I let out the mainsheet and Gretch turns the wheel back to run in front of the wind.

The slow sail home is peaceful. We have reached a détente, an understanding. It is clear to me, under other circumstances each of us might have looked for more in a mutual friendship, but the circumstances are what they are. Our plan tonight is to go for a drink at Ray's where Doc has agreed to meet me at 7:00 p.m. for dinner. If we time it right, Doc will catch us in the parking lot kissing goodbye. One thing we both know about him is his obsessive punctuality. If he says 7:00 p.m., he'll be parking his car at 6:55 p.m.

We motor into Shilshole with time to spare so commence a thorough cleaning. *Repose* has salt from stem to stern. We watch the time, leaving an hour before the curtain rises on our little vignette at Ray's. At quarter to the hour, we finish our wine and head to Gretch's car, which she has parked near the lot entrance in the best spot for our charade. As expected, Doc pulls in right on schedule. We've seen him coming down the road and lock lips for a long stage kiss but keep an eye open to make sure he sees. He drives right by us, pretending not to have noticed, but we can both tell he does. As Doc pulls into a parking place across from where we stand, we break our embrace, but Gretch holds my hands and gives me the deep sensual look I saw that first night and then leans in for one last chaste kiss. Doc will read it as true affection, I realize, because that is what her kiss is, the kiss of a friend.

~ ~ ~

I walk back into Ray's a minute behind Doc. He is waiting for me upstairs and chatting up the cute blond hostess. She can't be a day over eighteen.

"Pace yourself," I say as I walk up behind him.

He turns and laughs, "At my age, I like to start by jogging a bit before I go for a run."

I look at the hostess, who has no clue we're talking about her, and ask to sit outside. She hands a couple of menus to one of the girls standing by her, and we are led out onto the deck. This girl flashes a nice smile to say that, unlike the hostess, she has followed our parried joking. I catch her smiling at me a couple more times over the course of the evening. She has long, bleached-blonde hair and dark-brown eyes above a full figure. Curly's "built for comfort" phrasing passes through my mind. She's quite a bit older than the hostess but still can't be much past her mid-twenties. What do these girls see in middle-aged men? I ask Doc his opinion.

"Damned if I know. Damned if I care, either."

No help from that quarter, but maybe he's right. Why should I care? And when I think about it, I find I'm not opposed to sleeping with younger women, I just don't know why they'd want to sleep with me.

Our meal passes with no reference to Gretch and me but with lots of talk about the settlement, the details of which are as Gretch said they would be: condo, boat, no mortgage, and $5 million. The reason they caved in so easily, once they knew I knew what they knew, is that Gretch told Carole's lawyer she was advising me to keep my one third of the business; there was no stipulation in any of the partnership papers that I must participate in its operation. In other words, I could sit on my dead ass collecting my third of the profits for the rest of my life, while the two of them worked themselves to death. If they had called her bluff, I would have settled for less, but I suppose there was too great a risk for them to take that chance.

As we sit having an after-dinner cappuccino, Doc finally gets up the nerve to broach the subject he has been worrying over. "So," he says, and I watch him searching for the right way to begin, but he chickens out, asking, "How was the sail?"

I'm not going to help him out, so laying it on thick, I tell him how exciting it was to race across the Sound, all sails hoisted and the rail in the water, and how Gretch was ferocious in her intensity, moving hypnotically with the boat, lifting and driving in unison with the waves. I let my excitement show, watching him watch me, building it up slowly then bringing him back to earth with, "And you know, Doc, women who love sailing are hard to come by."

Doc doesn't respond, and at first I think I've overplayed the sexuality of sailing bit, but then he says, "I don't think this is such a good idea, Deke. I mean she's Larry's wife, for Christ's sake."

"So?" I respond, remaining in character. "It's not as if she's in love with me. Were just friends."

"Just friends, huh? I saw the 'just friends' kiss she gave you earlier."

"Okay, so maybe we're fuck-buddies," I answer, using Gretch's strange but descriptive term. "We sail and we screw. Isn't that what you've been trying to get me to do?"

I can see the defeated look on Doc's face. He knows

this whole stupid thing was his idea. It just backfired on him. Then he admits it. "Look, this was my idea from the beginning. I put Gretch up to it and I needled Larry into going along. It's my fault it's gone so far. It never occurred to me Gretch would actually fall for you. Shit. Has she?"

I knit my brows in thought. "God, Doc, do you mean you think Gretch is in love with me?" I ask, and it takes every ounce of control I have not to burst out laughing.

He throws his hands in the air and says, "I don't know, but I've never seen her like this. She's not acting like the Gretch I know. And Larry said the same thing."

He's reading my expression but now I have no trouble keeping it serious and quizzical. Has Gretch said something to Larry to further our plot against Doc, or has Larry seen something there that is real?

"Look, Doc. I guess I don't know what Gretch is thinking. But I know I'm not ready for a serious relationship with anybody. It's too soon. I just want to forget about Carole. Gretch is good at taking me to a different place. I'm not giving that up right now. I need her." Again, most of this is true. Doc is completely taken in. "But I've agreed to go out cruising with you and Larry and Curly tonight. Isn't that enough?"

Suddenly, he smiles ear to ear and replies, "Nope. Not enough. It's not enough to come out with us. You have to score."

"Score?" I ask, rejecting his lame word as both puerile and out-of-date.

"Yes. Score. As in participate, join in the fun, play the game. If a girl asks you to dance, you have to accept. If she sticks her tongue down your throat on the dance floor, you have to kiss her back. If she takes you by the hand and says, 'My place or yours,' you have to go with her. No objections, no excuses, no turndowns. Deal?"

I lean back in my chair and smile at him, my friend for so many years: Doc the instigator, Doc the diabolical dwarf, but Doc the friend in need as well. For tonight I'll let him off the hook, I'll play it his way. Tomorrow is another day.

I reach across the table and we shake. "Deal."

A deal with the devil? Perhaps, but I know Doc is just trying to walk the ever-so-fine line without falling off. He would like things to go back to the way they were, but he simply can't resist playing it out instead of just telling me to back off. Oh, rest assured, Doc wants some naughty lady to take my mind off Gretch, and he has played me into a concession, a deal as it were. I'm thinking if I don't look approachable, I won't be approached. But, at Teddies? Maybe I'm wrong. Maybe I'm in for a rude surprise. But maybe, just maybe, a rude surprise is exactly what I'm hoping for.

~ ~ ~

I follow Doc's car to Teddies. He says I'll get lost otherwise, but I think he just wants to make sure I don't change my mind. The public parking lot is down under the Alaskan Way Viaduct and Teddies is carved out of the hillside halfway up. From the outside it looks small. The cement block exterior has been painted hot pink, and the small "Teddies" sign by the entrance hangs from the hand of a manikin with a blonde wig and a see-through teddie, faded and mildewed. We enter through an anteroom with a coat check. The girl behind the counter is also wearing a teddie, though hers is both newer and less revealing than the manikin's. It's quite warm this evening, and neither Doc nor I have coats, but he drops a five-dollar bill into her tip jar anyway. The girl says, "Thanks, Doc," and leans across to give him a peck on the cheek.

He leads me to the back of the dimly lit room where Larry and Curly are already ensconced in a booth. I can feel eyes on us as we walk among the tables, and I don't make it to the booth without being patted on the ass a couple of times. Curly rises from his seat and shakes my hand. Larry salutes then spreads his arms as if to hug all the women gathered here and says, "Welcome to my humble abode."

I have to admit he does look at home, leaning with arms draped across the back of the red leatherette banquette. As I slide into the booth to sit opposite him, Curly asks rhetorically, "Sooo, what do you think?"

What do I think? I think I'm not in Kansas anymore. As I glance around the room, many of the women look back appraisingly. I have the uneasy sense of being sized up the way a lioness looks at her prey before deciding when and whether to leap. The place is quite crowded, but it extends back out of sight into side rooms, which may not be as full. The booths and tables of the main room where we sit are arranged in a horseshoe around a twenty-by-thirty dance floor with the bar itself taking up one long side. The bar counter is a rough-hewn, single slab of Douglas fir coated thickly with urethane. Behind it stand two teddie-clad bartenders. The long mirror on the wall shows them to be wearing sneakers instead of the stilettos that complete the waitress outfits. Here and there are couples talking animatedly, gesturing to be understood above the loud rock music, which is blasting from wall-mounted speakers in every corner. Most of the tables, however, are occupied by women: lots of twenty-somethings, fewer thirty-plus, and nearly no women my age or older.

"Where are all the guys?" I shout across at Curly by way of answering his question.

"Other rooms mostly." He points down a long hallway to them. "It's quieter back there. Can't hear yourself think in Larry's room."

Larry is still lounging and watching as newcomers enter the bar after leaving their outer garments with the coat check girl. It's obvious now why a coat check is necessary on such a warm night. Most of the women arrive in clothing that would get them arrested out in the street. Not that they look like hookers, though a few actually do, but the assortment of nighties, teddies, and various other undergarments wouldn't pass for decent exposure. As I continue to observe, I begin to realize most of the women sitting at tables are engrossed in their own private conversations. When guys walk through, they get the once over, but for the most part the women seem to be here for the fun of hanging out together.

Larry refers to Teddies as a "hook up" bar. Clearly, he means a place to meet someone of the opposite gender for a night of casual, uncommitted sex. These joints used to be called "pick up" bars. I think I like the shift in meaning. Pick up implies an uneven playing field where the male chooses the female. Hook up sounds more like a binary star system, each star circling the other, ruled only by mutual gravitation.

Doc and I order drinks, once the waitress, who is clad in a frilly black teddie, finally makes an appearance. The prices are exorbitant, but since ladies in sleepwear drink for free every Saturday, the guys are supporting the bar. We talk and drink and girl-watch for an hour or so, with my settlement the main subject. That, and Curly's successful detective adventure. "You owe me, big-time," he tells me and I allow as how I probably do. I ask what kind of flowers he likes, and my riposte is met by guffaws from Larry and the comment, "The kind delivered by a naked woman."

It's after 11:00 p.m. when a shift occurs. The dim lights become dimmer and the music changes pace. A moment later there's a hand on my shoulder. I turn to see long legs standing by my side. I look up. "Dance?" she asks, though it sounds more like a command than a question.

She holds my gaze as I rise, take her hand, and follow to the floor. She is tall and lean with boyish hips, and young enough to be my daughter. She is wearing high heels and seems only an inch or two shorter than I am. She is in her underwear. When we step onto the already crowded dance floor, she turns and wraps long arms around my neck and nuzzles in. I put my hands low on her back in the space where the camisole leaves off before the low hip briefs begin, and we sway back and forth to the slow, sultry music, unable to go very far in the crush of bodies surrounding us. Her close-cut, red hair is pixie-ish and smells of bruised lavender.

As we move together, she presses into me, softly at first, then with more force as she senses my physical response. I move my hands up and down her sides and she does the same. The spell cast is both sexual and sensual. I risk breaking it by quietly asking her name. "Ssssh," is the only reply I receive, followed by her hands moving to my flanks. I follow suit, tracing the soft curves of her buttocks then upwards flowing into the sacral dimples I can barely feel, yet they are there, I am sure of it. This reminds me of Carole, and my thoughts stray. The girl senses my drift and lifts her face to look into my eyes. Carole disappears as the girl kisses me softly, her tongue the faintest brush on my lips then mine on hers. She settles back and nuzzles again, kissing my neck; butterfly kisses that flutter just above my skin, not quite touching.

We cling together like this for what seems an eternity, then, in the pause between songs, she breaks contact, smiles, and leans in to whisper, "Christine." I begin to reply, Andrew, but decide against it. "Deke," I say, but she has already turned and is walking away. I watch her go, and swear I can hear the click, click, click of her heels above the music, now playing again. I suspect I will continue to hear them for some time to come. Dreams are made of just this sort of moment.

I begin to walk back to the table, but suddenly there is a hand on my arm and a voice, "Whoa, Tiger, where do you think you're going?" I turn to see a short, roly-poly blonde in a Stetson who has a hold on me. The hat is set back on her head and tied under her chin, the string disappearing into the deep folds beneath. Having successfully prevented me from exiting the dance floor, she now wraps both arms around my waist and jiggles seductively against me. She is wearing a rose-colored, knee-length, cotton T-shirt, the sort of thing Carole often slept in during winter months. Her abundant rolls of flesh shimmy gelatinously underneath the T any time she moves. She can't be even five feet tall and is barefoot, so my arms aren't long enough to reach down past her waist, not that I want them to.

At first, I'm a bit self-conscious and a little turned-off by her obesity, but after a while as she laughs and jokes about what she'd like to do to me, I accept her word play as just that, play. She tells me her name is Billie, Billie the Kid, hence the diminutive cowboy hat. "A one gallon hat. Just the right fit for a pint-sized cowgirl like me."

I laugh at her effervescent energy and frank appraisals of what she calls my "hard body." She is half-teasing and half-serious, I realize. "You're a good sport," Billie says at some point, referring, I suppose, to my apparent willingness to continue dancing with her, but the fact is I'm enjoying her company. She's a hoot.

"Just wish I was a little taller so I could look into those dreamy blue eyes."

I bend down to kiss her then reach under her buttocks and lift. Billie locks her short legs around my waist and we dance face to face, kissing occasionally, then she puts her head on my shoulder and I swing her and spin us until the end of the song.

Back on her feet now, Billie says in a fake Texas drawl, "Thanks, Pardner. Enjoyed the ride high up in the saddle." She laughs at her own joke then hugs me tight. We dance to another song then part company, but not before a long deep kiss that elicits a groan from her and from me as well. That girl knows how to kiss, I think, as I walk back to join Doc and Curly. I see Larry is missing, and when I ask where he went, Curly nods toward the back rooms then repeats his earlier question, "So, now what do you think?" His question is still rhetorical. He can't imagine any guy not liking this scene. And while I think it would get old and sordid pretty quickly, I have to admit it's interesting.

"I don't know, Curly. Dancing with half-dressed women half my age? What do you think?"

He laughs, and Doc, who has been watching me dance and measuring my reaction, laughs too, but more sincerely, almost fatherly in his satisfaction that I seem to be relaxed and enjoying myself. And I've been watching Doc and Curly watching me. Neither of them has been up dancing yet. I guess they're just amused at my novice status at Teddies. They use phrases like "new blood" and "fresh meat" to describe my supposed popularity. Or maybe there is some vicarious or voyeuristic pleasure I'm providing them.

Our waitress brings another round, but I hardly get a slug or two before I'm hauled back out on the dance floor. This time the woman is closer to my own age. I'd have guessed Billie to be early thirties, but Margaret, who is quite literally dragging me behind her, looks to be well into her forties. She may even be older than I am. She has chosen not to wear clothing appropriate to Second Saturday at Teddies, but her short, skin-tight, lilac tube dress reveals more of her soft curves and long legs than many of the looser-fitting outfits scattered around the room. And it rides up so high it barely covers the essentials. Throw in her black, stiletto, fuck-me pumps, and, while her outfit may be inappropriate to Teddies, and age inappropriate as well, the overall effect is hot.

"Thought it was about time you danced with a woman for a change," she says as we begin swaying. The floor is still packed and there's nowhere to go, so we dance in place leaning away from each other at arms length. Margaret has her hands linked behind my neck and I have mine linked at her waist. Our groins are glued together, and as we move our legs with the music, we grind into each other deliciously.

As we dance, I catch Margaret stealing glances behind me occasionally and making faces. I don't let on I've noticed but slowly maneuver us in a circle so I can see with whom she's communicating. Her girlfriends, I suppose, but when I finally manage to turn us amidst the crush of gyrating torsos, I see Christine watching. She averts her eyes at first, but they drift back and lock with mine. She is sitting at a table with a short, slender, young woman with long, straight, brown hair. They are both watching. Margaret, now that she can no longer see her friends, has moved closer and put her head on my shoulder and dropped her hands to my waist, linked loosely. Her long arms cling to me gently but firmly. She is quite tall and I can feel her warm breath on the side of my neck. And, as with Christine, the odor of bruised lavender issues from her hair.

I keep my eyes on Christine, but begin to caress Margaret's back. Margaret raises her hands and repeats my caress, tracing either side of my spine. Christine smiles in obvious response to this, as does her girlfriend. Then I see her mime speaking. My expression must register confusion about what she is trying to say, so she repeats the words until my face shows surprise. Christine is saying, "My Mom."

Love Hurts

We continue to dance in place, holding each other close. The song changes and I recognize the intro to *Love Hurts*, an old Roy Orbison heartbreaker. But as the singer begins, I realize this is not Roy's tenor but Emmylou Harris's plaintive contralto. With her head on my shoulder and lips turned toward my ear, Margaret sings along quietly, matching Emmylou's emotion-laden tones sound for sound and putting extra emphasis on the refrain.

When the words approach that she is too old to repeat, Margaret stops singing. Neither of us is young. Nor can we feel that first pang of lost love any longer. But it is true for me that I am still hurting from my loss of Carole. I'm doing my best to deny it and, in part at least, this is why I'm here right now with my arms around a stranger. But then, I think, Margaret is not really such a stranger, after all. Her soft, sad voice and Roy's words tell me she feels the same way.

As the song finishes, we both open eyes, which have been closed. Still holding me, Margaret asks, "Would you like to go rest for a while? These heels are killing me."

We find a quiet table for two in one of the side rooms and Margaret slips off her shoes and breathes a sigh of relief.

"Your daughter's?" I ask, flashing a wicked smile.

I'm rewarded with a sheepish grin and shrug that confirms my suspicions.

"The whole outfit, right?"

"Ohh," she moans dejectedly. "I told Chris it wouldn't fit. My hips are too big and that's her and her sister's fault. Just wait until she has her first kid, then we'll see how well this silly thing fits her."

I bend to one side and look under the table at her dress. It has ridden way up, exposing her upper thighs and revealing her likely lack of underwear. That's probably Chris's idea too. I disguise my reaction and say, "You have wonderful hips."

"Ohh," she moans again, but this time in delight. "You're very sweet, but I know better."

She's fishing for more, I realize, so I reach across the table and take her hands and hold her gaze for a moment then say, "I'm being entirely truthful. You have a beautiful body." And it's true, she does. I imagine there will be some stretch marks under her dress and maybe a little pouch of a tummy, but otherwise she's a knockout in this dress. Christine knew how to transform her mother into a vamp.

Margaret closes her eyes, smiles, and radiates satisfaction in my words. This is going well, I think. Like Christine's, Margaret's hair is cut short and of the same dark-reddish color but appears sophisticated rather than pixie-ish. High cheekbones are the difference, I realize. That and the age lines around her eyes and lips and the soft furrows above her brow. With eyes closed and facial muscles relaxed, she could almost pass for her daughters' late twenties or early thirties, but in the brighter light cast from above our table, I can see she is well past fifty.

We continue to hold hands and look into each other's eyes, then she lets go and straightens. "This is silly. I saw you with Chris. You don't want someone my age."

I frown dismissively and begin to contradict her but can see mistrust written on Margaret's face. She won't believe me. And I have to admit there is some truth in what she has said. No, I didn't come to Teddies to meet someone my own age. I came to bolster my ego, not to work on someone else's. And there is nothing like the attentions of a Christine to make a middle-aged guy feel young again. So, instead of denying Margaret's casual dismissal of what could become something more than a few dances, I ask, "All right, why did you come here? Why did you let your daughters talk you into this?"

She looks down dejectedly then up again, and I think she will answer, but she just shakes her head and doesn't speak.

"What? What could be so bad? My wayward, single buddies drug me here to have a little fun. And I am having fun. I'm most of the way through a divorce but still miserable she left me. My friends are just trying to cheer me up. Tell me that's not what your daughters are doing."

Margaret still doesn't say anything at first but then opens her mouth and closes it again. She is trying to find the right words, but all she finally blurts out is, "It's not."

I wait for her to go on but she doesn't. "It's not why your daughters drug you here?"

"No...I mean, yes, that's why they made me come with them." Margaret motions to the room. "They love this place. They love the anonymity. They love that they can tell their friends they *hooked up* without giving any of the details. They can practically make love on the dance floor with a total stranger and feel what that feels like then go home alone. But don't you think you and I are a little old for this sort of thing?" Her sad, confused look now both beseeches me to agree and hopes desperately I will not.

I smile a smile that will seem both wise and wistful. "No, we are not too old. Too old-fashioned, maybe. But not too old to find comfort in each other's arms. There's no age limit for that."

Margaret smiles back, her eyes weary. "I suppose you're right. I enjoyed being held again like someone meant it. It's been a while. I…" she answers, stopping short of saying everything she wants to.

"I what? I need, I want, I hope? What? Why are you here? And I don't mean why did you agree to come with your kids like I came with my buddies. I mean, what are you here for?" Then, realizing I am pushing too hard, I rephrase my question, "What did you hope this would make you feel?"

"Wow. Good question. I thought I knew the answer when we were dancing. So close, so separated from the real world. Feels good to let go, I suppose. I guess I hoped I could let go."

"But here we sit talking instead of doing. Would you like to dance some more?"

Margaret stops to consider. Do I want to dance? she seems to ask herself. Do I want to just be held again?

"I don't really know what I want," she answers after a moment. "But I know I don't want to go back to face my daughters. I may not know why I'm here or what I came for, but I do know why they brought me. They want me to hook up with some young guy just like you, to go home with him and have him screw my brains out all night. Stupid, huh?"

"Not stupid at all. That's why my buddies brought me here," I answer then it's my turn to pause to find the right words. "Okay, what we need is a plan. Here's what we do. First, you put your killer shoes back on. Second, we walk back through the bar without talking to or even looking at my buddies or your daughters. Third, we rescue your coat so you don't get arrested for wearing that edible dress you're wearing."

I pause again for effect and am rewarded with a shy but appreciative smile. "Fourth, you follow me back to my condo in your car," I continue. "I'll put on some music and we can dance. Or we can sit out on the balcony and just talk. You can sleep in my guestroom. Then tomorrow, when we each have to face our separate inquisitors, we can just smile when they ask what happened. We will have *hooked up*, and, as you said earlier, we can tell them we did that and refuse to give any of the details."

~ ~ ~

We ride up the six floors to my door in awkward silence. It's something about elevators. We have just finished skipping merrily across the parking lot like a couple of teenagers who have ditched their friends, leaving them speechless and amazed, and, in fact, that is exactly what we've done. The looks we got as we marched past them and out through the coat checkroom were priceless. Doc was wearing a bemused grin and looking over at Christine, Curly was doing a little victory dance in his seat, Larry aimed two fingers of his right hand at me and fired, Christine gave Margaret a thumbs up, way up gesture, and her sister looked like a deer caught in headlights. Altogether a very rewarding reaction we tell each other, laughing all the way to the elevator. But once the door slid shut, our mouths did too, laughter replaced by shy smiles. What's next? we seemed to be thinking. It's just something about elevators.

"Wine?" I ask as Margaret removes her coat and drapes it across the back of one of my kitchen barstools. "White or red?" I continue before she gets a chance to accept or decline.

"White, I think."

"Your choices are a Sonoma chardonnay or a Marlborough sauvignon blanc."

"The Marlborough. It's my favorite. How did you know?" she asks in jest, but I see a darker thought play across her face.

I finish pouring the wine and hand her a glass. "What?" I ask as she continues to look at me, an unasked question between us. Then I understand. She's thinking this might be a setup. Christine has arranged the whole thing in advance just as Doc had set me up with Gretch.

"You've got to be kidding. You don't really believe this is a setup, do you?" I search her expression for a sign. "The Kiwi wine is my ex's. She's from Australia and went to prep school, or whatever the Aussies call it, in Christchurch. I like it okay but prefer chardonnay."

Margaret smiles and shrugs, then says, "I guess not," but she still looks as if she doesn't believe it.

"You know, I could say the same thing. Maybe

Christine knows my buddies and you're the setup. I mean, look at it from my perspective. They drag me into this place with promises of casual sex and wild young girls, one of whom comes on to me, then there's the old bait-and-switch to a real woman, a gorgeous lady from my own generation who might be able to take my mind off my ex. And the fact she happens to be the only woman present anywhere near my age is pretty suspicious, no? And what about the you-and-I-are-a-little-old-for-this-sort-of-thing obvious ploy you used to get me to ask you back to my place? What about that, huh?"

Margaret is smiling dreamily and crosses the distance to melt into my answering embrace. "Gorgeous?" she asks, and I realize that was the last word she heard of my speech. Then she steps back, takes a sip of her wine, looking over the rim into my eyes. And remembering a few words that came before "gorgeous", repeats them, more statement than question, "Casual sex?"

~ ~ ~

Like Gretch, Margaret preferred being on top, and like Gretch, she enjoyed the view from the windowsill and the slow motion undulation lips-to-lips that brought her to orgasm. We lie entwined and I have no wish to disturb her sleep. Neither of us will reveal these details to our inquisitors tomorrow morning. No, this morning, I realize as I look at my alarm clock. It's 2:00 a.m. We won't share the details, but it feels great to actually have some to withhold.

Earlier, after we were both spent and immersed in rebounding sensation, Margaret had continued what she had stopped short of saying at Teddies. Unlike me, she does not want a divorce and neither does her husband. Christine's plot was to help her get even, one affair to cancel out another. Margaret apologizes profusely for what she sees as deception on her part, but I hush her with a question: "How long did his affair go on?"

She looks at me, worried, knowing exactly why I'm asking, then answers, "A few months, I think."

"And how long will it take to get even?" I ask, sparing her the effort to find the words to continue. "Is this it?"

Margaret's silence answers my question.

But when I wake at noon to the sun streaming through and to Margaret's not-so-gentle caress, I can tell she has changed her mind, for the moment at least.

Later, at my door, we kiss goodbye. I lean against the doorjamb waiting for the elevator to arrive. Margaret waits with her back to me and turns only after entering. Then, just before the door slides shut, she blows me one last kiss.

We both understand the risk implied in breaking Teddies' rules. Relationships do not come from hookups. That is the whole point in meeting and mating without attachment, Gretch tells me. If Margaret and I continued to see each other, her marriage would be over. Neither of us is the type to start something we have no intention of finishing.

"Compartmentalize," Gretch says. "Keep your love life and your sex life separate."

How is that possible? And why would you want to? I see it works for Gretch and Larry, but at what cost? It is not a cost I am willing to bear; the price is too high.

~ ~ ~

Next Saturday finds me back at Teddies anyway, chastened by my experience from a week ago, but, having decided Gretch is right and having decided I'm not yet ready to begin a new relationship, I find I am ready for round two in the hook-up match. What Doc calls "good clean fun." I've even stocked in a selection of condoms to help with the "clean" part, filling my nightstand with festive colors, glow-in-the-dark, ribbed and ringed, with and without lubrication.

Larry and Curly have gone off to other venues tonight, and Doc insists I need a wingman to keep me safe. Teddies is less crowded on its off-Saturdays, and many of the women are dressed in either jeans or party attire. A few teddies and other sleepwear outfits are sprinkled among the half-full tables when Doc and I arrive, and the crowd assembled is still lively, but there is a subdued sense to the revelry.

As before, we have come directly from Ray's, though it is later, nearly 11:00 p.m., and we are well-fed and well-lubricated from the pints of beer we've consumed. We pick a table-for-two on the back wall that offers a good view of the already-crowded dance floor and order a round of drinks when the waitress stops by. We sit scanning the room for girls looking back. I recognize Billie from last Saturday. Doc tells me she's a regular. She waddles over to say hello and pulls me away to join her for a slow dance. She can tell I'm not as much into her as I was last week so, after a couple of tunes, lets me go.

Doc is asked to dance several times over the course of the night but I am not. Maybe I don't look approachable. The main house ordinance at Teddies is proclaimed by a large neon sign above the bar: "Women Rule;" they do the asking, not the guys, and no means no. We wait to be asked. We can make eye contact all we want but we have to be invited to dance, ballroom courtesy turned on its head, Sadie Hawkins every day. There is one extra rule for all Saturdays: if asked you must accept.

But I am not asked. Doc says I don't look happy and no one wants to dance with a guy who looks pissed off. "Try smiling," he suggests.

I know I'm still thinking about Margaret, and Gretch too, if I'm honest. I guess I have a hard time letting go, or maybe it's rejection I don't like. By 1:00 a.m., both Doc and I are fairly soused. More girls have arrived, and I'm beginning to get second looks from some of them. I see Christine and her sister come in, pair up with a couple of young studs, and hit the dance floor. The two girls look vaguely sisterly, but Chris is at least six inches taller and her close-cropped red hair juxtaposed with her sister's long brown tresses make them seem more like friends than relatives. Each wears a tube dress, Chris in lilac, probably the same dress Margaret was wearing last Saturday, and her sister in carmine. The couples dance side by side.

The two guys they are with spend most of the time pawing them but talking to each other. It has the look of ritual rather than lust. It's as if the guys know it's expected of them but they'd be happier in a sports bar watching a game. The same is true of the girls, who are chatting away, oblivious to the hands running up and down their bodies. I ask Doc his opinion. He dismisses them. "No imagination. They'll hop in bed later to get it over with. Then it's, 'See ya next week, sayonara, adios'."

When they decide to sit it out for a while, they take up the empty table next to Doc and me, the guys with their backs to us, and the girls sitting across from them. The conversations guy-to-guy and girl-to-girl continue unabated. For all intents and purposes, the two pairs ignore each other. I wonder if this is a generational difference, a continental divide between sexes that erodes as we age. Or maybe men and women are always on opposite sides of that mountain range. As the metaphor succumbs to my inebriation, I imagine a king-size bed at the summit, the only place where the two sexes meet, couple, then say, "That's all for tonight, folks."

Too much beer, I think, or maybe not enough. I see our waitress approaching with a full tray and signal with my hand to catch her attention. She nods to me as she passes and says she'll be right back but in doing so fails to see one of the two guys push back in his chair. When she runs into him, she tries to keep the tray from falling, but she is off-balance so the entire tray flips over, spilling its contents. Chris and her sister have seen it coming and jump out of the way in time but the guys get a beer bath. The waitress runs for towels as the two guys stand there dripping. Chris and her sister have broken into hysterics. The guys look pissed off. Pissed on, I think, but keep the thought to myself. Doc has busied himself picking up the tray and broken glass. The bar towels the waitress returns with do little to sop up the mess, and both guys stomp off to the restroom. While the waitress does her best to clean up, the girls join Doc and me.

When the guys return, they look disgusted and

bedraggled, and the girls crack up again. The guys do not see the humor in this. One of them says to the other, "Let's get the fuck out of here." His buddy waffles. I can tell he's wondering whether something can be salvaged from this debacle. He's thinking a quick shower before hitting the sack is all it would take, right? But his friend stands there defiantly, hands on hips, so he gives in.

I watch the two of them walk across the bar and out through the coat check, arguing and gesturing animatedly. I shake my head and turn to Doc. "Kids," I say, summing up the whole tableau in a single word. The girls turn to look at each other and, at exactly the same moment, say, "Old farts," and break into hysterics again.

Doc and I sit watching the two girls as their laughter rises and falls only to rise again when I say, "It's not that funny."

When they finally settle down, Chris looks at her sister and asks, "Well?"

"Why not," she answers then puts her right hand behind her back.

Chris does the same. "One, two, three," then both whip their hands into the middle of the table, Chris's index and middle finger spread out to represent scissors and her sister's fist rests alongside.

"Rock breaks scissors," she says, eyes sparkling.

"Okay, you win again. Which one do you want, Sis?"

She scoots her chair over next to mine. "I get the young one."

That sets me off in a paroxysm of laughter. Doc looks fit to be tied. The girls are bemused but seem pleased to have gotten me to laugh, though they haven't a clue why. And the fact they don't only makes me laugh harder. Doc's stature and premature gray make him look older, and though he knows this, he's sensitive about it. This is the one way Curly can get to him, and to Larry as well, since Curly's shaved head is taken by women to be youthful, while Doc's gray and Larry's male-pattern baldness mark them as old farts. By contrast, I have a full head of blonde hair with no gray yet.

I'm still laughing when Doc pulls out his wallet and plunks down his driver's license. Chris picks it up. Doc taps his finger on the table in front of me to indicate I have to produce mine. "Okay, okay," I say, still chuckling then hand it to the sister.

"Forty-two," Chris says.

"Forty-five," her sister answers. "That's alright, he still looks younger."

"That's just because he dyes his hair," Doc says.

Both girls look at me then back at Doc. "Liar," they say in unison. "But maybe you should try it."

I laugh some more while Doc sputters. Then he adopts a fake pout and folds his arms across his chest for emphasis.

Chris rises from her chair and sits in his lap. Then she begins running her fingers through Doc's hair. "Aw, there, there now. I'll make it up to you."

I look at the sister. "What do I call you?"

Chris turns and they exchange a puzzled look. "Weren't you listening?" they ask, again in unison, but this time it seems staged, a well-worn routine.

I think back and cannot remember hearing her name. And I have been listening for it. I hate it when I can't remember the name of a person I have met and am nearly anal about this. I have had too much to drink, but still…. Then I get it. Chris called her "Sis."

"You want me to call you 'Sis'?"

"That's my name. Ask me again and I'll tell you the same."

So, this is a routine. I think for a minute then remember something Margaret said. "Okay then, what's your middle name?"

That stops her and she pouts. I have not asked the next expected question, which might have been, "But I'm not your brother so why do you want me to call you 'Sis'?" The answer would have been the same, "That's my name," etcetera, etcetera, etcetera.

"So," I say when she doesn't answer, "I seem to have spoiled your game. I can only conclude your name really is Sis. Yes?"

"That's my name. Ask me again and I'll tell you the same." She's smiling again.

"I think that's not quite true. Since you wouldn't answer when I asked your middle name, it must give away your first name, yes?"

The pout returns, but she repeats her answer, "That's my name. Ask me again and I'll tell you the same."

"Sissy Spacek Saunders," I say then lean back in my chair.

Both girls give me an open-mouthed questioning look as if to say, how did you guess? Doc looks befuddled too.

"Pretty smart, huh?" I fold my arms across my chest in triumph, but when their expressions change, I realize I've overplayed my hand.

"Mom!" they say in unison, and Sis starts punching me in the arm.

I cover up, feigning injury. "Uncle, uncle. Margaret told me her last name and she mentioned that Sissy Spacek was her favorite actress. I just connected the dots."

Sis stops hitting me and climbs into my lap. Then she looks over at Chris. "This is going to be fun. I can tell."

She turns back to fix me with a penetrating stare and salacious smile.

I say to myself, "Yes, this going to be fun."

Continental Divide

We say goodbye in the parking lot. Doc and Christine leave for his place in separate cars, and since the girls drove together, Sis walks with me to where I've parked my old Saab 900. I unlock her side first and hold the door open for her to get in. She laughs and makes a comment about my chivalry, but I look down at her dress, which has ridden way up, and say, "Just taking in the sights," and am rewarded with that salacious smile again.

Riding the elevator and standing opposite, we look each other up and down, then, when the door slides open, Sis takes the key ring from my hand and walks over to unlock. While she searches the dozen keys for a likely candidate, I run my hands down her flanks and nuzzle the back of her neck. Once again, bruised lavender. Sis turns and leans against the doorjamb and pulls me to her, lips brushing in soft, fleeting, dry kisses that promise what they do not immediately deliver. I press into her for more, but she breaks away laughing, skipping inside, and kicking off her high heels.

I close the door behind me and watch as she wanders about the living room, picking up each small thing that pleases her, a soapstone statue of a sea otter, a triptych of my parents, my older sister, and me, a surf-polished rock brought back from the Indian ruins of

Mamalillaculla in British Columbia, my farthest north sojourn to date. Sis studies each item carefully, her expression showing interest and her small hands caressing the surfaces of the statue and the stone and tracing the outlines of the subjects in the triptych. She replaces each item exactly the way she found it then moves on to another. Her perusal feels intimate, exposing some part of me I never thought of as having an existence.

The kitchen is next, with the dining area adjacent. It's a chef's kitchen with a large rose-granite island composed of prep sink, built-in cutting board, and six-burner gas range top with a powerful vent hood. Sis circles the island, pulling open drawers and examining contents, picking up an occasional item and asking its purpose. It is clear to me I know more about cooking than she does, and when I tease her about it, she just replies, "Yes, but I know more about other things," and gives me a melting look. I'll just bet you do, I think to myself, returning her gaze with an amused but expectant smile.

Sis continues along the wall from right-to-left and each time she arrives at a doorway to another room, she goes through it and explores, again right-to-left. I follow her silently. Back in the living room, she finds my rogue's gallery: all those photos of Carole and me on vacation, or on the boat, or at parties with friends or relatives. Sis removes a photo of Carole from an early trip we took to her parent's vacation home in Queensland. Carole stands under a palm tree on the beach in a blue and green string bikini. She is deeply tanned and her long blonde hair is sun-bleached and blowing in the breeze. Her amber eyes smile back at me. This is my favorite photo of her.

"She's beautiful," Sis says, her voice trailing off to a whisper.

"I know."

"You miss her, don't you?"

"Yes, I do." My look must seem sad but I hold her gaze.

Sis turns away and hangs the photo back where it came from, taking care to level it properly. "That's okay. You never forget your first love."

Then she walks over and puts her arms around me and her head on my chest. "There will be others. Some you will love less, but some you will come to love more."

Sis's words strike me in tone and tenor as prophetic. She is not speaking about herself, I know, but about women unknown to either of us, ones she can see in her mind's eye. Wish I could see so clearly.

We stand in embrace for a while, then Sis lets go and walks away through the next doorway. It's the guest bedroom. "I like my room," she says, teasing again to get me to smile, and I do. She checks the huge walk-in closet and whistles. "Sure hope you can afford all the clothes it will take to fill this up."

"As it so happens, I can. So, when are you moving in?"

"Hmmm, be careful what you wish for," she answers and flops backward onto the queen bed, lifting her knees to put her feet up. Realizing she is not wearing underwear, I quickly avert my eyes.

"Ooops, a Britney Spears moment, wasn't it? Too much, too soon?"

Before I can think of an answer, she launches off

the bed and walks out.

The master bathroom is next. It opens both onto the living room and onto the master bedroom, an odd arrangement that dates from an earlier renovation neither Carole nor I thought worth correcting. We supposed the guest room with its *en suite* bathroom was once the master. Its huge closet with all the built-in compartments suggested this too.

Sis walks through, fondling the soft towels and closing the seat and lid on the toilet with a sidelong glance at me to feign disapproval. Then she opens the medicine cabinet and takes out each item, smelling my aftershave ("Yummy," she says), noting my various containers of lotion, toothpaste, shave gel, and first aid unguent, and reading each pill container out loud, "Ibuprofen, baby aspirin, multivitamins…oh, and oxycodone. Party time." She smiles at me and says, "Just kidding."

Moving down the counter now, Sis opens Carole's cabinet. It is empty except for a half-empty tube of KY jelly. "This all she left you?" Sis asks, teasing me gently then adding in a saucy voice, "We won't be needing any extra lubrication, I promise." She drops the tube in the wastebasket and steps back to admire the barren cabinet shelves. "Plenty of room for my things," she says then walks out into my bedroom.

I stand in the doorway and watch her examination of its palatial dimensions and wall-to-wall glass looking out on Lake Union. Again, she whistles. "I want this room."

"Okay, but you'll have to share."

Another mischievous glance then Sis sidles over and knee-walks up the king bed until she is looking out at the water. She looks over her shoulder at me for a moment. It's an odd look I can't read. Then she turns back to the lake outside. It is backlit in city-light amber glow, and all along the edge, dock and boat lamps twinkle. The otherwise-dark bedroom is awash in reflection and refraction.

"Did my mother see this?"

Her voice is just above a whisper. What must Sis be thinking? Did Margaret provide details? No, I think not. My guess is Chris and Sis probably compare notes on lovers, and I imagine it will be Doc and I whose cries of passion are wryly examined when next the two of them are together, but I believe Margaret will have kept her own counsel. Or perhaps they hadn't asked her, not really wanting this sort of intimate knowledge of their mother. But they set it up, so maybe I'm wrong.

"What is it you want to know?"

"That's enough."

My broader question implicitly encompasses the underlying truth, that her mother and I had shared a bed. I search for something to say but understand that no words are looked for. I decide to leave Sis to her thoughts and take a few steps back into the living room. Maybe I'll go sit on the balcony for a while until she composes herself. Or maybe she'll curl up and fall asleep. That would be all right. Then from behind me, her voice beckons, "Don't go. Come here."

As I approach what has always been my side of the bed, the left, Sis scoots over and says playfully, "Oh, no. This is my side." She pats the bed next to her, I lay down, and we face each other.

"Are you okay?" I ask.

At first Sis says nothing. In the dim light I can still

see her face well enough to understand this simple question is costing her something. Then she sighs. "Look, you gave her what she needed. It was written all over her face the next morning. I just wanted to hear you say it."

That stops me. Is tonight just a review or some sort of test? "Is that why you're here?" I ask, an edge I don't like creeping into my voice.

"No, nooo." She takes my face in her hands and kisses me. "I'm here because I want to be. I... I don't want you to think it's for any other reason."

Then kisses replace words for a while. We hold each other and just kiss, nothing more. This is a new experience for me. It is deeply sensual. It is sexual as well, but the sensuality of slow kisses with no more than the most evanescent and occasional brush of tongue through parted lips is overwhelming. Some of her kisses are more warm breath than touch. Some offer the slightest pressure to part mine then back off when they succeed. Some begin in a flutter followed by the tip of her tongue grazing from one side to the other. And some are just tongue, no lips at all, a lingual caress, delicate beyond belief.

At some point in our kissing, I realize I want nothing more than this tonight. To hold her and kiss her is all I want. My focus must have drifted, because she pauses and pulls back to look into my eyes.

"What?"

"This is what I need, this is what I want now. Just to kiss you. Is that all right?"

"More than all right." She closes her eyes and begins kissing me again.

We alternate between kissing and holding each

other, Sis lying across my chest, her warm, earthy breath on my neck, mine in her hair, until she drifts off to sleep, and sometime later I fall as well.

When I awake the next morning, she is gone. Not again, I think. Then, as my head clears away the nighttime cobwebs, I hear water running. Sis is taking a shower. Well, I think, that's not the guest bathroom shower, that's mine, and it's a double. Room for two. Hmmm. Okay, I just can't resist. I drop my clothes next to hers at the foot of the bed, slowly open the bathroom door and peek in. Sis has her back toward me and with the water running won't hear. The shower is one of those no-door installations, so I could walk up and grab her from behind, but I'm not sure what sort of reaction I'd get, so I just turn on my control, letting the hot water cascade over, and enjoy the view. At some point Sis senses my presence and turns. She looks me up and down; that lascivious smile is back. Then she walks across, reaching her arms around, and rubs belly to belly sexily.

"That feels nice," I purr, but as I do, she leaps back, and icy cold water spews from the showerhead. She has adjusted the control.

Her mistake is that there is only one way out and I'm blocking her path. I motion with my index finger for her to come to poppa. She feints to one side and tries to run past on the other but I catch her around the waist.

"So, you like cold showers, huh?"

"No, no," she says, struggling to escape.

I begin to move her toward the downpour, still raining cold water, but then she shouts, "I'll make it worth your while." A moment's hesitation loosens my grip just enough for her to escape, but I'm close behind and tackle her once I'm sure we'll end up on the bed.

We wrestle for a minute, Sis squealing softly, "Rape, rape," but laughing the whole time. Then the struggling subsides and a gentler, mutual exploration begins. We kiss each other dry, taking care with all the places some water might be hiding. We end up in the embrace that during the 60s sexual revolution was called the "69" for its bent-body symmetry, and we continue that way until we are both satisfied. Then we kiss again, sharing each other's taste.

~ ~ ~

At 11:00 a.m., ensconced in a booth at the Blue Star and drinking coffee, we watch the cars and cyclists whiz by on Stone Way in nearly equal numbers. By mid-winter only the stalwarts will be left pedaling by to and fro from local jobs, but on any warm Sunday morning, two-wheelers nearly outnumber four-wheelers. I love this place. It's the only pub I know where you can get a beer with breakfast. Along the far wall opposite the bank of windows on the street runs a bar with honest-to-god stools. On tap are several microbrews as well as a few good mass-produced ales and pilsners, like Mack and Jack and Stella Artois.

We make an odd couple, Sis and me. I'm wearing jeans, sweatshirt, and boat shoes. Sis is back in her tube dress and heels. We get looks from the other patrons that suggest amusement at my expense, and sensing their amusement, Sis plays into it, bending toward me to show some cleavage and crossing and re-crossing her legs to flash two young guys sitting at a table by the window. Their breakfast girlfriends across from them are not amused.

The waitress arrives to take our order and gives us both the once over. I can imagine her thoughts. Breakfast at Tiffany's this isn't. More like Breakfast at Teddies, I think, or worse. The waitress probably wonders how much a night with Sis costs. I'm brought out of my reverie by a cell phone ringing. Not my ring tone. Sis pulls a bright-red Blackberry out of her clutch purse, checks the caller-ID, and answers.

"Hey, Chris, how was your *date*?" she asks, infusing the word "date" with obvious innuendo for the benefit of our neighbors. I don't know whether to crawl under the table or laugh. What comes out of my mouth is a self-conscious chuckle, which could be read by anyone as an admission of guilt. Do I feel guilty? I search my feelings but find no guilt, just a little embarrassment, mostly about the way we look sitting here together, but I have to admit I'm a bit embarrassed about hooking up with someone half my age, or close enough anyway, since I really don't know how old she is.

Sis is laughing at what must be Chris's description of her night with Doc. The one-sided conversation is filled with exclamations of surprise, both feigned and authentic. "He did not," "You're kidding," "He didn't really say that," and the like are interspersed with laughter, shrieks of disbelief, and the occasional, "That's gross" or "No way." Ordinarily I would be irritated by a non-stop cell phone connection in a restaurant, and I would definitely be embarrassed if the culprit were with me, but I can tell from the faces around me, who are pretending not to listen but are engrossed anyway, that this has all the hallmarks of a floorshow. And the fact is I'm enjoying the performance as well.

"He did not," Sis says, but without humor. "Please tell me you're kidding."

She listens quietly then repeats herself, "He did not really fall asleep…before." Then, remembering her audience, she adds, "After is okay, but before is really not good, Christine."

Then Sis breaks up in laughter. "Ohhhh, you meant the second time," she says in a voice loud enough to carry across the restaurant. "Well, what do you expect when you pick up old farts?" She gives me a devilish wink then winks the same way at the two guys she's been flashing. I look around at the other tables and see some of them suppressing laughter and no longer pretending not to listen.

"Wait!" Sis says. "Make that noise again." Then she parodies it back into the receiver, "Ooo…arrarr…unhunhunh…ahhhhh," and mimes post-coital collapse onto the booth and slides partway under the table. This is too much for the entranced audience. Hoots and roars fill our part of the room. I'm laughing too but can feel the color come up in my face as I realize all assembled must be thinking I'll be treated to the same sort of condescension later. Screw it, I decide, the guys are just jealous, and, no offense intended, their dates don't count.

"No, he didn't," is the next thing Sis says, but the questioning tone is gone from her voice. This is a statement. I'm confused at first, but when she adds, "I fell asleep first," I realize I am now the brunt.

The conversation continues, peppered with the same sorts of exclamations but softer in tone. "No, we didn't," "I would never do that," "He didn't," "Yes, he did," and the like are again interspersed with laughter, shrieks of dismay at the questions put to her, and, again, the occasional, "That's gross" or "No way."

This time I really am embarrassed but there is nothing I can do but put on a fake smile, grin, and bear it.

Then I hear her laugh and say, "I'll never tell." And for a change I can hear Chris answer, "Oh, yes you will." Sis just laughs harder.

"Okay. How shall I put it?" she begins, but not before turning on those dark brown eyes and smiling luridly at me. "We had a great conversation...we started from two opposite viewpoints...but we reached the same conclusion...and...at nearly the same moment too."

I glance away and see the audience decoding what Sis has said. A woman at a table opposite breaks up first in whoops and belly laughs that confound the husband sitting across from her, until I see the color rise in his cheeks as well, and until the older woman sitting next to his wife, who might be his mother-in-law, looks away out the window. But there is a smile on her face that belies her embarrassed gesture.

Our meal arrives before I am subjected to more ribaldry and discomfit. Sis signs off her call. We eat in silence but steal glances at each other. Sis looks a bit chagrined but otherwise seems pleased to have provided so much entertainment. I imagine my expression is more pained, but I do smile once in a while when she looks up. I sense she is both testing me and begging forgiveness in her own way. A barrier has been erected between us that waits for one or the other to speak, but neither of us do. Our audience is quiet. They wait for the wall to come down as well. I hear hushed conversation, the sounds of cutlery scraping, and the sipping of coffee. A pall of tenseness has fallen around where we sit.

Sis sets down her fork, dabs at her mouth with a napkin, and then rises to walk around the table. She steps in on my side, places her left knee on the banquette and her right between my legs, then leans in to kiss me. The kiss is long and deep, the first yet of this kind we have shared. I return it, my hand on her bare thigh.

"Am I forgiven?" she whispers in my ear after she breaks the kiss.

We are nose-to-nose as I answer, "Yes."

The spell lasts a few moments then the applause begins around us, first the sound of one pair of hands but rising slowly to take in the whole restaurant. I am certain those sitting across the room have no idea what they are clapping for, but as in all such public displays, repetition rules.

~ ~ ~

We return to my condo and spend the rest of the day in and out of bed. But in deference to my maturity, we leave long periods of cuddling and quiet conversation in between sexual romps. Sis is both gentle and energetic, and, perhaps in contrition, seeks to please me.

In the late afternoon, sun streams through my windows and washes the bed in enervating heat. Sis falls asleep prone with her face toward me. I have been drifting in and out of numbed satiation but take this opportunity to look at her more closely. Her long brown hair has fallen across her face in tendrils, so I remove it deftly, taking care not to disturb her slumber. Her face in repose reveals much it would not when animated. I study the small creases around her full lips and the faint lines at the corners of her closed eyes. She is no longer a girl. Probably in her early thirties, a few years older than Christine. At first I had presumed Sis to be the younger sister. But her face, now absent of makeup, tells another story.

As I continue my close inspection, I count the small scars, remnants of childhood horseplay or fights with her sister. There are seven of them: two are low on Sis' neck just behind her left ear, one creases her right brow, another two are high on her forehead and normally covered by bangs, one is a small puncture just below her lower lip on the left side and the other splits it. These last two suggest Sis has been bitten by someone or something many, many years ago. The side of her head I cannot see remains un-inspected, but since her left ear has three pinholes I presume her right does too. One is in her lobe. The other two are high on her ear just below the bend. She has removed the studs she wears in each high pinhole and the single loop she wears through each lobe. I can see them scattered across the nightstand on what she still insists is her side of the bed.

Her torso is marked here and there with moles and freckles, and I find a bright-red birthmark the size of a dime high up on her inner thigh. A strawberry. I'm surprised I haven't noticed this before considering our early morning sex play, but after thinking through the physics, I realize it would have been hidden. I find no further scars until I reach her feet, which sport several pigment free blotches on her right and left ankles. Curious. It is almost as if they had been burned at some point. I touch them with my fingertips and the skin feels no different than the surrounding unmarred areas. Sis stirs and uncrosses her ankles but does not wake. Too bad I can't get her to switch from prone to supine, I think, and as if she has read my thoughts, she turns onto her back.

~ ~ ~

I watch with strangely voyeuristic pleasure as I move up her body to inspect her breasts. They are, after all, the best part. Any guy will tell you that. We are all fixated, and any woman who wants to indulge herself in the fantasy about men going back to their first nipple with mom can be my guest. I have to say, though, that's just Freudian nonsense. He once quipped, "Sometimes a cigar is just a cigar." Yes? He might well have added, "Sometimes a tit is just a tit." But nothing feels better in your hand, the creamy, malleable flesh, the coarser areolas with those little bumps that respond so wonderfully to the touch, and the nipples, which draw themselves up like little soldiers rising erect for battle. If we are delighted to look and touch, women should just lay back and enjoy it, even if they don't understand what all the fuss is about. Or ask a lesbian. I'll bet they love breasts every bit as much.

Sis's breasts are perfect. They are still high on her chest but pendulous enough to belong to a woman, not a girl. For me the distinction is important. Imagine it like waiting patiently for tomatoes to ripen. If you pick them before they reach the perfectly red-ripe stage of soft fleshiness, they are simply not as sweet. And besides, young girls give them too freely; any pimply boy can cop a feel. There's something to be said for the thrill of pursuit and its rewards. It's a guy thing.

~ ~ ~

I kiss each nipple softly then take one between my teeth and tug gently. Sis makes a small noise, not a moan really, more of a whimper. I raise my eyes without letting go to watch her reaction then give another tug. "What are you doing?" she groans sleepily with eyes closed. I gave her nipple another tug then bite down.

She comes off the pillow with an, "Ouch! Stop that, you pervert," but she is laughing now. "Two can play that game you know," she says and lunges to grab me. But I scoot back and tumble off the bed and onto the floor. It's a long drop from the elevated platform. Now I'm the one who's moaning. I look up to see her face looking down at me. "Serves you right," is all the sympathy I get.

Then she slithers off the bed on top of me but puts most of her weight on her hands, one to each side. The view is wonderful, her nipples just grazing mine. Then she sniffs a couple of times and says, "We need a shower," and rises to stand above me. Hands on hips, she grins.

"Are you coming?"

Breast Reduction

On Monday, I beg off work. Brian doesn't need me anyway, though he asks that I make sure to come in Thursday through Sunday since he'll be away on a long weekend with his family. "No problem," I tell him.

I spend the morning going back over my thirty-two hours with Sis. Pathetic, I think, that I have actually counted them. After our long shower, soaping, rinsing, then drying each other, and for me, after the wonderfully sensual experience of shampooing her long hair while she sat cross-legged on the shower floor and I sat behind her, legs to either side, hot water cascading over us, Sis had once more donned her tube dress and walked out, bright and cheerful and giving me one last kiss goodbye. Is that all there is? I'm left wanting more but not expecting it. This leaves the feeling of limbo; I can neither let her go, retaining the memory of our idyllic interlude, nor anticipate a future reprise.

I ask myself what I really want from her and find no answer. Sis is far too young for me, but even if that weren't a barrier, there is nothing in what she said or did to make me think she has any interest in a long-term relationship with either me or anyone else. And the truth is I'm not sure I want anything long-term either. Someday, maybe. But for now I'd be quite content to have a girlfriend and no responsibilities. This thought seems reasonable to me and more consistent with the way I feel, until I realize that underlying what I mean by girlfriend is exclusivity. That may be what I want, but I doubt it's what Sis wants or is ready to concede. And there is nothing I have seen in her character that makes me believe concession is even a part of her vocabulary.

"I'll call you," she said, just as the elevator door slid shut and she was whisked away. I had watched earlier as she took my phone and called hers then deleted the record of her number. Control freak, I think. But no, that's not right. Sis loves the feeling of being out of control, the excitement, the surrender, and the sensuousness of it. I mentally compare her lovemaking to my night with Gretch and know this is true. Gretch is all about control. That is why she seems, and is, so good at it. She thinks her way through sex. Sis abandons herself to it, no thought, just feeling. This is why she may never be anyone's mate, I realize. That requires thought and planning and a degree of control that would kill her free-spirited embrace of whatever's next.

So the question, I suppose, assuming she actually does call me, is will I accept what she gives, enjoying it for however long it lasts, watching her flit in and out of my life, or will I beg off, knowing that since nothing will ever come of it, my pursuit of her is simply a waste of precious time?

But is time so precious, really? Not to a thirty-two-year-old girl with a long life of love and commitment somewhere out there waiting in her future. But at forty-five, I already understand myself well enough to know commitment is what I want, even if it's not what I need at the moment. Long life and love are partly in my past, and the future is neither so certain nor so distant anymore. The clock is ticking.

This is a circular argument, I know. I'm back where I started. Sis is too young for me and she is not ready for any sort of commitment. Fine then, it is what it is. I may not be young but I'm not over-the-hill either. Think I'll just wait to see what happens. That's some sort of decision anyway, short-term maybe, but enough for the moment. Sooner or later she'll call or she won't. In the meantime, I've got my buddies and maybe I'll ask Gretch out for a friendly dinner. She may have an opinion or two along the lines of the "get it out of my system" she has already recommended. But then I remember she also said she'd be happy to be my "occasional fuck-buddy," if only I didn't count it for too much. Is this what I might be for Sis? That just isn't enough, and I know it.

~ ~ ~

Doc calls at 4:00 p.m. and asks me out for a burger and a beer at the Blue Star. My pub is one of his favorites too. He orders a Pilsner Urquell and I ask for a black-and-tan, half Mack and Jack, half Guinness. Our waitress is the same girl who served Sis and me yesterday. She has a smirk on her face she is trying unsuccessfully to hide.

"What's so funny?" Doc asks when she returns with our beer then shuffles away, covering her mouth to keep from laughing.

If I could reproduce Sis's imagined imitation of Doc's climax and the noise he made, I would, though the words "you had to be there" cross my mind.

"Sis and I were here yesterday. She put on *quite* a show," I answer.

Doc begs me for details, and I finally relent, describing Christine's call and making sure Doc is sorry he asked by repeating her accusation that he fell asleep before satisfying her.

"I did no such thing," he sputters then adds sheepishly, "Oh, yeah. She went to use the john after…well, just after. I drifted off…"

"I did too," I say, omitting the part about Sis falling asleep first. No sense kicking him when he's down, and I have to admit I would never have met Sis except for Doc's constant nagging, so I owe him.

"So…give me the details."

But I don't owe him that much.

"Oh, no. You'll have to use your vivid imagination. But it was definitely a pleasant way to spend the weekend."

That draws a chuckle and a "Fine, but you don't get any details either."

I start to drop it but cannot resist. "Not necessary, we already got the details from Chris. In fact, it was too much information."

At first Doc frowns then I see the light come on in his eyes. "Just so happens Chris and I are having dinner at The Metropolitan on Friday. I'm sure she'll be happy to fill me in."

Just like Doc to wine them and dine them. He probably *will* get the details. I can't imagine Sis would withhold much, if anything, in her rehash to Chris. But I know the intense sensuality will be lost in translation so the details that matter most to me will remain personal. It does interest me that Doc is seeing Chris, and I comment on it. After all, it has been Doc's assertion that Teddies is for one-night-stands, just casual sex, no commitments.

He shrugs and gives me a non-committal answer. "What can I say? I like young women and I don't have many opportunities to hold one anymore. Most of the breasts I get to touch have seen better days."

His answer shocks me. It seems rude and shallow, and while I might expect this sort of thing from Curly, I would never have expected it from Doc. This is his profession, I think. He's talking about his clients, for god's sake. Then it dawns on me. This is downside of plastic surgery. In my entire life I have fondled the breasts of fewer than ten women. I add them up and the number shrinks to six, and one of those doesn't count since I was drunk and got my face slapped for it.

Doc has touched hundreds. The novelty must have worn thin a long time ago. For all his joking about having the world's best job, it has cost him dearly. In a sense, it's Doc who's had the breast reduction, his over-exposure inuring him to the very thing that excites the rest of us. And so he seeks younger and younger women, not because he likes them younger and younger, but because he is getting older and likes them the age at which he remembers their perfection. What a sad fate: to watch your middle years go by, knowing this will be taken from you, that no matter how charming you are, eventually there will not be a young woman willing to allow that intimate touch. And even sadder, I think, to be caught in this downward spiral by mere obsession.

As I continue to put myself in Doc's place I finally understand his serial monogamy. It has the same root.

Doc's loves are the same age, more or less. He gets older but they remain fixed in time, their bodies retaining their firm youthfulness while his slowly shrivels. When that ceases to be the case, he moves on. What irony; a plastic surgeon who disdains his own efforts. Able to repair time's ravages for others, he is impotent to repair those of the women he has loved.

~ ~ ~

The week goes by slowly. I get calls from Doc, Larry, and even Curly, all trying to coax me back to Teddies but I'm not in the mood. I've been reminiscing about Carole again and am disheartened and somewhat disgusted with myself. This is what comes of hooking up with girls half your age, I think. Since I can't imagine a relationship with Sis beyond the bedroom, it makes me long for what I have lost. Even though I know I don't want Carole back, and even though I know I could never love her again the way I need to love and be loved in return, she remains fixed in my mind as the ideal.

Fine, then. How do I go about getting another Carole? I want one to magically materialize in front of me. Poof, instant lover and best friend. Internet dating looms on my horizon, I know. I have already responded to Match.com's come-on, "It's okay to look." Talk about daunting. My first search was for women 35-55 within twenty miles of Seattle. I figured it would give me plenty to look at but all nearby. I checked the photos only box, figuring anyone who wouldn't post a photo must have a reason for not doing so, and any reason I could think of was scary. That search returned exactly 512 hits. That was okay, though; I didn't really want to mess around with women ten years younger or older than I am. So I narrowed my search argument to 40-50 years old. Same result, 512 hits. Must be a mistake, I thought, some programming error. But when I compared a few pages of each search result, I saw immediately the photos were different. The wider range search had produced some women with gray hair. The narrower had not. Then it dawned on me. Thirty-two pages of sixteen photos on each, 512 in total, must be the Match.com maximum. There were women within my search criteria who were not in my results.

That gave me pause. If there were over 500 women in the 40-50 range, there must be over 1,000 in the 35-45 category. My next search, ages 42-48, also returned 512 hits, as did ages 43-47. I had to narrow my search to a ridiculous, age 44-46 to end up with twenty-seven pages, 482 women. For the fun of it, I tried searching for women exactly my age and got 160. Doing the math, at 160 for each age, there must be around 1,600 women between five years younger and five years older than I am, and 3,200 if I want to look as far out as ten. Narrowing the search to a year younger or older would be ridiculous, and I'd still have to look through almost 500 candidates.

I began skimming and selecting the faces I liked best. I quickly determined that in order to go beyond a face I would need to create my own profile. The only information provided by clicking each photo was hometown. About halfway through the thirty-two pages, I noticed hometown changed from Seattle to some of the outlying communities. Maybe if I narrowed the distance from Seattle to ten miles, I'd get only Seattle residents. Assuming that Match.com was drawing a twenty-mile circle, halving the radius would result in dividing my headcount by four. Cutting the radius to five miles might reduce it even further, but only looking for women who live within biking distance isn't much more reasonable than looking for women exactly your own age. But you have to start someplace so I settled for a search of plus or minus three years within ten miles of 98117, my Shilshole office ZIP code. That still gave me nearly 500 possibles, though only half were in Seattle proper, the other half lived in towns like Bellevue or Kirkland. As long as I stayed on my side of Lake Washington, I'd have fewer to consider. I'd also avoid the commute back and forth across the lake. In all my years here, I have never warmed to the idea of floating bridges, and when a few sections sank a while back, it only strengthened my conviction.

~ ~ ~

By Thursday, I'm past ready to stop staring at my walls and go to work. No word yet from Sis, so I'm also ready for female companionship. I call Gretch's office and leave a message inviting her to dinner on Friday or Saturday, my treat. Later in the day her assistant RSVPs with a time and place and the stipulation, we're going Dutch. Gretch has chosen Wild Ginger downtown, an excellent Pacific-rim fusion restaurant that I think of as Thai. Their satay bar has won awards. I haven't been there for a while since the boys don't care for its couples orientation, their assertion not mine. As I imagine the various entrees I've tried, I'm salivating. Good choice, Gretch. See you Saturday at seven.

I arrive at Wild Ginger promptly, coming straight

from the marina in business casual and boat shoes. I'll be a bit underdressed but hope Gretch won't care. There's a short wait in the lounge while our table is cleared and reset, and in that space of time, Gretch arrives. One look tells me I should have taken the time to change. Her little black dress and string of pearls make me look foolish. I start to apologize, but she wraps her arms around my neck and shuts me up with a long kiss that is definitely not just friendly. Once I get my breath back, I begin again to offer my explanation for not dressing more formally, but she waves the apology off.

"You're not underdressed, I'm overdressed. I had a cocktail party to go to first. It was a Bar Association thing. Totally boring but Larry insisted on attending. Now he's off with the boys. So…why aren't you?"

Before I can answer, the hostess rescues me, showing us to the table Gretch has reserved. Gretch doesn't let it drop though. "I'm told you fell in love at Teddies," she says, picking up where she left off and leering at me with glee in her eyes. "And with someone half my age."

Way more than half your age, I think, but before saying it, I reconsider. Time to change the subject a bit. "Doubtful. She's probably not much younger than you are. How old are you anyway?"

I'm certain she won't answer. In my experience women never do, once they clear the thirty mark. But I'm wrong.

"Fifty-two." Then when that leaves me speechless, continues, "This is the part when you tell me I don't look a day over forty."

I fumble with my words but manage, "You don't."

Gretch motions aggressively with her hands for me to elaborate. I laugh at her histrionics. "You can't possibly be fifty-two. And you don't look forty either. Maybe thirty-five. Here all this time I've thought Larry was a cradle robber, and now I find it's the other way around."

Gretch shrieks with laughter and delight. "You have to promise me to call him that. It happens once in a while and it really makes him crazy. But, you see now, your new love really is half my age."

"Well, not quite, but I get your point."

"My point? I have no point. I'm just teasing you. Earlier I was teasing Doc. I told him I had a hot date tonight with someone he knew and loved. He looked pained and said, 'So that's why he wouldn't come with us to Teddies.' I just flashed a wicked smile."

"Maybe we should let old Doc off the hook. "

"Old Doc? Now who's having trouble with chronology? Seems to me you have a few years on him."

"Three. But I think he's taking aging more to heart. Just a few things he's said make me worry he's beginning to think of himself that way. I still think I'm a kid."

"Obviously. Otherwise you'd stick to women instead of playing with girls."

"*Mature* women like you, you mean?" I ask.

Gretch switches from mischievous to lascivious and leans across the table until her face is so close I can feel her breath. "I may not be a girl anymore, but I still fuck like one."

I hold her gaze. "Better."

And she does too. There's something in her

intensity or her expertise. Or maybe it's appetite. In any event, the movable feast, Wild Ginger to Wild Gretch, brings me to my senses and erases the blues. She departs before midnight this time, concerned to make sure neither Larry nor Doc nor I take our sex play too seriously. We agree we'll both let Doc off the hook and assure him our relationship is just about sex and will be intermittent. No fault. No foul. I can't really imagine why Larry has accepted this nor do I know what has changed Gretch's mind. Maybe nothing. Or maybe she thinks I can handle the fuck-buddy thing since I have more than one now. Not sure I do, of course, since Sis has yet to call, but Gretch is certain I'll hear from her soon. But I find I can't understand what Gretch wants. Before, she said she didn't even see how we could be sailing friends, that I'd be "unable to go forward" toward establishing the kind of relationship she believes I need. But tonight, she was the same lioness, seeming to abandon her former idea of what I really want.

And curiously, Gretch wanted details from my thirty-two hours with Sis. She thought it funny I had counted them. I had expected derision but received only an amused and endeared, "Ohhh," followed by what felt at first like a maternal hug but lapsed into something quite un-maternal. When Gretch insisted, I tried to describe the difference between her intensity and Sis's abandon but failed to draw a distinction. That seemed to worry her. It was as if she was sizing up the competition and wanted to steal from the playbook. Problem is, Sis doesn't seem to have one. I think it would be much easier to explain Gretch to Sis than the other way around. But I find I don't really want to.

~ ~ ~

On Sunday morning, Sis calls. "How would you like to take Chris and me sailing this afternoon?"

"I'd love to but I can't. Have to work. How about an evening sail?"

There's a pause while I listen to the muffled give-and-take then Sis comes back on.

"What time?"

"I close the office at five. Only takes me a few minutes to walk down the pier."

More muffled conversation then, "It's a date. Later, Dude."

Dude? Later, Dudettes, I think. Then I wonder if either of them has ever been on a sailboat. Hope Chuck is there this evening. I'd love to see the look on his face. A twosome of teenagers. He'll probably think I've been hanging around with Larry and Curly too long.

Then it hits me. Oh, shit. Please tell me they're not planning a three-way for later. I stop to imagine and find the thought very distressing. I really don't have either the self-confidence or the stamina for that. And I don't want to screw up whatever relationship Sis and I have going, assuming we have one at all. The image of the two girls kneeling on the bed on either side of me, naked and laughing, floats through my mind. Then the image shifts to add Margaret on top of me while her daughters watch, a waking nightmare that makes me shiver. The image shifts again. Chris and Margaret have disappeared. It is Gretch astraddle now while Sis watches then joins in the play. My shiver is quickly replaced by a stirring in the loins.

~ ~ ~

A few minutes before five, I close up the sales office and wander down to my dock. No girls at the gate. Either they're late or I've been stood up. "Yoo-hoo," they call from the boat, waving and clowning around on the foredeck. Keep that up and I'll be fishing one or both out of the water. Chuck is standing lifeguard dutifully and smiles as I approach.

"Didn't know you had any kids."

I can tell he's joking. Didn't know Chuck had a sense of humor.

"Your nieces here have been telling me stories."

Nieces, huh. I give the two of them a wilting look.

"Oh, I could tell a few stories myself. These two are dangerous."

My tone sets Chuck back on his heels a bit. I don't sound much like an uncle, unless you mean Uncle Molester. Then I laugh. "Just kidding. They're really great gals," I say in what I hope will sound like a fatherly voice. "They even offered to help me wax *Repose* next weekend. What do you think of that?"

Chuck is completely taken in. Chris and Sis have gone from grinning to deadpan to hesitant smiles in a moment's span. They can hardly play the parts they've cooked up and tease me back. I look at them and ask, "Isn't that right, girls?"

They look at each other and shrug; then they turn back and in syrupy-sweet voices say in unison, "Yes, Uncle Andrew."

~ ~ ~

Chuck helps us cast off and we head out of the marina. This will be the laziest of sails. The breeze is almost non-existent and the Sound is rippled. Once we are far enough offshore, I turn west-southwest into what little wind there is, flip the switch to raise the mainsail, and pull out the genoa by hand. Then I add sixty degrees to the autopilot heading, and *Repose* turns to fall off the wind into a close reach roughly west-northwest. The sails fill and *Repose* heels over slightly to starboard. The girls have been watching me in rapt attention, but as I settle in to let *Repose* sail herself, they ask, again in unison, "That's all there is?"

"That's it. What did you expect?"

"Well, more fiddling around with all the…whatevers. I mean, look at all this…nautical stuff. And you don't even have to use the steering wheel. It turns by itself."

I laugh at her supposition that sailing is difficult. It would be impossible to explain the intricacies of racing, which is probably what she imagines sailing to be. I've crewed a few times and it's fun, but I'm really just a cruiser. I appreciate all the computerized electronics of today's sailboats that have robbed Sis of the frenetic activity she's been expecting. To emphasize my point, I lean back, put my feet up, and close my eyes. "Let me know when we get near that island way off in the distance or if you think we're going to hit another boat."

Neither girl says anything. I keep my eyes closed and wait. Then I hear some shuffling and feel *Repose* move through the wind and heel to port. One of them has been fooling around with the autopilot. There are no other boats nearby so I keep my eyes closed. I know the genoa is hung up and chafing against the shrouds and mast, but the breeze is too light to do any damage.

Then *Repose* turns again and heels to starboard.

"Would someone like a sailing lesson?" I ask, eyes still closed. As I lay stretched out, Sis straddles me and begins a rocking motion. I keep my eyes closed but say, "That feels nice."

"I'm sure it does," she says. My eyes pop open. It's not Sis.

Chris hops off and the two of them laugh at my surprised expression.

"We want to steer," they say together like petulant children.

"Thought you already were," I reply and close my eyes again. I know I'm teasing them into asking nicely, but they deserve it for the Uncle Andrew routine back at the dock.

"Okay, *please* can we steer?"

"Say, pretty please and I'll let you."

That did it. Now both of them straddle me, Chris closest and Sis on my knees. "Ready to say uncle?" they ask in unison.

"Nope," I answer but Chris starts tickling me. I'm quite ticklish. This is fun, I think, then I feel Sis unzip my jeans. "Okay, uncle, uncle!"

They clamber off and give each other a high-five. "First dibs," Sis calls out.

~ ~ ~

We spend the rest of the evening tacking back and forth. I teach them how to come about gracefully and after a couple of sloppy turns they get the idea and even direct each other while I lean back and watch. Holding a steady course, however, is another matter. Neither has the feel for it. We do a lot of flopping around, get becalmed twice when one or the other turns too close to the wind, and there are several jibes. But in the five-knot breeze, nothing bad can happen, so I let them do what they want and make my criticism very gentle and my praise generous.

By 8:00 p.m. we are back near Shilshole, and I start the engine and have Sis steer into the wind so I can lower the mainsail and pull in the genoa. She asks if she can motor back and I let her, explaining how to keep her speed down by shifting in and out of neutral and how to allow for the current and southwesterly breeze that sets us a bit to starboard in the channel. She follows my instructions pretty well, and I only have to adjust her course slightly on occasion. Like most novices, Sis has a tendency to over-steer.

I take over the helm as we approach. I enter the fairway between docks, stop *Repose*'s forward motion, and then back into the slip. My propeller turns clockwise in reverse so *Repose* will prop-walk to starboard. This has the tendency to make the bow drift to port, so I have Chris hop off and take the bow line to pull us in at the forward dock cleat while Sis handles the boat hook to prevent the stern from scraping, and while I turn the wheel over all the way to starboard, shift to forward, and goose the throttle to stop our backward motion. We make a good landing and the girls both seem pleased to have been instrumental.

After *Repose* is tied up securely, we head for Ray's. They offer to treat me to dinner and I accept the invitation, but insist on paying. Both are students at UW, Chris just finishing up a graduate nursing program, and Sis in a delayed bachelor-of-arts after which she hopes to teach. In neither case can they afford much entertainment. That must be one of the reasons they like Teddies, free drinks for dressing down. They also like the no muss, no fuss, commitment-free fun they have. Neither has time nor interest right now in working on a relationship, and the two of them are quite vocal and matter-of-fact about their hook-ups. A little drinking, dancing, and sex play go a long way to loosen them up after an intense week of classes and cramming for exams. The abandon I have seen in Sis is the flipside of her pursuit of a goal.

Both girls have been wearing tube tops and tight shorts that are hardly more than briefs. That accounts for Chuck's interest. Mine too, if I'm honest. They threw on sweatshirt tops when the sun lost some of its edge, but shed them after we docked. The evening is still quite warm and the breeze has dropped to a whisper. They head for Chris's car once we get to the lot. It's parked way out in the middle and Chris beeps open her trunk as we approach. Each hands me a spaghetti-strapped sundress, red print for Sis and violet-streaked for Chris. They exchange their gum-soled sneakers for heels then each takes a sundress, slips it over her head and down to her waist, pulls the tube top off, using me as a shield from anyone who might notice, and adjusts the dress and straps. Next, each reaches up under her dress and slips off the shorts. The whole process takes less than a minute.

Quick-change artists. I say, "That was entertaining. What do you do for an encore?"

Sis gives me a sly smile. "We'll see," she answers, and I begin to worry again the two of them have something planned. My concern must register in my expression, because Sis gives me a questioning look then it dawns on her where my mind has wandered off.

"You wish! We don't even share clothes."

Both girls break into peels of laughter and I'm left standing there looking foolish. While they amuse themselves with whispers, glances at me, and play-acting that ranges from polar extremes of haughty disdain to animal lust, I just grin and bear it. They are really wound up. When they finally wind down again, Sis grabs her overnight bag and Chris locks the car, but they continue to cackle.

"Where are you parked?" they ask, a moment apart, then in unison say, "Jinx," and launch back into another fit of giggling.

After dropping off Sis's bag, we walk the two blocks to Ray's and up the stairs to the casual section, one girl on either side, arms linked around waists. The looks we get suggest the observers are trying to make up a story to account for the three of us. Maybe I'm a celebrity photographer with two of his models. Or maybe I'm a young-looking dad being taken for a birthday dinner by his daughters. Or maybe I'm a pathetic old sugar daddy with his two bimbos. Or, I suppose, I'm just a clueless chump being mercilessly teased by two clever young women. But I guess for tonight I'll be Uncle Andrew home from an evening sail with his nieces.

Falling

By 11:00 p.m., Sis and I stand on my balcony sharing a bottle of wine in the warm night air. The half-full bottle and our untouched glasses rest behind us on a small wrought-iron table between teak Adirondack chairs. To the south, the Seattle skyline sparkles and wavers in the shimmering air currents. To the southwest, the Space Needle pierces the darkness. Wafts of salt-laden air flow around us in the light westerly breeze. We lean against the railing side by side taking in the traffic on the opposite shore, still coursing steadily with unknown purpose. On Lake Union, a few commercial boats continue to cut the water, but for the most part, all are tied securely for the night. Every ten minutes or so, a jetliner flies by on the way into SeaTac airport, landing lights blazing and wingtips blinking a red heartbeat.

"What are you thinking?" Sis asks after a while.

I pause before answering to consider the purpose behind her question. Her tone is level and serious; none of the flippant or teasing nature it commonly has filters through. "I'm happy being here with you." Don't know if this something she will want to hear or not.

She takes my hand without withdrawing her eyes from the distant parade of cars.

"I am too."

We stand a minute in silence, then she turns and

slips into my embrace, threading her arms slowly over my shoulders. At first she does nothing more than look quietly into my eyes, considering. I stare back, waiting for her to decide whatever she needs to. Then she leans in and kisses me softly and repeatedly, delicate kisses that make the rest of the world flow away. We stand like this for several minutes before Sis pulls back. "I love the way you kiss."

"That should be my line. I never want to stop."

As I say this, she nestles closely, her head on my chest. "That's what I'm afraid of." Her admission is mostly to herself. "I'm afraid you need me in a way I will never need you. I do want you, but I don't need you. Do you understand the difference?"

Knowing this is a turning point of some sort, I pause before I respond. Sis may be right but she has also attributed more need to me than I really feel. I'm not sure how to explain exactly where I am right now. Then I remember a line from an old Neil Young song and reverse it, "It doesn't mean that much to you to mean that much to me."

"Yes," she answers evenly, not recognizing the words. "That's exactly what I mean."

"But it must mean something or we wouldn't be here together talking about this."

She begins to answer but I cut her off gently, "Let me finish." Sis drops her arms to my waist and hugs me, waiting for me to say what I will say.

"I'm in a strange place right now. I don't honestly know what I want or need in the long run. Right now I want you, and it's true at some level I need you as well. But I don't know what I will feel a year from now. Maybe the same. Maybe not. Certainly it would make more sense for me to be meeting women my own age. But there's a lot to be said for not listening to the part of me that judges what makes sense and ignores what feels right. And I'm not. Not listening, that is.

"Look, Sis, I know very well you don't want an exclusive relationship. And I imagine you're worried if we continue as we have been, you may hurt me. But there's nothing I can do to prevent that. I can't tell you I won't be hurt if you leave, whenever you leave. I probably will be. But I can tell you truthfully the hurt you leave in your wake could never match the hurt Carole's departure inflicted. I cannot believe I will ever love anyone so completely as I once loved her."

We stand holding each other and not speaking for a long time, so long in fact that I cannot stand the silence any longer. "You know, when I said I never wanted to stop kissing you, that's just what I meant. I didn't mean I never want you to leave. I love your soft kisses. They are so much more intimate than sex." I pause again then take a lighter tack. "Not that I want to substitute kisses for everything else."

I feel Sis relax and cuddle closer. She makes a happy noise that sounds like, "Hmmm," with a small laugh tagged onto the end then asks, "Do you remember your first kiss?"

Yes, I think, I will always remember. But what I say is, "That was Carole."

"Wow. You married the first girl you kissed?"

"Well, not right away. We dated a long time. And we'd been friends for a year before we started going out. She was dating other guys. I was library guy, always there when she walked in. It became a joke. Then we started studying together after we found we shared the same business classes in different periods."

"Wait! You met in college? You never kissed a girl 'til college?"

Her tone is utter disbelief. She has pulled back to look at me, unwilling to accept I'm not joking.

"I was painfully shy in high school. I never dated. And I was younger than most of my classmates. Besides, lots of guys don't really begin dating 'til college."

"That is *so* not true! Most guys have had sex before college. My first kiss was at twelve in seventh grade. I was dancing with this guy I had a huge crush on and just planted one on him. I had sex first when I was fifteen and most of my girlfriends beat me to it."

I shrug. "I was a little afraid of girls. I did go to dances, but I hung out with the guys on our side of the gym floor. I didn't know how to dance, so was only asked for the slow numbers occasionally. Those girls were pretty aggressive. Made me nervous. I guess...I just wasn't popular."

"Wow," she says again. "I saw that photo with your sister and parents. You were adorable. I'd have been all over you."

"Yeah, well, if you're shy, having girls all over you is pretty intimidating."

"I'll bet they thought you were gay."

"No, they thought I was stuck up. They thought I thought I was too good for them. And since I wasn't comfortable with any of the girls who tried, I just let them think what they wanted. After a while they all left me alone. Then, in college, Carole and I started hanging out together, so I guess the other girls thought we were a couple."

"Huh. Still hard to believe. You mean to tell me none of those pushy teenage girls ever tried to kiss you? I would have."

Sis is smiling warmly as she says, "I would have," and at first I smile too. But then my mind wanders back to my first kiss and I can feel the pain and tears.

"What? What's wrong?"

At first I cannot speak. Tears course down and, once begun, resist my attempts at control. "It was a long time ago, that first kiss."

"And you still love this girl? I don't get it."

I have never told anyone this story. I have carried it with me my whole life and have never had someone I could trust with the knowledge. Why do I trust Sis? Somehow I do. I can feel it. But, why?

"It was the summer before I entered ninth grade," I begin slowly. "My sister, Jess, was three years older. Our parents had gone out of town for a few days and said we could each have a friend stay over but no big parties. Jess and I tolerated each other but knew the other would rat out any serious infractions. I opted not to ask any of my buddies. Jess invited three of her girlfriends and bartered future chores if I kept my mouth shut.

"I'd met her little clique. They were annoying but tolerable, so I agreed to the deal. We watched TV together for a while that night, but when they wanted to play music, I left them to dance together. One of them teased me and begged me to stay in the soupy, insincere way teenage girls have, but there was something unsettling about the way she asked and the way she looked at me. I went to bed to read until I got tired, then fell asleep.

"Sometime in the middle of the night, my door clicked open and shut. At first I thought I was dreaming, but then I saw her standing alongside my bed. As I watched, she removed her pajamas. Then she stood there looking at me. She could see my eyes were open. We just stared at each other for a minute before she climbed into bed with me and rolled on top. All I was wearing were boxer shorts. I could feel her breasts pressing down on my chest. Then she kissed me, softly at first, but soon she pushed her tongue into my mouth and began groaning. I felt myself become erect even though I was fighting her now. She felt it too, reached into my boxers, and slid me inside her. Within seconds I came.

"And then she laughed, and kept laughing as she put her pajamas back on and left me there in my sticky puddle. For the whole school year, anytime she passed me in the hall, she'd say, 'Hey, Quick Draw,' and I'd look away, unable to meet her sneer."

Sis has remained silent while I spoke. Tears have filled her eyes to mirror mine. "Jesus, you were raped."

"She wasn't that strong. I could have pushed her away," I answer, the same defeat in my voice I had felt each time I heard "Quick Draw" that one miserable year.

"God, it's worse. You were raped and you blamed yourself. You're still blaming yourself."

"A girl can't rape a guy, Sis. It takes two to tango."

"Oh, bullshit. A grown man couldn't control an erection under those circumstances. Teenage boys have no control at all."

My defeated expression is all I offer in my defense.

Sis shakes her head sadly. "It's no wonder you

didn't date 'til college. And it's no wonder you're still in love with Carole. This is so screwed up. You poor guy. I've known women who were date-raped and worked their way through it, but at least they had someone to talk to. You've never told anyone else this, have you? Not even Carole."

"There was never anyone to tell. And with Carole, any time I thought I might, I remembered all the years I had kept it from her. I…I just couldn't."

She gives me a look drenched in pity but doesn't speak.

"Don't pity me," I say angrily, all vestiges of the morose gone. "It's been thirty years. I'm not a clueless teenager any more. I don't need you to feel sorry for me." Then, as if to call me a liar, the tears come back, but they are not for my fifteen-year-old past, they are for what might have been my forty-five-year-old future with Sis, a future that even if I believed unlikely, still might have existed. But now I have ruined it. I have let her see just how needy I am, and my few angry words are only anger at my self-pitying self.

Sis leaves my fading words unopposed but takes me by the hand and leads me to bed. We hold each other, kiss occasionally, and hold each other some more. At some point, I fall asleep. When I wake she is no longer lying beside me. I listen for some sign she is still present someplace in the house, but hearing none, get up and go looking. The kitchen clock reads just past 3:00 a.m. Sis is sitting out on the balcony. I stand in the open doorway behind her for a while. She is quiet. I think she knows I'm here but she startles when I speak. I ask the same question she first asked me, "What are you thinking?"

"I'm still happy to be here with you."

"Good. I'm happy you are."

"I've been sitting here trying to decide what I want. I think I know what you want and I guess I could just go along with that, but I'm not sure it would be good for either of us. I want us both to want each other but not need each other. I don't know if you can do that, and I want you to think about it for a while before you try answering."

She pauses and sighs. She sounds unsure when she begins again but manages to work through it. "Here's what I think I know: you want me to be here with you, yes?"

"Yes, you know that's true," I answer, more sure of what I say than Sis seems to be, but hesitant to commit too much.

"And I'll accept for now that you think I won't hurt you any more if I leave sooner than if I leave later. I also believe you need time alone as well as time with me. You like your time alone but you don't want to *be* alone. Does that sound right?"

"Yes, it does." This feels like the heart of it right now; I don't like being alone. It reminds me of what I've lost, and it makes me fear that, unlike what Sis has claimed, I will never love again at any level close to the way I have loved Carole.

"There's something you don't know about me," she says. "I don't like Teddies. I occasionally go with Chris but that's just to humor her. Teddies is Chris's place, not mine. I find guys to hook up with on the Internet. Match.com. I look for the ones who say they're currently separated or recently divorced or give the impression they're just looking for company not commitment. That way I know I can't do much damage. I sleep with them and leave them. They are happy to be bedded and only a little pissed-off to be dumped. And I never lie to them."

Sis pauses and I wonder if she's waiting for me to say something. Up to this moment I've thought of Match.com and its competitors as purveyors of single souls desperately seeking to be coupled again. I have imagined a storefront business with two doors, ladies and gents, just like the signs you might see in a bar above the restrooms. Walk in and get matched up. But Sis is saying that for her it's walk in and get hooked up. Then I understand she is hardly the first person of either sex to think this way. And I can easily see how it could be misused. It's no wonder I've heard internet dating called, "Entering Match.com hell."

"But I've been lying to you," she resumes slowly. She speaks in a voice that sounds sad but accepting of what she feels she must say. "Or at least misleading you." Then she stops again and turns in her seat to face me.

"That night at Teddies…Chris had a deal with your gnome-like friend. She'd sleep with him on condition he'd find someone perfectly safe for Mom. He told her about you and said he was pretty sure he could talk you into coming, and you wouldn't suspect a thing. Was he right?"

"Sadly, yes. I had no idea. But I should have suspected. Doc seldom if ever does anything straightforward. He loves cross-woven plots."

She nods her head. "I guessed as much. But as I watched you dance first with Chris then with the little cowgirl then with my mother, I could tell you were into the whole thing. I suspected Doc had double-crossed Chris and brought in a ringer. Not that it mattered as long as you were a good actor and Mom didn't catch on. So, when I came here with you, I thought you were a player, someone I couldn't damage. By the time I figured out you could easily be hurt, it was too late."

She pauses again and looks into my eyes for some sign of agreement. Too late for what? Too late to avoid the hurt she knows she must inflict now? Or is it too late to leave without hurting both of us? She can see my question hanging in the empty space between us and turns away. I follow her gaze and watch the lights play across the lake below us.

Sis remains quiet for a long time then continues, "That first night when I walked in here, I thought to myself, this is pretty nice. Great-looking guy, fantastic bachelor pad, obviously has money, even has a good shy-submissive act. So I let myself go a little, let myself play along. Big mistake. Now I realize you're falling in love with me, maybe not head-over-heels, but it's more for you than just casual, isn't it?"

Sis rattles on, her rhetorical question hanging in the air, but I stopped listening at "falling in love with me." By the time I tune her in again she's staring at me in silence. "Sorry," I say, "I lost you at the 'falling in love' part."

"That's just what I'm afraid of. You'll become fixated and I won't be able to live up to your expectations." Sis rises then and comes over to the doorway where I'm still standing. She takes my hands and locks eyes with mine. She is waiting to hear the words to convince her not to run away. Her posture is all flight, no fight. Am I falling in love with her? If I admit it will she run? Or maybe if I admit it she will believe me when I say I know the risk and will be free to stay.

"I am falling in love with you," I say, simple acceptance of the fact in my voice. "But that would have happened no matter who was the first woman to be here with me like this. I want the feeling of falling in love again. Losing Carole has left a big hole I need to have filled. I think it makes me more open to it. And it's also true I haven't stopped being in love with Carole. So, what does that mean? How can I be in love with two women? And why stop at two. Maybe I could fall in love with three or four. I suppose the truth is I want to be free to fall in love with you without worrying about you worrying about it. And I love the idea of you being here, someone to come home to. I know you're teasing me about moving in, but I want you to know I'd love you to. I also know it's foolish to tell you this because we've known each other for a week and you're probably ready to run right about now. But it doesn't matter to me when, or even if, you feel comfortable enough to consider that. It's an open offer."

During the entire time I have been speaking, our eyes have remained focused on each other. In the silence that follows, we hold the same gaze. After a while it begins to seem like a contest. If I break away first, will she turn and run? But when the break comes, it is Sis who closes her eyes and says, "Alright. I'll stay. But we need some rules. If we're going to be together, we need to have boundaries."

At this point I'll happily agree to any rules she insists upon. "Okay, shoot," I say with a big, stupid grin.

She doesn't like my anything-goes smile and gives me a weary look, as if to say this is a bad idea, but she goes on anyway, "First, I will move in with you. Truth is I'm tired of never having someone to come home to. But separate bedrooms. Deal or no deal?"

"Deal," I say, nodding first and thinking a little before I continue. "You need your own space. So do I. Makes sense. You are still planning to sleep with me now and then, aren't you?"

In response Sis gives me a withering "Don't be stupid" look that melts into an answering grin, and she touches me in a way that removes all doubt. I just keep grinning foolishly.

"Second…in response to your silly question…neither of us beds anyone else under our shared roof. *But*, we can do what we please elsewhere. *And*, I'll expect you to find other women to sleep with. No exclusivity on either side. I cannot be the only woman in your life. That's too big a responsibility. Deal or no deal?"

I think for a minute, but since this is clearly a requirement and since it makes sense of a sort, I answer, "Deal. But I don't like Teddies either. Can you help me find women on Match.com like the guys you find who won't be hurt?"

"I think so. We can look through profiles together. With some it will be clear they're not looking for anything permanent. We'll try to avoid the ones who are."

I think I can do this, I say to myself. But then I realize the truth: I want to think I can do this. That's not at all the same thing. But I don't have time right now to think it through so I answer simply, "Alright, then."

Sis is unconvinced. It's all over her face. So, her last caveat is the clincher. "Third, if either of us thinks this is getting too strange, or too intense, or too personal, we say so and talk it out. No holding back. No secrets. Deal or no deal?"

Even as the word "deal" leaves my mouth, I understand I have violated her third rule. I know I'm holding out on her. But then she knows I'm in love with her. There's no secret between us. And I will need some time to weigh my feelings before I can tell what I mean by love and whether those feelings are too intense or too personal. Who knows, I think, maybe I'll like what Sis has proposed. And, since everybody who has expressed an opinion recommends I take my time before jumping into a serious relationship, maybe that's just what I should be doing. And even if I find I've only been fooling myself, at least for now they'll all stop worrying about it. My foolish grin has faded, replaced by a deeply satisfied but wistful smile. Sis smiles the same way. Then, having made up her mind to let it be, lifts to kiss me and give me a nip on the ear.

"Let's go back to bed."

Smile, and I'll Send You a Wink

Three days later, Sis arrives at my door dragging several suitcases behind her. She takes her time unpacking and organizing her walk-in closet. It has cubbyholes, hanger units at different heights, pullout drawers, and strategically placed hooks. When she is done she calls me to admire her work. A place for everything and everything in its place, I think. Her self-satisfied look seems to agree. I like it that she's pleased to be standing here, and say so.

"What is really pleasing is to be out of the parental estate." She's teasing me, but honest as well. I get a nice hug to show her appreciation.

"All moved in?" I ask.

"Not quite. Still have to fill the bathroom with my stuff. Takes a lot to make me beautiful every day." She picks up a huge case that presumably contains all her cosmetics and begins lugging it to her bathroom.

"Obviously," I respond, referring to the imagined contents of the case.

"Oh, really?" She gives me a sidelong glance. "Then maybe I'll clutter up your bathroom instead."

By the time she is done, I really do regret teasing. Her side of the double sink area overflows into mine with brushes, combs, bottles and jars, and two fuzzy cubes, one holding a lifetime supply of Q-tips and the other filled with facial tissue. The cabinet and most of the drawers are overflowing as well. She leaves me one side of a medicine cabinet and two drawers out of the six. She goes back to her room and returns with a furry pink bathrobe, hangs it prominently next to my beige terrycloth, and places a pair of ratty-looking, matching-pink, hausfrau slippers below. Then, pleased with herself, she stands hands-on-hips and flashes me a smile. "What do you think?"

"I think you're too adorable for words. I trust you realize, however, this bathroom doesn't have a lock on the bedroom side, just a pocket door. You can forget about privacy."

"Hmmm. Cuts both ways, doesn't it?"

Then, as I watch, she kicks off her shoes and begins a deliberately slow process of unbuttoning her blouse and removing her brassiere. She stands languorously, barefoot, bare-chested, and blue-jeaned, hands held behind her back enjoying my rapt attention. Then she says, "Seems a shame to waste water when we could both shower at the same time. Want to join me?"

~ ~ ~

We settle into a pattern. Sis continues to spend some nights at her parent's home, some nights with me, and some nights, she claims, with men she's hooked up with. She makes a point of showing me their profiles on Match.com and continues to insist I make an effort to find other women. We look together at possible matches for me and she tells me to work on my profile. Two weeks later, I haven't even begun. Sis arrives back from an evening out to find me watching TV.

"Get that profile done yet?"

This makes the third or fourth time she's asked.

"No. Just can't think of what to say."

"You mean you don't want to think of anything to say."

"I guess."

"That wasn't our deal. You have to hold up your end of it."

I suppose I knew I wouldn't get away with it. I look up to see Sis watching me and waiting for an answer. "Okay, I'll do it. Can you help?"

"Sure. Get your laptop."

"Now?"

"Right now."

I kill the TV and find my computer buried in the closet. I'm not much of a technophile. But I'm not a technophobe either; I know how to find my way around the Internet. I sign onto Match.com using the ID I made up: *cmdeaconblues*. Then Sis takes over.

"So, here's the first question. What brings you here today to Match.com?"

There are several possible answers. I choose, "A friend found someone great on Match.com, so I'm giving it a go."

Sis tells me she's found many someone's but none of them was really all that great.

"Why look then?"

She ignores me. "Next question. What is your relationship status, currently separated or divorced?"

"You know I'm not divorced yet. There's a ninety-day waiting period after the paperwork is accepted. I think the clock started ticking last week."

"Well, either you tell the truth and limit the number of women who might be interested or you tell a little white lie."

"Let's stick to the truth for now, okay?"

"You're the boss."

"Doubtful. What's next?"

"What is your gender? I think I can answer that one and the next as well: are you looking for men or women? I think I'll say you're looking for women between the ages of thirty-two and forty-seven."

"Why not forty to fifty?"

"Women always lie about their age on Match.com. Good rule of thumb is to automatically add three years. And younger women are less likely to be looking for long-term."

"Okay, you're the boss."

"And don't you forget it either. So, let's say women within twenty miles of your ZIP code, which would be…?"

"98117 is good. That's Shilshole."

"Fine, next come the physical attributes. Height?"

"Six foot nothing."

"Body type? Let's call it 'about average.' Don't want to make you sound like a gym rat. When your date gets a close look, she'll just think you're modest. Very endearing."

"So, astrological sign?"

"You're joking, right?"

"Right. We'll leave it 'no answer.' Continuing on, we have eyes: bluest of blue; hair, beach boy blond; body art, none that I've found yet. Here's one for you to answer: 'Brag a little. What's your best feature?' The choices are: arms, butt, calves, chest, eyes, feet, hands, hair, legs, lips, neck."

"I'm not answering that."

"All right, but then I get to choose. Deal?"
"Fine."
"Lips it is. And I should know."

I begin to protest but Sis cuts me off. "It's not an answer they'll expect. It will be intriguing. Next question: what do you do for fun in 250 words or less? I can start with sailing. What else?"

"I don't know. Um, movies, plays, dining out, the occasional Mariner's game."

"How about concerts, beach walks, dancing, romantic dinners at home, cooking with a friend. You have to look at this from the woman's perspective."

"Yeah, but I thought you wanted me to sound like someone for a date not for a lifetime, right?"

"Good point. Alright, here's what I'll say: I like most outdoors activities and quite a few indoor activities as well. I'm a sailor and have my own boat. I like quiet dinners out on the town, concerts, plays, movies, a walk on the beach, or anything else you can convince me to do. I'm easy."

"You're way too good at this."

"Lots of experience."

"Right, that's what worries me."

Sis gives me a look but can see I'm just teasing so goes on to the next question: favorite local hot spots and travel destinations.

"That's easy. The Blue Star and Ray's Boat House. The only place I've ever traveled out of the country is Australia, Carole's home. And British Columbia in *Repose*."

"Okay, but where would you like to travel?"

"You name it. It's Carole who wouldn't go anywhere."

"Let's try this: Haven't done much traveling yet so I'll turn the question around. Where would you like to go with me? Europe? The Caribbean? China? India? Or someplace closer to home, like a cruise up the coast into British Columbia. I'm open to suggestions."

"Sounds fantastic. When do we leave?"

She looks at me and knows I'm not really joking. "Someday...someday."

The next question is: favorite things. Kind of hokey but we manage to create a list: foods—just about anything but Brussels sprouts; music—just about anything but rap; books—just about anything that's not too serious, too violent, or too long; ditto for movies; and TV—just about anything on PBS or the Discovery channel, is there anything else worth watching?

We've been sitting a while so we do a seventh inning stretch then Sis continues, "What was the last thing you read?"

It's been a while since I read anything. "My divorce settlement," I say.

"I like that. Very clever. How about a book?"

"Last book I can remember is *The English Patient*."

"When? Ten years ago?"

"Maybe," I answer without a trace of chagrin. Not everybody reads books.

"Pathetic. All right, here's what I'll say: The last thing I read was my divorce settlement, an engaging little story with a happy ending, unlike the last book I read, *The English Patient*, which while engaging, was definitely not happy. Took me long enough to get around to reading it, huh?"

"Very funny. Misleading too."

"Only a little. We can be a trifle loose with the

details without lying, can't we?"

Her question is obviously rhetorical so I don't comment. Sis goes on chatting while filling in the check boxes for describing what sports, exercise, and general interests I have. She marks some that I have no interest in like museums and art, and discussing politics, which I avoid like the plague, but otherwise she is truthful. I nod and go along with whatever she suggests.

Then she gets to the lifestyle section and answers the first question: how often do you exercise, with "three to four times a week."

"Why," I ask.

"Five times or more is obsessive gym rat territory and one to two times a week probably means you never get off the couch. This is one of the things guys lie about."

The truth is I don't exercise at all though I walk a lot. I just don't count it as exercise. Nor do I count the regular thrashings I get from playing tennis with Doc, but he runs me around the court like a squirrel after acorns, so I suppose I do get some.

Sis ticks off the other items. Apparently, I eat healthy (though that's a stretch), I don't smoke (true, unless you count the occasional cigar with the boys), I'm a social drinker, keeping my consumption to one to two drinks a day (let's call it two to three, or more if I'm out with Doc), I'm in sales and marketing (true), I live alone (not true but since we've already agreed to no hookups at home, they'll never know), I don't have kids (true), and I don't know if I want them (I think that's true but the fact is I never gave it much thought since Carole never wanted any). Oh, and I like cats and dogs (who doesn't?). In the background/values section she puts me down as Caucasian, spiritual but not religious, college-degreed, English-speaking, and middle-of-the-road politically; all perfectly good answers and close enough to the truth, though the right-shift we've done during the Bush administration has me way left of center now on most issues.

She leaves my income as a "no answer," but cannot resist asking.

"I probably spend less than $50,000 a year." Cagey answer, but she just smiles and waits. I haven't discussed the details of my settlement, but I'm no good at keeping secrets and I really don't mind sharing the information. It just never came up.

"I really don't know. I probably spend about as much as I make selling boats when I put in the hours. Haven't been doing that lately. The rest is investment results. Maybe $300-400k most years once I find a decent broker to manage my money."

Her incredulous expression makes telling her worthwhile. "You're shitting me."

I shrug in apology for my unearned fortune.

Sis continues on to the next group of questions about what I want my prospective dates to be like, but she is clearly distracted. She inputs generally open answers so as not to discriminate based on race, religion, ethnicity, height, weight, education, marital status, the presence of or desire for children, drinking habits, eye and hair color, and income. I insist only that non-smokers are all I can deal with.

"Okay, your turn," she says, handing me the laptop. "You just need a 'Dating Headline,' something catchy, and you need to write your introduction—what you are looking for right now in your life. I'm off to my nightly beauty regimen. Call me when you're done."

I imagine it will take me longer to write this than it will take her to do whatever it is that women do with all the cosmetics, but I'm wrong. When I go looking for her, I find she is still at it. Her face is covered with something that looks like guacamole or pea soup.

"Lovely."

"Don't make me laugh," she spits out clench-jawed. "And, by the way, you asked for this, if I remember correctly."

"What was I thinking? I'm done with my intro."

"Well, go get your laptop and read it back to me."

I do as I'm told. It occurs to me that doing what I'm told may become a regular habit. But the possibility only makes me smile. I return to find Sis waiting patiently. She looks like a petite female version of the Incredible Hulk. That thought elicits a chuckle from me and a sneer from her when I say it out loud.

"I made the headline, 'Call Me Deacon Blues...Come Sail With Me."

Sis has heard the explanation of my nickname. She looks at the ceiling with a "Why me?" expression then motions for me to continue with the intro.

"I've lived in the Seattle area since I graduated from UW. The Pacific Northwest has become my home. I like any outdoor activity that includes being on, in, or under water: sailing in my boat on Puget Sound, diving in the Caribbean, cruising in BC, kayaking in the San Juan Islands, whatever you'd like. I even work by the water since I sell boats for a living. That said, I'm happy hiking up in the Cascades as long as you understand I'll be looking for a view of the Sound."

"I'm just going through my divorce now so I'm not

looking for a long-term commitment, just someone to hang out with and share my passion for sailing. Someday I'll want more, I know, but I guess I need to leave my baggage behind and that just takes a while. I know from looking at some of your profiles that most of you will probably pass on mine, preferring guys who have been out there long enough to know what they want. Trust me, I get it. But maybe some of you don't know what you want either right now. If so, maybe we can find out together. I make a good friend, one who will always think of you first. All we have to lose is some time. What do you say?

"That's it." I wait for her expected disapproval, but she nods and holds out her hands for me to give her the laptop. Within a few keystrokes, my profile is on the way to the Match.com censors. Then she turns to the mirror and begins to wash away the green goop, but not before removing her bathrobe and halter-top to avoid staining them green. I relax and enjoy the show. She seems to have no sense of modesty, a pleasing attribute.

"Still need some photos," she says after she finishes washing her face and begins to dry it. "We can take a few at the boat, unless you have some already. And I want a good professional headshot, so you need to find a photographer tomorrow."

"Is what I said okay?"

Sis continues drying and looking for any missed spots. I watch her in the mirror looking back at me. It's a serious look, too serious for the circumstances, and I worry I'm missing something.

"Is what you say what you really think?"

She hangs her towel back on its hook. "I mean, you don't really know what you want?"

"Yeah, that's true. And I think I need to get to the place where I'm happy I don't know what I want. That's going to take a while, but it's where I have to be before I can go any further."

Sis closes the distance between us, puts her arms around my neck, and kisses me. "Time for bed," she says.

~ ~ ~

Next morning, as Sis and I sit having coffee out on the balcony, we discuss whether I should write to some women or wait until they write to me. I sense something different in her, some worry or reticence. She is calmly watching the boat traffic out on the lake but seems abstracted, lost in thought. When I ask what's wrong, she thinks for a moment then says, "I'm reconsidering one of my answers in your profile."

"Which one?"

"How you feel about kids. I know you shouldn't say you don't want them or definitely want them, and I think you shouldn't say, 'probably not', either. The way you wrote your intro in combination with the 'currently separated' answer is going to limit the number of women who will write to you, though you'll still get lots of emails, trust me. The question is whether you should say 'not sure' or 'someday'."

My turn to ponder. I try to put myself in the position of the women who will read this. The younger ones will still be of childbearing age, and many of the women in my stated range will already have some children. This will be an important piece of information, one way or the other. Maybe not for hanging out together, but if they have any thoughts about what they want in the future, they might skip my profile if I say I'm not sure. On the other hand, if I say "someday" and happen to meet someone I really do like that turns into something more than just friends, the lie will be in place to trip us up.

Would it be a lie? I search deep inside for the answer and find I have always wanted children. This surprises me at first, but the longer I think about it, I begin to understand it was Carole's decision, and like all the other decisions in our marriage, I had let her make it unopposed.

"Someday," I answer minutes later and explain my thought process. "If it's a toss-up, the winning answer should be the closest to the truth, right?"

"And the truth is you want to have children some day?"

"Well, I know I'm a little old to start a family, but I think I always wanted to have kids. Carole didn't, so that was that."

Sis reaches over and pats my hand. "You're not too old. It's a better answer anyway. 'Not sure' is too wishy-washy."

~ ~ ~

On Saturday, Sis shows me her date's profile. He's twenty-two and I comment on her cradle robbing. She laughs and reminds me I'm that much older than she is and then some. Then she leaves me to try a few Match.com searches while she dresses for the night. So far, I've refused to publish my profile. She took some good photos and added them and we're both content with how it looks and reads, but I'm still stewing about the whole thing. What's my problem? I suppose it's the whole "starting over" idea that intimidates me. And I'm torn between the fear that no one will write or even send me a wink, and the fear that, as Sis claims, I'll be inundated with responses.

While I'm stewing, Sis returns, dressed to kill. She's wearing a slinky, short dress the color of chili peppers, heels, and a matching clutch. Parrots on large hoops dangle from her earlobes. "Salsa dancing," she answers, gyrating sexily under my nose when I ask where she's off to. "Don't wait up."

Nothing to do but continue my rummaging among the other "currently separated" losers, I think. I do feel somewhat deserted by Sis but know she's right I have to start someplace, and besides, her consistent presence in my life has been a positive force, only detracted from by her full social life outside my four walls. I could resent her weekend absences but find that I don't. She has been generous with her time and patience, and with her body as well. There's a lot to be said for regular sex.

I suppose she must feel the same way. She can choose to sleep with her dates or not, knowing full well I'm waiting back at home and available at her beck and call. Neither of us is suffering from want of a physical relationship. What I miss most is the feeling of exclusivity and companionship, the unwritten understanding that the most important person in my life is the one who shares my bed. Sis is not that woman, and I cannot foresee a time when she will be.

So my search continues, though I'm not looking for a "soul mate," a "life partner," a "significant other," or any other aphoristic Match.com catch phrase connoting an active interest in finding a long-term relationship, an

LTR, and certainly not an "until-death-do-you-part" or "share life's journey" sort of commitment. No, I have my marching orders from Sis: currently separated women who are not looking for a mate right now are the ticket out of my rut, or into it, and she should know; she's the master of the one-night hookup. So I dutifully return to my foraging, weeding out the profiles that seem to want more than I can offer right now, and searching for telling phrases like "seeking fun-loving guy to hang out and have a good time with," or "not looking for wedding bells and babies," or "recently single woman new to the dating scene and looking for a nice guy to spend time with," or "looking for someone to coax me out of the house," or my personal favorite: "neither a one-night stand nor a lifetime commitment; there's room in the middle, right?" You get the picture, other "currently separated" losers.

There is poignancy to my search, brought on by page after page of both heartfelt and hipster ramblings. Some are well-written, filled with witticisms, while others languish in cliché and sappy phrasing. But underlying all are the simplest of motives: the pursuit of happiness, whether ephemeral or lasting, and the touch of another human, both emotional and physical. And so we go on together, my women and me. Sometimes I read a few lines then click the back key on my browser, saying, "Next," but with others I take the time to give them a fair chance. I know the effort involved in creating this wish we publish, this hope for more than we have, laid out in carefully worded lines whether we are any good at it or not.

The "true love" seekers are the easiest to dismiss. Maybe they've watched too many unimaginative TV shows or soupy PG movies. Their profiles are littered with phrases like "hopes and dreams," "stable and grounded," "share the rest of my life," "not looking for a fling," "life is too short for games," and other trite reflections on what they do or do not want. Still others endeavor to draw me in with promises like "friend and lover" or "companionship and more" or "friendship and intimacy." And laced throughout is the repeated quest for "honesty" and "integrity." This last is the saddest story of all: so many of these women have lost the ability but not the desire to trust. Are we men not trustworthy?

This is the battle cry for women in our war of the sexes. I've heard it often enough. But their pleas and demands here on Match.com are both more strident and more sincere than I have heard before. What comes across in a TV sitcom as dismissive and humorous lies here on my screen as accreted wisdom: they do not expect to find honesty in us, but they have not lost hope.

By the time I surface from beneath the pile of the "currently separated," it's nearly midnight. I have unearthed a handful of candi-dates, our flippant designation for what I seek, or at least what Sis seeks. I've added them to my "Favorites" list, and Sis can check them out tomorrow. All eight are attractive in different ways, from quirky to outright gorgeous. Ages vary from thirty-seven at the youngest to forty-four at the oldest, and I know I will catch some shit from Sis about that, but I didn't really choose them on the basis of looks or age. I chose them for what they said, either because they were upfront about not wanting anything too serious in a relationship right now, or because they have written something engaging or clever that reveals a person I might like to know.

Who wouldn't write back to a woman who said, "I've left my baggage in the trunk, cleaned out my closet, buried my skeletons, and washed my dirty laundry," or the one who was looking for "someone who will let me read the front page of the paper first?" And what about the woman who said, "I consume dark chocolate like others eat vitamins—daily," or the one who warned, "I play Scrabble for blood not pleasure?" How could I fail to answer them? Then there was my favorite reason for looking for a partner: access to the HOV lane during rush hour, conversation optional. Add a couple of women with pithy one-liners: "I'd like to meet you sooner rather than later; weeks of emails are for pen pals," and "It's not the crap you're dealing with that matters. It's how you're dealing with the crap." Throw in one more with a philosophy of life based on years of doing the opposite: "I have found in life that I never regret the things I do, but often regret the things I neglect to do," and you have a quorum: eight women I'd like to meet. Now if only they'd like to meet me.

~ ~ ~

I wake to my front door opening and closing gently. I'm a light sleeper. I glance at the clock. It's 1:00 a.m. She's back early. I've learned to expect Sis to return before 10:00 p.m. if she's just been out for a meal, or not at all. I wonder what happened. Hard to imagine a twenty-two-year-old turning down a night with Sis or just about any other woman; those boys are walking hard-ons, every one. Then it occurs to me that maybe there was nowhere for them to go; maybe the kid couldn't afford a hotel room, and back to the dorm wasn't cutting it. The idea brings a smile to my face.

"You awake?" I hear next and open my eyes. Sis is kneeling alongside the bed, naked as a jaybird.

"Nope," I answer but lift the covers so she can crawl in with me.

"Bet I can change that." She disappears beneath, feeling her way.

~ ~ ~

We sleep in on Sunday until nearly noon then go out for a late breakfast at the Blue Star. Sis seems to like my pub as well as I do and promises to behave. We talk a bit about my Match.com finds. I can't answer all her questions, but the gist of what she recommends has us creating a priority list based on lack of interest in a serious relationship. I readily agree to let her choose since I have no vested interest in any of them. Later, after reading each profile carefully, Sis decides to discard four. Three are too long she says; the women have taken a lot of care in describing the things that are important to them, things Sis claims that indicate they are definitely looking for a long-term relationship, even if they don't say so. When I point out I want that again too some day, she says, "I know. But not now, right?"

Her words and tone are matter-of-fact, but her look says something different, something softer, gentler. I know she wants me to take it slow and not become involved too quickly. It's kind of like having a kid sister who looks after you, though the likeness falls apart when you consider that we're sleeping together. Maybe I should say best friend instead. Except that was Carole's job. Still, Sis does have a way of insinuating her way into my life, and I like that she does.

"What about the other one? You know? The one who said she's not looking for wedding bells and babies."

"No smile," Sis answers. "It's my rule: no smiles, no winks, no emails."

"I don't get it."

"Think about it. Why isn't she smiling in any of her photos?"

"She is so," I say and point out two shots with nice smiles though not the typical open or goofy ones.

"No teeth."

"So what? Maybe there was nothing that funny to smile at."

"No teeth."

She mimics the perplexed look on my face then explains. "I had one three-hour dinner date with a guy whose profile had a great photo with just that sort of smile. Longest date of my life. He was missing his front teeth. Every time he smiled, I stared."

"You're shitting me."

"Nope."

Rebekah

We spend a few more hours searching using keywords to look for sailors and hikers, extending both the age range and distance from Seattle, and reconsidering the children issue. Then I leave Sis searching and go for Asian take-out. Neither of us is interested in cooking. By the time I return, she's signed off. We sit out on the balcony sharing from several cardboard containers, drinking beer, and discussing the pros and cons of the six remaining candi-dates whose profiles Sis has printed out and is now shuffling through.

"Any you especially like?" she asks nonchalantly, or as nonchalant as you can be with a mouth full of fried rice.

"How about the one who said she'd rather meet sooner and skip all the emails?"

"What did she look like? Was that the tall blonde?"

"I think so. 5'-10". A little tall for me."

"You like'em short, don't you?" she says, and smiles in a self-satisfied way. I've made no secret of my attraction to her petite but perfectly proportioned features.

"Oh, I don't know. Maybe a little variety would be fun," I joke and get kicked for it.

She pulls out one of the profiles and hands it to me. "Okay, how about this one?"

Sis has chosen a short, close-cropped brunette with an equally short profile. She's the youngest of the lot, thirty-seven, and she looks younger. No kids but would like one or two some day. She also has a sense of humor. She's the one who is looking for an HOV lane partner, conversation optional, just someone to hang out with.

"Sure. She's cute," I say. "Good choice. Are you going to write to her?"

"Don't tempt me. Think I'll leave that up to you, though. Go give it a shot."

"Now?" Her withering look answers and makes me throw my hands in the air in defeat. "Okay, okay, I'm going."

~ ~ ~

I work offline to formulate a message. I'll do a cut-and-paste later when I have said what I want to. It takes me two hours of writing, deleting, rewriting, editing, more deleting, more rewriting, and a lot of talking to myself before I give up and say, "Screw it. It'll have to do."

Sis wanders by now and then, but I close the lid to my laptop each time. I'm not sharing. Once she pulls it away just after I snap it shut, but the laptop enters sleep mode before she can open it again. She doesn't know my password and I refuse to surrender it no matter what dire consequences she threatens. Her "I'll cut you off" is met by my laughter and a "That's likely." I get punched in the arm once but grab her hand before she can dodge away and she ends up in my lap. Her kiss tells me I'm right.

"Okay," she says, getting up and walking off, "but we'll see who has the last laugh."

I watch her to make sure she really is going, then flip open my laptop again. I start my browser and sign in to Match.com. I'm just about to click on "My Favorites" when I realize I have twenty-three emails and sixteen winks. Shit, Sis must have unhidden my profile. Wait, that's only four hours ago and I have thirty-nine women already? I hurriedly mark my profile hidden again then go looking for my little troublemaker, who, when I find her, bursts into hysterics at the look on my face.

"Told you I'd have the last laugh. How many?"

"Thirty-nine, including the winks."

That sets her off on another giggling jag. I walk away, but she trails behind me to review the incoming mail.

"Hit refresh."

"I hid the profile again. There won't be any others."

"Hit refresh."

"Fine." When the screen fills again, there are two more emails and one more wink. "How?"

"It's Sunday night and every woman's heart goes wandering."

We exchange looks then she continues, "Just kidding. Look, as soon as I opened up your profile for general viewing, all sorts of automatic matches tripped from Seattle to Bellevue and beyond. Most of those women haven't even seen your smiling face yet."

"Great. That's just great. Are you going to help me answer all of them?"

"Nope. Just send automatic thanks-but-no-thanks messages to any you really aren't interested in. It's a one-button click to reply. The rest are up to you."

I choose one and Sis shows me how to do this. Then

we go through the roster, eliminating about half as too serious or not attractive enough and adding a few to my favorites list. Two of the emails I have received are from women who I had already made favorites, one chosen by Sis and the other by me. I suggest these two are probably the best to begin with and Sis doesn't comment. I take her silence as concurrence. One is the feisty redhead who warned, "I play Scrabble for blood not pleasure." The other is the little HOV-lane-seeking brunette. I write back to make dinner dates and each accepts.

~ ~ ~

My first date is Friday evening, the little brunette, Adele. Not a common name though Sis seems to find it endearing for some reason. Adele suggested meeting at the Blue Star for burgers and beer, Dutch treat. I'm surprised by the coincidence but happy to have such an informal place for introductions. I'll feel right at home. The Dutch treat idea amuses me since the total probably won't be much over forty dollars, but maybe she has something to prove. On the other hand, my previous dating experience happened twenty-five years ago, so for all I know splitting the bill is commonplace. That said, my date for Saturday, the feisty forty-two-year-old redhead, Rebekah—Hebrew spelling she tells me—hasn't specified who pays and has chosen Palisade overlooking Elliott Bay for our dinner. There are more formal and expensive venues in Seattle, but not many.

I return from work on Friday to find Sis waiting. She's laid out what she wants me to wear on my date: khaki Dockers, my newest pair of boat shoes, and a blue plaid, button-down Oxford.

I laugh. "You really want me to look like a nerd?"

"I want you to look like you just stepped off your yacht. I couldn't find an ascot so this yellow tie will have to do. What do you think?"

Her question is sincere, or at least faking sincerity.

What I think is I'll look like Capt. Crunch, but what I say is, "My plan was to go in jeans. It's the Blue Star, not Ray's."

That draws a pout, which isn't even slightly sincere, but I can tell she wants to get her way, so I give up without a fight. "Okay, you win. If you insist on making me look foolish, I'll play along."

Her answering smile tells me I've made the right decision.

~ ~ ~

Stone Way is lined with parked cars, so I find a space on a side street three blocks away. As I approach, I can see Adele waiting for me outside on the sidewalk. She's wearing a creamy-yellow halter-top and designer jeans, which look like they were applied with a paintbrush, and pastel flip-flops. She looks more like late twenties than late thirties, and I wonder if she's understating her age. When she sees me she brings her hand to her mouth to cover up a laugh.

"I know, I know, I look like I just escaped from a regatta. My niece's idea."

"Your niece?" Her smile is incredulous.

"She's visiting but I may have to throw her out. She gives bad advice."

That draws a raucous laugh. Adele laughs all the way to our table.

"It's not that funny," I say, but keep the smile on

my face because I suppose it really is funny, to her anyway. But as the evening goes on, I begin to realize Adele laughs easily and not always when I expect her to. She thinks it's a riot my thirty-two-year-old niece is living with me and helping me find dates, but when I describe Larry's and Curly's antics, she just smiles. The other odd thing is she seems to want to know more about my purported niece than about my divorce from Carole. She asks bluntly whether either of us brings dates home for the night, and I answer we've agreed not to. But mostly she chatters away brightly about her work as a waitress and her daytime classes. She's attending UW in the nursing program and hopes to find work locally after she completes her degree. I tell her I know a younger woman, Christine Saunders, who is in the graduate program, but UW is a big school and Adele hasn't met her.

After dinner, she insists on paying her half, even when I complain. I offer to walk her to her car, a courtesy she laughs at but allows me to provide. There's an awkward moment when we get there about how to say goodbye. Adele says, "We could have a hug," and wraps her arms around me for a few seconds. I wave as she drives off and stand for a minute thinking about my first date. She's cute enough and pleasant enough, but I could tell she was just going through the motions. She's not really interested in me. "No chemistry," another Match.com catch phrase. I don't know if I'm supposed to write to thank her again for a nice evening, and if I do, whether I'll be expected to offer to get together sometime in the future. I'm sure Sis will have an opinion.

And she does. I barely make it through the front

door before I'm inundated with questions: "So, how did it go? What's she like? Did you get a thank-you kiss? Details, details."

I stand, hands on hips, looking askance at her. She stares back expectantly. I shouldn't tell her anything after making me dress up the way she did.

"Adele was wearing jeans," I say and wait for an apology I know will not be forthcoming.

Sis laughs and shrugs. "So, is she hot?"

Good question. Like Sis, Adele has a nice firm body with everything in the right place, but she is more cute than hot, just like Sis.

"She's cute. Like you."

At first Sis laughs, but then she stops abruptly. "Wait a minute. You don't think I'm hot?"

I fumble around with some "Uhhs" and "Umms," before confessing I don't think of her that way. To me hot means overtly sexy. Her warm, open, playful demeanor precludes this. "Look," I say, trying to dig myself out of the hole, "I find you very attractive, and you're great in bed. I love being with you. But hot isn't a way of being; it's a way of looking. You look cute. You look adorable. And when the light is in your eyes, you look beautiful. You don't look hot."

Well, you really screwed that up, I think, as I continue to hold her gaze and see the hurt in her expression. I'm an idiot. What must it feel like to a thirty-two-year-old woman to have a middle-aged guy say she's not hot? I expect her to turn and walk away. I imagine she will pack her bags and walk out of my life. But her face softens, hurt replaced by…what exactly? Sadness? Acceptance? I cannot read it. Then she closes the distance between us and melts into my embrace. We stand this way a while, Sis softly crying, me saying I'm sorry over and over again until she lifts to kiss me.

~ ~ ~

The next morning, it's as if nothing has happened. Sis returns to her barrage of questions and I answer as best I can. Sis seems surprised when I tell her there was no goodnight kiss, just a goodbye hug. And when I tell her I doubt Adele is at all interested in me, even as a casual date now and then, Sis assures me I'm wrong, that Adele is just playing hard-to-get.

"She sure didn't seem interested," I say, but when Sis insists, I agree to call to ask her out again sometime. As a reward for my compliance, Sis offers to make us an omelet. She's been out shopping. I watch her prepare it and have to admit she looks like she knows what she's doing. The end result is delicious and I tell her so. "Have to keep you around for a while."

She gives me an odd look but it softens into a smile. "Great. How about a year's lease?"

"Deal," I answer, very happy to think we've gotten past whatever hurt she felt.

~ ~ ~

My Saturday date begins at 7:00 p.m. I've reserved a table by the window overlooking the bay and marina. When I arrive, Rebekah is still not there, but she walks in promptly at seven. I have chosen to dress myself this time and have decided to wear a pale-blue pinstripe shirt, lightweight dark suit, and black dress shoes. Not taking any chances at looking under-dressed tonight. Sis commented that I looked nice but definitely not hot. "Just teasing," she said, and her look was sincere so I accepted it at face value.

Rebekah is also wearing a suit, sleeveless bright-green silk brocade and high heels to match. The jacket top flares at her hips, and the matching dress underneath is cut low in front. Her only jewelry is a pearl necklace; her ears are not pierced. The effect of all that shimmering green contrasting with her red hair is stunning, and she knows it; she can see it in my eyes. As she walks toward me, she smiles wickedly and holds out her hand for me. I reach hesitantly to take it. I never know just what to do. Should I grip a woman's hand gently or give it the firm shake I would with a man? I decide to give her a firm handshake and am rewarded by a broadening of her smile. Halfway through the shake, I realize her eyes are the same shade of green as her dress. Mesmerized, I just keep shaking. Her laugh breaks the spell and I let go.

I turn to speak to the hostess, who has been taking in our little tableau, and she smiles shyly. "This way," she says and leads us through the crowded room to our table. As we approach, I try to decide if I'm expected to pull out Rebekah's chair for her. She gives me a knowing look but pulls out her own seat. It's clear she finds my discomfit amusing, and though she smiles to let me know this, it is a warm smile nonetheless. My best hope is that she thinks my apparent ineptness is cute and endearing rather than clueless and cloddish.

Once seated, Rebekah turns those eyes on me again. "Don't you love first dates?" she says after another few moments of awkward silence. She seems so sophisticated and self-assured. I'm out of my league.

"I feel like a kid caught with his hand in the cookie jar," I answer without thinking about the implications.

She laughs. "And what kind of cookie am I?"

I can feel the blush overtake my face but recover quickly. "Ginger snap. Spicy and hot."

"Great answer." Her eyes sizzle with both intelligence and sex. She really is hot, I think, and make a mental note not to reveal this to Sis.

We spend the next two hours comparing our respective divorces and trading stories of intrigue and betrayal. Hers is due to be finalized soon. Mine will be another two months or so. Divorce is a good thing to have in common. We each know the other's pain. We each know the other's sense of freefall, part relief, part fear, part emptiness. Our meals come and go, and though we eat them, we are so engaged in conversation we hardly notice the chef's perfect palate and presentation. We are lost in each other. At some point we stop speaking, and in the silence that surrounds us, we both look out the window, but darkness has turned the plate glass into a dim mirror and we each see the other looking back.

"Shall we?" she asks.

I nod, take out my wallet, and tuck three fifty-dollar bills in with the check our waitress has left. We walk out and across the parking lot slowly, Rebekah leading, her heels' click-click-click keeping pace with my heartbeat.

"Do you keep your boat here?"

"I did once but switched to Shilshole years ago. That's where my broker's office is."

"Can I see her?" Rebekah's reference to *Repose* as "her" brings a smile to my face.

"Sure, anytime."

"How about right now?"

I'm not ready for that answer and it makes me hesitate. "It's a mess. You should really let me clean it up before you see it."

"Don't be silly. I'll follow you over. Which is your car?"

"Oh, it's back there," I say and point behind me. "I thought I was following you to yours."

"And I thought I was doing the following, or do you prefer to be led?"

We have both stopped and are facing each other. She leans in to kiss me then, a soft brush at first but shifting to press more firmly and ending with her teeth plucking at my lower lip.

"That's enough for now," she whispers. "I don't want to scare you away."

~ ~ ~

I arrive back home at midnight. Rebekah and I have walked around the marina hand-in-hand and shared a long kiss goodnight. Sis is reading in her room where she does her actual sleeping. As I walk past, I wave. Once in my bedroom, I strip off my suit and hang it. Then I begin unbuttoning my shirt and turn to engage the gaze I have felt focused on my back.

"A little late for dinner to be ending." She leans in the doorway.

I ignore her gambit. "Lots to talk about."

She pushes off the doorjamb, walks over to where I'm standing, and reaches up to trace the skin around my lips. "I like this shade of red lipstick. Get that talking?"

I'm tired and don't like her tone. After all, this whole thing is her idea. Is she just teasing or is she jealous? I decide not to let myself be dragged into an argument, so I don't answer.

"Is Rebekah hot?" Sis asks, enunciating each syllable in her name as if it were a separate word.

Now I'm pissed. This is none of her business. Sis and I have a deal of her own making. We live together, we sleep together when we both want to, and what happens elsewhere is none of the other's affair. That's what I should have said. What I say is, "Very."

~ ~ ~

I toss and turn most of the night. Sis had spun on her heel and retreated to her room after my verbal slap in the face. I expected a door-slamming exit but watched as she shut it ever so slowly, delaying a final click, which sounded louder and more fatal than any door-rattling closure could have been. Her door is still shut this morning when I leave for the marina. Rebekah has suggested a sail that I readily accepted.

As I drive around Lake Union, passing Gas Works Park, already filled with morning walkers, and proceeding toward the Chittenden locks, I try to solve my puzzle. Why was Sis so pushy, so sarcastic? She was amused by my Friday date with Adele, so why did my Saturday date with Rebekah bug her so much? Maybe it's because she chose Adele while Rebekah was my choice. That and the whole "hot" issue. But it still doesn't make sense. Sis goes out all the time and sometimes doesn't come home until the next day. And she's been open about which guys she wants to sleep with. She even teases me about it, though I never give her the satisfaction of reacting. That was the deal: sleep where and with whom we want, no recriminations.

I decide not to worry about Sis for now and concentrate on the sail ahead. When I pull in, I can see Rebekah waiting by the gate. Chuck must not be around this morning, I think, smiling to myself, and when we get to *Repose,* I see his boat is gone. It pleases me to think he's off cruising someplace, and I remark on this to Rebekah, then end up explaining my relationship to him, as well as Larry, Curly, and Doc's badinage both with Capt. Crunch and among themselves. I suppose my rambling portrayal must seem as nervous to her as it does to me, so she leans across the cockpit to kiss me and holds it long enough for the kiss to mean something. That shuts me up. When she breaks away, she is wearing the same amused smile she trained on me most of yesterday evening. Then she laughs. "So, are you taking me sailing or what?"

I'm still a bit flustered but manage to tease back, "Think I'm more interested in the "or what" part, but we can go sailing first."

~ ~ ~

We spend the day lazily cruising back and forth across the Sound on autopilot. We talk and kiss and cuddle, paying attention to the sail only long enough to execute each tack. In mid-afternoon the wind freshens to ten knots then drops off to a whisper later. Our last tack is under power. Rebekah teases me about going for a motor, not a sail, but by this time I've become comfortable with her and gently tease back. She suggests Ray's for an early dinner and I agree. By sunset we're walking out, chatting away like old friends, sated by a good meal and a shared bottle of wine, and, having parked side-by-side earlier, we both know where we're going. Literally anyway, figuratively I'm not so certain. My place is out of bounds and Rebekah hasn't told me whether or not she lives alone, and to be honest, I'm not sure she's even ready for the next step. But I decide to accept her comment from last night: I'd prefer to be led, so wait for her cue. It comes as soon as we reach the cars.

"I'm beginning to think I won't scare you away after all," she says, taking both my hands and leaning out. "You seem less nervous."

I nod and answer the implied question, "I'm not nervous. Well, maybe just a little."

She drops my hands and wraps her arms around my neck, bringing her face within a few inches of mine. "And now?" she whispers.

Rebekah has lifted up and moved in so we touch along our whole length and radiate heat into the cool night. I suppose I should be nervous, but the intimate feel of her body flowing into mine relaxes me.

"Now I'm not nervous at all."

Her kiss then is deep and seeking, not hot and passionate, a warm, sensual kiss that gives breath rather than taking it away. Then she pulls back to look into my eyes for an answer to her unasked question and, finding it already there, says, "Follow me."

We retrace our path from Ray's to Palisade, crossing the Ballard Bridge and running the gauntlet between Queen Anne and Magnolia then begin the climb to Magnolia Bluff. Her home is on the Boulevard with an unobstructed view of the Sound and the majestic Olympic Mountains beyond. By Magnolia Bluff standards it is modest, but by nearly any other standard it is palatial. A shack with this view would qualify as a palace.

I get out of my car and look out to the shipping channel, where two huge container vessels are passing, one fully-loaded, heading south to the docks, the other, now unburdened of its cargo and riding high in the water, beginning its 120 mile run up the sound, through the Admiralty Inlet, and out the Strait of Juan de Fuca to the Pacific, and from there to another port to load up before sailing across the ocean back to from wherever it came.

"Nice view." My tone suggests what an understatement this is.

Rebekah walks over to stand alongside and rest her head against my shoulder.

"Yes, it is."

This is a voice I haven't heard from her, a voice with a faraway forlornness that marks an ending not arrived at yet, but one that is not too distant. I guess the house must be sold to allow for a fair division of assets. Not surprising in this neighborhood of very expensive homes. Still, while hers is probably worth more than mine, the difference is likely to be no more than a half million.

"I'm sorry."

"I am too. It was my dream house, close enough to the city with all its bustling activity yet perched here as sentinel to the sea below." She is quiet for a moment then sighs and continues, "But life goes on whether we want it to or not. It will be listed and sold soon enough. I get to keep it until then."

We stand looking out at the water for a long while before she says, "Come. Let's go in."

Once inside, Rebekah locks the door behind us then

takes my hand and leads me up the turn-of-the-century oak stairs to her bedroom above. One small lamp is lit and casts shadows across the four-poster queen bed and armchairs beyond and onto the far wall, where photos of distant ancestors wait and watch.

We kiss but neither of us can dispel the solemn mood that has enveloped. The sense of impending loss is potent. We pull back and begin speaking at the same moment. This makes each of us smile wanly.

"You first," I say.

"I was about to ask if you wanted a drink."

"And I was going to suggest we have one."

She walks over to the side table on which the low light is burning. There are two cut-glass tumblers and a bottle on a silver tray.

"Single malt. It's all I have, I'm afraid. It's the one thing he forgot to take."

She pours to fill the glasses halfway and hands one to me. That's a lot of good scotch, I think.

"Let's sit outside," she says and walks across to the French doors that open onto a small, enclosed porch.

The late evening cool has descended and dew has begun to cover any flat surface, but warm air still rises up the high embankment and rolls over us in soft waves. The contrast is invigorating.

We sit quietly sipping and lost in our separate thoughts. I think how sad it is she will lose this house she loves so much. And I think how easy it would be for me to buy it for her. Yet I know the timing will be wrong. It will be gone before we ever reach that point, and I'm not sure beginning a new relationship in another man's home is such a good idea anyway.

I reach across to lift the hair that has fallen between

us and tuck it behind her ear, and she turns to face me and seems to be reconsidering the wisdom of my presence here.

"Would you mind—?," she begins but I hold up a hand, nod then rise from my chair.

"Another time."

"Yes. I...I thought I was ready..."

"I'll let myself out."

I bend to kiss her cheek. She remains still. I walk back through the doorway and across her bedroom. I turn to take one last look and see Rebekah lift her glass to take a sip. Then I quietly close her bedroom door and walk away.

~ ~ ~

I arrive home before 10:00 p.m. On the ride back from Magnolia I've been wondering whether Sis will still be there. We've had our first argument and it didn't end well. Then we did what you should never do, go to bed angry. I barely get the key in the lock before the door swings open and she steps through to wrap her arms around me.

"I am so sorry. I was such a hormonal bitch last night."

It strikes me as funny so without thinking, I laugh and say, "Yes, you were."

She pulls back to measure my response, straight-faced, but her expression changes quickly to the same amused look I'm wearing.

"Don't be mean."

"I'm not. Well...I guess I was...I mean, last night when I said Rebekah is hot."

"Very hot."

"Hmmm, she is, you know. She's also conflicted and maybe a little bit broken like me, not really done with her twenty-year marriage. I doubt either of us is ready to start over again. We both want to, but not quite."

Sis watches me as I work all this out in real time. I can feel confusion and self-doubt playing across my face.

"I don't know what that would feel like," she says. "I've never had a long enough relationship to need getting over with."

I think how sad this is and how contemporary. We have *con-ed* ourselves into thinking that *temporary* is what we really want. We have lost our sense both of permanence and innocence, the latter given away of our own free will, the former lost in the sound bites of our peripatetic lives. But I can feel it inside me, the want for the immediacy and impermanence of a lover wrestling with the need for the companionship and stability of a best friend. And while I can imagine Sis being both friend and lover, I cannot imagine her committing to it. So perhaps I should be looking for a Rebekah, a woman who has tasted enough of permanence to want it again, but not one so innocent as to imagine it comes without a price.

Mount Beth

Monday morning I head off to work and Sis leaves for the university. The fall semester begins soon, and she needs to buy the books that go with the classes she has already signed up for online. I try Rebekah's cell phone but it immediately rolls to voicemail. Either she's talking or has it turned off. Probably the latter.

The week flies, and by Friday I haven't heard from her yet, though I've left two more messages, the last suggesting Rebekah call me when she is ready; no pressure, I understand about hesitancy and indecision. Sis, however, does not. She's been wearing me down with frequent cajoling and occasional demands that it's time to go back online. Meanwhile, Doc and company nibble away at my reticence for a return engagement at Teddies. Sis is also irritated that so far I've refused to call Adele. The confrontation arrives Friday night.

"What are you waiting for?" she asks when I turn down her latest offer to help me resume my Match.com search.

"I'm not. I'd just rather stay in tonight."

"You've been in all week. Not even a lunch with Adele. If you won't look past Ms. Very-Hot, why not go out with the boys, at least? What do you have to lose?"

"Apart from my sanity, you mean?"

This draws no verbal response, but Sis is not happy with my flippant dismissal. Her body language speaks for itself.

"Look, I'm sorry. I just don't want to."

"Fine, but you're in violation of our agreement," she throws over her shoulder as she walks away.

Am I? I've been trying to date, and I've been looking online, and I just want to take this more slowly than Sis wants me too. Why is she in such a rush? Why can't I wait until Rebekah is ready to call me back? Can't I let a couple of weeks go by?

I yell after her that I want to let some time pass to see if Rebekah calls me. This brings Sis marching back to where she left me standing.

"And that's the other way you're violating our agreement. You're getting involved too quickly. We agreed to no entanglements."

Did we? I don't remember agreeing to any such thing and say so.

"You don't remember me saying 'no exclusivity on either side' and I expect you 'to find other women to sleep with?' You accepted that deal."

"Yeah, I do remember. But I *have* found another woman to sleep with, she's just not ready to return my calls."

"Right. But I said women, not woman. That's part of what I meant by no exclusivity. And since your one woman hasn't called back, and may never call back, you aren't even beginning to hold up your end of the bargain."

Her words bring me up short. I don't know if I can do what she wants me to and I'm not sure I want to try. But it's also true I don't want to lose her. I'm not ready to close the door, I think, but I find myself closing it anyway. "Maybe I'm just not built like you. Maybe I can't sleep around as if it meant nothing. And maybe I want someone like Rebekah, not for one night, but for as long as it lasts."

I watch my implied ultimatum shifting and twisting in her expression, her eyes steely. If I were to look behind me at this moment, I would see the chasm jawing open to swallow me whole. But then her eyes soften and she sighs. Having reached some sort of equilibrium, Sis offers a compromise. "Ten more days. No more. If she doesn't call back next weekend, we find someone else for you to write to. And you go out tomorrow night to Teddies with Doc."

"Okay," I answer, but she's not finished. I don't get let off so easily.

"And I'm suspending my 'no other women under our roof' rule. I expect you to bring one home tomorrow. I'll spend the night elsewhere. And no cheating. Chris will report back if you leave alone." She is deadly serious. I'm about to accept her terms reluctantly, and wondering whether even this will be enough to please her, when she adds, "I'll be expecting details," and adopts a coy look that lets me know the battle is over.

"Deal," I say, relieved, then tease back a little, "Just how much detail do you want? Should I take notes?"

"Nope. Just make it interesting. Entertain me."

~ ~ ~

Doc seems beside himself with pleasure when I call to accept my place in this week's SSFC entourage. Maybe he's been worrying about me again, or maybe Sis has been worrying him. In either event, I've relaxed and decided to "go with the flow," as Curly says. So, before our respective bedroom-nights-on-the-town, Sis and I head to Ray's for an early dinner and sit chatting aimlessly about everything and nothing until just before 9:00 p.m. Then we leave to go our separate ways. While we wait for the valet to bring around her car, I complain I might strike out, but she just looks askance and replies, "It's Teddies," then adds, "Don't be good. I won't be."

I find my three-horsemen-missing-their-fourth seated at Larry's accustomed table in the back. The place is hopping, and once again I can feel the open stares I get as I weave between tables toward them. They already have a beer for me and say, "Drink up, you're way behind."

I do as I'm told but think I should have skipped the two beers I've already had with Sis. Then it occurs to me to wonder if her part of the plan was to give me a good start toward the relaxing of inhibitions. Okay, chill out, I say to myself and begin to scan the room for women looking back. The idea is to avoid seeming obvious. I get a few returned looks, but it's early and only a handful of couples are up dancing yet. Maybe I'll keep a low profile for now. Then I see Christine watching me from across the room and remember my deal with Sis.

As the evening progresses, so does my state of inebriation. Larry and Curly have already paired up and headed out, leaving me and Doc to sit alone. I've been remembering my first time at Teddies, and this memory has led right back to Carole of all places. Then I stew for a while and become disgusted with myself for stewing, after which my thoughts drift to Rebekah and I stew some more. And it doesn't help that neither of us has been asked to dance yet. Doc says, "The night is still young," but I remind him, "Yeah, but we aren't."

The crowd at Teddies has swelled, and now there do not seem to be enough tables to accommodate everyone and the dance floor is jammed. One of the new arrivals is a behemoth of a woman, sitting with a beanpole, who only makes her look larger by comparison. She keeps stealing glances in a deliberate and obvious way. I start looking back just for the hell of it. She is simply too large to be attractive, but she does have a pretty face and long, straight, blonde hair. She reminds me of Mary Chapin Carpenter with a second-story addition. No, wait, a fourplex. I can hear her voice booming across the floor occasionally and it has the same deep, breathy pitch MCC is famous for.

While we sit nursing our beers and watching the dancers, I see Christine break away from her partner and walk our way. I'm expecting her to drag me out for a dance and lecture, but she takes Doc's hand instead. Doc acts surprised by this, and I'm surprised as well. I thought Chris had already dumped him. But then I realize this may be another setup and Doc's act is just that, an act.

Alone now, I see the behemoth rise and lumber in my direction. She's obviously been waiting for her cue, Doc's departure. She grabs his empty chair, flips it around, and, after hitching up her long cotton nightie to expose the silk boxers she's wearing underneath, straddles it. Then she rests both knee-sized elbows on the table and leans forward to set her chin between her two meaty paws.

"So," she says in a back-woodsy drawl. "You like big girls, or are you just curious?"

Her voice may lack sophistication, but I can see a sparkle of humor in her stare that belies the coarse front she's putting up. I decide to try for an answer in kind.

"Don't rightly know, ma'am. Never had me a big girl before."

"Hah," she shouts, rising from her three-point stance and swatting the table. I'd swear my half-full beer lifts an inch off the surface. "Well, all right then. Let's you and me go find out."

I follow her to the dance floor, dwarfed by what must be her 6'-4" stature. She is easily the biggest woman I have ever seen. She would make two of me, maybe more. She takes me in a bear hug and begins to move slowly wherever she wants to go. She is Moses in this Red Sea of dancers; they part before us. I put my hands on her hips, since I cannot reach any farther around, and hold on for dear life. She ought to be wearing a sign: "Caution, wide load." After a loop around the floor, she says, "My name is Beth, Honey. What's yours?"

"Deke."

"Deke, huh? As in, short for Deacon Blues? Boy does that fit you to a T. You could freeze steaks with the scowl you've had on your face tonight. What happened? Momma leave you for some rich stud?"

Beth's perceptive, or well-informed, guess makes me pause in our repartee for a moment, but she's not the kind of gal to let a quiet moment pass.

"Cat got your tongue, Sugar?" She laughs at her own joke as she continues, "No more Momma's milk for you."

Beth's laughter shakes the two of us in the way a volcano shakes the ground when it erupts. I decide there is nothing for it but to play her game.

"You got that right, Sweetie. And you know Beth," I say, lisping her name into a superlative.

That brings on another eruption of laughter from Mount Beth, and she reaches down to smack me on the ass.

"You don't know the half of it, Honey. I am the Beth. You juth don't know it yet."

~ ~ ~

It's 1:00 a.m. before we cross my threshold. The "your place or mine" question asked by Beth is quickly answered after she tells me hers is in Puyallup, close to an hour's drive away, and the further question, implied by the look I give her, "Why would anyone live in Puyallup?" is answered with a shrug and the simple observation, "Puyallup's where the horses are. Seattle's where the action is." Hard to argue with the logic.

Earlier, I'd caught the amused looks from Doc and Chris when we passed them on the dance floor. They seemed too pleased with themselves to be entirely innocent, and when I ask Beth, she confirms this.

"Yeah, the dwarf and his butt-less filly set you up. But if you know that, why are you playing along?"

Good question, and it will take a while to answer it, so I beg off with a matching shrug and grab us each a beer. We head out onto the balcony to drink them. Beth's blunt cowgirl vocabulary is both refreshing and catching, so I guess I should say, "We mosey along to the balcony with our brews." In any event, I follow her, my shadow totally eclipsed by hers.

"Lots of reasons," I say, once we've settled into our seats and Beth has commented on the view. It's only the latest comment. She's been keeping up a steady stream of superlatives to describe my not-so-humble abode.

"Meeting expectations is probably top of the list. I'm guessing this setup concocted by Doc and Chris is actually a setup in itself. But I decided days ago to play the game. I agreed to go to Teddies and not come home alone."

"Second is more complicated. I'm halfway through a divorce and have no fixed idea about the future. I've got three buddies who want me at Teddies every Saturday, a woman my age who's been happy to fuck my brains out but who's just in it for fun, and a woman half my age who's living with me, sleeping with me, but insists I sleep with other women for some reason. That fucked up enough for you?"

Beth chuckles in a way I take for agreement that my life is probably more absurd than hers.

"The third you already guessed. I'm curious as hell to see what a woman your size is like in bed."

That draws a belly laugh from Beth and an admission.

"Not surprised, Sugar. Pretty much happens every time. You know, when I was in high school I never had a date, not even to Prom. At WAZU, though, the other AG students accepted me for the big cowgirl I've always been. And I got the reputation for takin' on any bull man-enough to ride this 300-pound heifer. You probably thought I'd put on the beef over the years but it's not so. I came out of the pre-teen shuttle at 250 and only grew a little afterward. I'd take first prize at the county fair, hands down."

Now we're both laughing. She's a hoot. I'm having fun shooting the breeze with her and have been honest when I said I was curious.

After our laughter trickles off, Beth turns to look me up and down.

"Hope you got a king with a sturdy frame. I need a lot of room in bed, and I like to tussle."

I weigh 180, but once back inside, Beth hoists me like a baby with no more effort than I'd put out lifting Sis. I cannot adequately describe the sensation, though I imagine most women can. They've been swept off their feet often in their lives. For me, it's a first since I was maybe six or seven. Loss of control comes closest, but there is no fear involved, only anticipation.

She tosses me onto the bed as if I were a sack of grain then proceeds to pull her nightie over her head. This action turns loose the largest breasts I (or anyone else, I should imagine) have ever seen. A Colonel Sanders Variety Bucket would fall way short of corralling one. But the truly amazing thing is that for all their weight they do not sag.

Beth is pleased by my open-mouthed reaction and says so.

"Quite a pair, huh?"

I still say nothing, so she adds, "They're a miracle of modern science."

That's when I notice the fine stitch lines around each nipple and tracing down to disappear in the slight fold of skin below each breast.

"Doc's work?"

"He may be a dwarf but he's a genius too. Wasn't for Doc, these beauties would be down around my knees."

I motion her closer and she obliges. I trace the stitches up and around each nipple, drawing an even more pleased response.

Then I motion her away again. I want to take her all in. Without coaxing, she strips off her boxers and does a 360 so I can appreciate the rest. Sure enough, Doc has sculpted her posterior as well. Huge, she is. Obese? Definitely. But she's also sexy as hell. And, most provocative of all, she is completely shaved.

I close my eyes and imagine myself scaling Mount Beth. I'd tell my Sherpa to begin the ascent on the left flank. There are a few more handholds on the slope and the left hip is slightly higher, providing a convenient ledge on which to establish base camp. Next would come the traverse behind the mountain, a steep slope above a yawning crevasse, a fall into which might leave you lost forever, but the risk is worth taking because you must reach the right-hand slope and bivouac before you prepare for the assault. To reach the true summit you have to climb the right-hand peak. It's slightly higher than the left.

"What the hell are you grinning at, Boy?" My reverie has left a smirk.

"I was climbing Mount Beth."

"Hah! You're welcome to try but you're not dressed right. Let me give you a hand."

I've been undressed before but have forgotten how delicious this is. And it's especially titillating when your body can be manipulated so effortlessly. Beth is not only big, she's strong. I'm expecting her to let me be on top but I'm wrong. She flips me over to face her then straddles me. I'm certain I'll be crushed, but her legs are so long she seems able to completely control the weight she applies.

"You're gonna love this, Sugar. I guarantee no woman's ever done this to you before."

Her assertion seems unlikely, but as she begins to move, the sensation is wonderful, so I don't argue. Then I realize she's right. I'm not inside her, though that's what it feels like. Instead, her labia are so long and deep it just seems that way. The image of a Vienna sausage in a hot dog bun floats through my mind but is quickly driven out by sheer pleasure. Beth makes small adjustments in her position until the parts, which do not normally connect, do so. Her enormous clitoris is rubbing head-to-head with my glans. We reach orgasm seconds apart.

Afterwards, we lay side-by-side fondling. Her breasts are truly amazing; areolas like saucers and nipples the size of my thumbs. I can't stop playing with them but do when Beth threatens to climb back on top. I beg off with an "I'm plum wore out, ma'am," but promise to make up for it tomorrow morning. At 7:00 a.m., she collects on that promise.

~ ~ ~

Sis shows up one hour after Beth departs, an unlikely coincidence. And when I comment on this, she laughs and asks if my bed is still intact.

"See for yourself," I taunt, having left the bed unmade and the sheets unchanged deliberately to test her reaction.

"Smells like a barn, but there's still some bounce left," Sis taunts back after a quick tumble from one side to the other. "Sooo, how was she?"

Sis is just too pleased with herself, so even though I know she's teasing, I decide to answer honestly.

"Might be the best sex I ever had. Certainly the most imaginative."

I go on to describe my night in detail, ignoring Sis's obvious discomfort. But when I describe the depth and breadth of Beth's genitalia, she bursts out laughing, and when I further describe Beth's clitoris as "a little man standing up in a boat," Sis collapses onto the bed in hysterics. My description had the same effect on Beth and she promised she'd remember that one for future use.

I lie down beside Sis and prop myself on my elbow to watch her laugh. Her whole body spasms for what seems like minutes. When her laughter subsides, she turns to look at me and then starts up again after I offer, "Entertaining enough for you?"

When next she ceases, I reach across and wipe away her tears of laughter. Sis closes her eyes and lets me. When I stop, she sighs and hoists herself onto her elbow then says, "I guess Beth is hot, too, huh?"

Her words are more statement than question but I answer anyway. "In her own inimitable way, I suppose she is. Mostly she's just fun to be with."

Again, Sis seems too pleased with herself for my liking. I know this whole setup was her doing, and while I did have fun, I really don't understand why Sis has made this happen. "Why?" I ask.

"Well, I guess I'm trying to figure out what you mean by 'hot' and why you don't think I am."

"That's not what I meant. Why did you set me up?"

I'm expecting Sis to deny it and put the blame on Doc and Christine, but she doesn't. "I know what you meant. My answer's the same."

"Maybe. But if that's true, it's just partly true. There's more to it."

Sis frowns and seems unwilling to answer at first. Then she sighs. "Look, it's like I told you before, I can't be the only woman in your life. It's too much responsibility. And you really don't know what you want yet. It's too soon after Carole. That's why I want you to go out with lots of other women. It's the only way to find out what you need. If that's true love and a life partner, fine. But I think you should try the love 'em then leave 'em thing first."

"Like Doc?"

"No! Like me!"

The force of her answer sets me back on my heels. Sis wants me to be like her, but she also wants me to be with her. The unspoken threat implied by her "fine," that she will leave if I decide what I want is "true love and a life partner," hangs thickly in the air between us. She is advising against getting involved too quickly and too deeply. This is why Sis doesn't like Rebekah. She sees Rebekah as the kind of woman who would make a good life partner for me, one I could easily fall for on the rebound from Carole. She's probably right about that, but her advice is self-serving. Sis needs me to remain in limbo, available to her whenever she wants, or whenever I want, but not joined at the hip, not fully committed. She doesn't want it to mean that much to me to mean that much to her. I don't know if I can live this way.

Girl on a Swing

Monday morning I call Adele and invite her to dinner again at the Blue Star. Mondays always seem like burger nights to me. She accepts immediately without comment and we agree to meet at 6:00 p.m. After my words with Sis last night, I've decided to follow her advice and keep things light, and since I'm not really interested in any sort of relationship with Adele, I can follow the letter of Sis's law without following the intent.

I arrive promptly, dressed in jeans and a pullover sweater now that the evenings have turned cool. Adele is similarly attired, though like last time her jeans are painted on. She greets me with a big smile and wraps her arms around me as if I were a long-lost lover instead of a second date. She makes full-body contact and rubs in enough to make it obvious but breaks cleanly and says, "I'm glad you called. I didn't think you would."

I stumble over an apology about time constraints but she waves them off casually. "No worries. You're here now. That's all that counts."

As the waitress escorts us to a table by the window, I replay the "No worries" part in my mind, recognizing the phrase from Carole's Aussie repertoire. But I know it's also British and wonder if Adele is a transplant.

Still, I can't detect any accent, so I'm pretty sure she grew up here locally. She chats amiably about her week, relating stories of problem customers and classroom drama. Gone are the questions about my niece and our living situation. Gone are the laughs at inappropriate moments. She seems focused on me in a way she wasn't on our first date. And she asks about Carole, and about Match.com, and about whom I've met so far. She also asks about *Repose*. I'm surprised because I don't remember mentioning I owned a sailboat. I was wearing boat clothes on our first date because Sis wanted me to, but I don't remember Adele commenting beyond her stifled laugh at the figure I cut. Still, I probably said something and it's just slipped my mind.

Adele's questions about Carole center around the usual: what happened, who cheated, why couldn't we reconcile, when is the divorce final, how am I feeling, and what comes next; questions that are easy to answer unless you want to delve deeper than the superficial. Her questions about Match.com and other women seem designed to gauge what sort of relationship and what sort of "match" I seek. I answer each of Adele's questions as honestly as I can without much detail but skip discussion of Teddies altogether. After each answer, I reverse her question and she replies in kind.

By the end of the evening, we both know far more about each other and have reached something like a friendship. My initial thoughts about Adele have been reversed. Now she seems interesting and engaged in the process of getting to know me better. There's even been some casual flirting and a few averted glances. And like Sis, Adele has the deep-brown bedroom eyes she can turn on at will.

After our meal, I walk her to her car as I did on our first date, but unlike that first time, there are no awkward moments when we get there. Adele loops her arms over my shoulders and leans in for a long kiss goodnight, a kiss that promises deeper kisses to come.

"Call me," she says as we part.

"I will," I answer and wave as I walk away.

As I drive back to my condo and to my impatient inquisitor, I review the evening. The change has been dramatic. Not that I'm really enamored of the idea of falling for Adele, but all my reservations regarding her have taken flight. And, we have a sailing date scheduled for Saturday, so we'll see how she does with that. I've also learned her age. She claimed to be thirty-seven in her profile but now insists she's only thirty-two. "Your niece's age," she says coyly, and her driver's license, at least, concurs. And since faking a driver's license these days would take some skill, I presume she's telling the truth. The purported reason for doing the opposite of what Sis says women on Match.com do is that Adele is looking for someone older, someone in his forties and already well-established. I take it to mean financially stable. I'm not sure I'm ready to buy this sales pitch, but it's amusing anyway, and I need to have a woman to date to avoid breaking Sis' cardinal rule.

I'm expecting the third degree as soon as I walk through my door and find I'm vaguely disappointed when Sis doesn't greet me. Her door is closed, so maybe she's taking a nap or maybe she's studying, since the semester has begun. Recently she's been buried in work and less available for hanging out. I opt not to disturb her. It's early, so I grab a beer and head out to sit on the balcony. Two hours goes by with no sign of Sis so I decide to call it a night, satisfied by my quiet interlude but not at all certain this isn't the quiet before a storm.

By the end of the week, little has changed. Sis has ceased her constant pressure on me to find dates. She has been busy with schoolwork, I know, but she has been breezy and light-hearted in the time we have spent together over meals or on occasional walks around the lake, and in this whole week she has not once asked me about Adele. I volunteered we were planning a sail Saturday and we had shared a kiss goodnight on Monday, but other than a "That's nice," Sis has failed to comment.

Friday night, as I sit out on the balcony examining my thoughts, I realize that for a change I feel relaxed about the future. I suppose this is because Sis seems relaxed as well, but it's also because dating or hooking up seems less threatening now I've done it a few times. Perhaps I've begun to invest less of myself in these meetings, taking more of a "not much ventured, not much lost" approach. Or maybe it's because Doc and the boys have dropped the pressure too; I've had no calls to make an SSFC appearance at Teddies tomorrow night. Of course, I wouldn't have been able to go since my date with Adele would conflict, but they don't know that. Or do they? Sis could have passed the information along, I suppose, but why would she? No reason, I guess, and it doesn't matter anyway. I'm cool with it.

Behind me, I hear the elevator bell first, then keys jangling, then our front door open and close as Sis arrives, followed by the sound of her high heels when she removes them as she always does, pulling off one at a time and dropping it haphazardly onto the marble entryway floor. This ritual brings a smile to my face. In a way it reminds me of my father, who would whistle every day as he came in through the garage to let us know he was home from work. It is the sound of the daily commonplace, a heart-warming gesture not meant to be a gesture, but succeeding anyway.

I have closed my eyes to savor the moment then open them to look up as I feel her hands of my shoulders. She gives me an upside-down kiss then swings around to collapse into my lap. "What a week," she moans. "I'm up to my ass in homework."

"Better than alligators."

Sis looks at me blankly at first then gets the substitution. "Right. Where are you taking us for dinner? Not the Blue Star. Adele's the burger-and-fries girl, not me. How about Trapezio?"

I've never heard of it and say so. That draws a "where have you been—on Mars" look from Sis.

"You must have. It's just down below Pike Place Market on the Hillclimb."

"Nope. Never have. Sounds Italian."

"Well, mostly Italian, but you can get fresh fish or a steak if you want. It's very hip."

"Hip?" I ask dismissively. "What makes it hip?"

"You'll see."

"You're the boss," I say and mean it, but I'm smiling and relaxed. Sis seems as pleased with herself as she did when she asked about my night with Beth, and I suspect she has some intrigue planned, but I'm up for whatever it is and happy to play along.

~ ~ ~

We arrive at Trapezio at 7:00 p.m. Sis's reservations prove necessary for a good table, since the place is packed. The entrance is anything but welcoming, but as soon as you open the door, kitchen smells waft up, setting off salivary glands, and the hostess waits invitingly at the bottom of the long stairway down. We hand over our lightweight jackets and immediately are led to a table for two in the corner of the main room. Waitresses bustle busily between the closely set tables, and the crowd assembled is vocal but not overpowering, and behind all the voices plays soft jazz. Suspended from the sixteen-foot ceiling is an eclectic selection of decorative bric-a-brac, most curious of which is a trapeze, from which, I presume, derives the restaurant's name. Also hanging down is a long loop of sturdy fabric held off to one side by a small hook. I can sense Sis watching me as I take it all in.

I comment on these, but Sis only agrees they are odd things to see in a restaurant. Her smile gives her away, though, so I'm not surprised when I see a very tall, young woman walk in wearing a top hat. She's about Sis's age, clad in fishnet stockings and a low-cut, close-fitting top. She bows to her audience and mounts the trapeze directly over our heads. There is something vaguely familiar about this face, I say to myself and frown, trying to remember where I might have seen her. Before I can come up with the answer, she bends backward nearly in half, flips over, and, in the same motion, removes her top hat. She hands it to me with an insouciant smile then begins her routine, moving seamlessly with deliberate grace from one pose to another, sometimes becoming so entwined in the trapeze ropes I can neither tell how she got there nor how she will disentangle herself. But she does. And each time she changes pose, she locks eyes with mine for a moment just long enough for me to understand she is doing this on purpose. And I look back. It feels a bit like watching a woman pole dance in a strip club. You're not sure where to look and feel self-conscious, but you look intently anyway. The show lasts a good ten to fifteen minutes, and I must confess to being mesmerized. Her body is sculpted in long, lean muscle and her face is devilish pixie. After she descends from her perch, she bows to the crowd and to Sis and me, then accepts the return of her top hat and gives me a wink.

Our drinks have arrived during the show, and we sit sipping now for a while before the waitress shows back up to take our order. In the meantime, Sis has been plying me with questions: how did I like the performance, doesn't she have a great figure, isn't she flexible, and the like. I assent to all, especially in regards to her flexibility, which she has demonstrated by the seemingly impossible feat of raising her leg behind her and touching the flat of her foot to the back of her head. My back hurts just thinking about it and I say so. Sis laughs and answers, "Yes, but imagine what other uses her flexibility might have."

That observation both silences me and makes me realize this must be another of her setups. Then the girl's face appears in memory. It's the tall blonde from Match.com. Has Sis written to her? Seems unlikely. What's more likely is Sis had her sign up on Match.com and write something that would fit Sis's criteria for dates for me. This seems twisted but well within the realm of possibility, especially for Sis. Again, it doesn't really matter; if my goal is to keep her happy, maybe part of doing that is pretending innocence.

After our dinner arrives, we savor our food and continue to chat about our high-flying contortionist. The conversation drifts away from her beauty and suppleness toward the more obvious questions of how she learned these techniques and how she can make a living performing them. By the time we have dessert and coffee, the second show begins.

This time she unhooks the long loop of fabric from the wall and swings it out to one side. But first she asks the guy sitting under it to move his chair back so she doesn't end up accidentally kicking him. For this act she is dressed in tights and a different low-cut, fitted top. She bows to the audience here and there to get their attention then reaches up and hoists herself by the fabric loop, which she then parts and uses as a trapeze, stretching and bending and turning and winding herself all the way up to the ceiling while we watch. She seems serpent-like in her ability to twist sinuously and bend backwards nearly in half. Again I watch with rapt attention, and Sis watches both of us as if I were a part of the show. After the girl drops down again, Sis motions her over and whispers in her ear. She smiles, reaches into her hat like a magician, and withdraws a business card then hands it to me, accompanied by a second wink.

Alayna, it reads. I smile back and nod. The two girls exchange a guarded look then she walks away.

~ ~ ~

By Saturday morning, the weather has turned nasty. Rain drives against my windows in sheets, and wind gusts upend the balcony table. I check the forecast and the next few days look the same, so I call Adele and beg off sailing. I offer dinner instead, but she takes a rain check on the sail for later in the week. We compare schedules and decide on Thursday afternoon. I'm not working that day, and Adele has morning classes then the whole weekend to catch up on study and assignments. Since I don't want to face down Sis over a Saturday night at home alone, and since I definitely don't want to join the SSFC, I decide to see if Gretch has anything planned. Unfortunately, she does, but she has the kindness to intimate she's disappointed to have to turn me down, and we agree to meet for a drink and dinner at Ray's tomorrow evening. I know Sis will be at the library all afternoon and spend the night cramming for a test on Monday, so she'll probably be happy to have the condo to herself for a few extra hours.

I suppose I can always fake a date, but I know I'm not imaginative enough to pull it off. I try calling Alayna instead. She probably works both weekend nights, but maybe she can join me for a late lunch or early dinner if she's free. We agree to meet at the Copacabana at 5:00 p.m. right after she gets off work. It's a Bolivian restaurant near the Pike Place Market and just a short walk from Trapezio, so Alayna can go right from dinner to her treetop stage.

I arrive early but find her already seated by the window overlooking Elliott Bay. I like the Copa for its great food and view and casual atmosphere, but since it closes at 4:00 p.m. most days and 7:00 p.m. on

Saturday, it's really just a lunch place. Alayna is wearing a ridiculously short skirt and her fishnet stockings, already partly in costume. I hope she gets good tips at Trapezio. The act warrants it, and her outfits don't hurt either.

When I get to the table, she rises from her seat and gives me a nice hug, then we settle in to talk a while about everything and about nothing. She's also thirty-two, and I'm sure she's an old friend of Sis's but keep the thought to myself. I suspect Adele is too, but I haven't caught her saying anything yet to give it away. The question, I suppose, is whether I care one way or the other. On the one hand, if I play along and it makes Sis happy, I should be happy too. But on the other, it feels creepy to consider sleeping with women who are close friends. I try to analyze what I mean by creepy and find I can't define it beyond a general discomfort with the idea of having them compare notes. But maybe I'm thinking further down the line to when Sis and I might be more than just lovers, a time when such memories of her friends' intimate knowledge of me might stand in the way of taking a deeper relationship seriously.

In any event, as I talk with Alayna and imagine a future night in bed with her, I decide against it. There is too much risk, and even though I would love to see her naked and can readily imagine the ways she might bend, I also sense, without being entirely certain why, that this would be a huge mistake.

After dinner we walk slowly to Trapezio. Halfway through our stroll Alayna takes my hand and, as we proceed, shifts her grip occasionally to interlace her fingers with mine then shifts back again to hold firmly but fluidly. Her hands are strong and have been toughened by her act, but there is a range of nuance in her touch that erases this distracting sensation. When we arrive at Trapezio, she enters through the service door and pulls me inside. The long kiss she gives is filled with soft brushing contact and tip-of-tongue promise, not unlike the way Sis kisses. My mind drifts, and I only become aware of our change in posture slowly. Alayna has been bending backward, pulling me to her, until we are molded together in an arc. At apogee, the furthermost point from our center of gravity, her back is arched and her knees spread wide in a stance you might see going under a limbo stick, but though she holds me tightly, she exerts no downward pull. If I let her go, she would not drop. She holds this nearly coital pose for a minute then slowly rises again effortlessly and breaks contact, dancing away. But before she disappears inside, she turns for one parting wink.

~ ~ ~

I arrive back at the condo before 7:30 p.m., and though I expect Sis to be out for the night, she meets me at the door. Her previous disinterest in the details of my date with Adele is now replaced with intent questioning and, oddly, with intense scrutiny of both sides of my neck.

"What are you looking for?"

"Hickeys," she answers in perfect seriousness.

"Aren't we a bit old for that?"

"You are, maybe, but not that child you were out with."

"She's not a child. She's exactly your age. Thirty-two is old enough."

"Is it?" She leans in to kiss me in exactly the way Alayna has, minus the theatrical dip.

"So, who's the best kisser, me or Alayna?"

"Hmmm, hard to tell. Think I might need more kisses from each of you for a conclusive study."

That comment earns me a smack on the ass and a huffy pout, but Sis can't keep a straight face and cracks up. Once she regains her composure, she comments breezily, "Take your time deciding. Don't rush," then she turns and pretends to walk away.

"One thing I can say, though. You're both better than Adele."

This comment turns Sis around and she gives me a wicked look. Clearly I've made her day. And just as clearly, this information will get back to both Adele and Alayna. I'm certain of it.

The rest of the evening is given over to discussion of my date with Alayna and with Sis's explanation of how she's come to know her, an admission obviously designed to steer me away from the idea they've known each other for a long time. I allow the pretense to go unchallenged. This is, after all, a game two can play. I even dutifully describe the back breaking position Alayna put us in, but try as we might to duplicate it, Sis and I end up on the floor each time. Then we try one last back bend and end up in bed.

Afterward, Sis tells me she likes being the beneficiary of my earlier sexual stimulation with Alayna, who, she points out, had all the work without the payoff. Once again, she is just too pleased with herself, so I can't resist answering, "Yes, but turnabout is fair play."

Lacrosse, Anyone?

We sleep in on Sunday morning until 9:00 a.m., then I rise, stretch, and head for the shower. Sis rolls over and lolls seductively, making certain her breasts are uncovered, and begs insincerely for me to come back to bed, and even though it's tempting, I know I'll be late if I don't ignore her obvious ploy. I cast a comment over my shoulder about her lack of "flexibility," enunciating every syllable, and am hit in the middle of my back with the pillow she throws.

"You really have to get your butt in gear," I say to myself. "No time for fooling around." Brian has asked for the day off, and since I have late-season customers to meet at 10:00 a.m., I have told him I'd hang in all day.

The weather this morning isn't exactly conducive to looking at sailboats and certainly isn't right for a sea trial, but yesterday would have been worse. October brings out the bargain shoppers, hopeful that a seller staring at the long winter of expensive slip fees and spring maintenance ahead will be amenable to big cuts in the asking price. And they're right to a degree, but they're also a nuisance to sell to as they delve deeper and deeper for the lowest of the lowball offers. I can spend many weekends showing boats they will never buy. Spring is better, with the excitement of the long

Puget Sound summer enticing buyers to jump at the first reasonable deal. The problem in spring is the sellers. They want top dollar and won't settle for less until June or even July, when they begin to worry all the buyers have already found what they're looking for.

At 10:00 a.m. sharp, my buyers call to say they don't want to fight the rain and wind, both of which have picked up now. Relieved, I tell them, "No problem, maybe next weekend," and close up shop after first hanging the "Back By" sign on the sales office door and setting the hands to twelve noon. Breakfast at The Blue Star is next and I enjoy the peace of eating alone, broken only by the infrequent appearance of the waitress to refill my coffee mug and the comings and goings of neighboring customers. Then it's back to the silent office for five hours of twiddling my thumbs and catching up on some paperwork and correspondence. I also leave a note for Brian to say I'll be taking Thursday off to go sailing. The forecast is decent but this is October, so 'expect change' is the rule. As I leave just before 5:00 p.m., I re-hang the 'Back By' sign and set the hands to 10:00 a.m.

~ ~ ~

I find Gretch waiting for me when I get to Ray's. I get a big hug and a friendly kiss and an equally friendly, "It's been a while. Great to see you."

"It's great to see you, too," I parrot back. "I need some advice."

This draws a surprised look that turns into a broad smile, when, after noting and decoding her confusion, I add, "Not legal advice. Girlfriend advice."

"Happy to oblige," she says and puts her arm

around me in a motherly gesture as we follow the waitress to our table.

We order drinks first, Tanqueray and tonic for Gretch and a pint of Alaskan Amber for me, and chat aimlessly until our drinks arrive. Then I launch into an explanation of my situation as I interpret it. I notice the intense concentration she applies and realize Gretch has shifted into "lawyer mode." I recognize this as a habit she has developed over the years and one which she probably has no overt control of, but I also recognize she will be able to repeat verbatim everything I am telling her.

The basis of my quandary, I say, is Sis and her demand that I not only date other women but also bed them. This problem, I tell Gretch, has been exacerbated most recently by the introduction of two young women whom I am certain Sis knows well. I have been uncomfortable all along with her insistence I sleep around, but sleeping with her friends is worse. It feels creepy, I say. That gets a laugh out of Gretch, but she correctly qualifies it as "stepping over the line."

Gretch asks me to describe Adele and Alayna. When I ask why, she dismisses my question with a wave of her hand. I say the two of them are the same age as Sis, thirty-two. Gretch raises her eyebrows. I go on to say they are both quite attractive, Adele is fairly short and Alayna is quite tall, and I go into some detail about Alayna's leg strength and coordination. Gretch then asks if Adele and Sis are athletic. I pause to consider this a minute then answer that both are well-muscled, and though I don't know if they are really all that athletic, they very well might be. This answer draws a sigh from Gretch.

In response to my quizzical expression, she asks, "Are they energetic?"

"I guess so. No trouble keeping up with an old guy like me anyway."

"Right. So, is Sis aggressive in bed or does she just let you lead?"

This time it's my turn to laugh. "Me, lead? Why do you think we're having this conversation? I'm being led around like I had a ring through my nose. Of course, she's aggressive in bed. Just like she is in every other way. She could give lessons in aggression."

Gretch shakes her head. "You're being triple-teamed."

"I know. I figured they knew each other. I just don't know what to do about it."

"What I mean is they're teammates. Probably played together in high school. I'll bet they went the whole three or four years, graduating from intramural to JV to Varsity. And it wouldn't surprise me if Sis were the team captain, whatever sport it is. So, the question is what sport? Can't be basketball if Sis and Adele are short." Gretch pauses a while to think it through then asks, "Are they quick on their feet?"

I remember back to the moves Sis put on me in our shower after she doused me with cold water, and as I relive that moment, I nod.

"Very."

"Soccer or lacrosse, most likely. Wait, how tall is tall?"

"Alayna must be almost my height so maybe 5'-10" or 5'-11"."

"And Sis is five-foot-nothing?"

"Yup, at most."

"It's lacrosse. Sis and Adele were probably defenders, either goalie or point, or maybe they were midfielders if they're really fast. They would have played both offense and defense. Alayna was most likely on attack. Her height and long reach would have been an advantage in shooting higher into the goal. On the other hand, if Sis is quick enough, she might have played best as a cutter."

As Gretch continues to expound, I watch her eyes glaze over in a very un-lawyer-like fashion. Clearly, she is reliving her glory days. What I know about lacrosse wouldn't take up a decent length paragraph, but Gretch has lived it. Maybe it was high school or maybe it was college. This is where she learned her own aggressiveness and where she honed her innate athleticism. She is speaking from experience.

I wait until she has come back down to earth then remark, "That was fun."

She blushes. I cannot believe my eyes. Do female lawyers actually blush, I wonder, especially those who are as aggressive in bed as Gretch has been with me, and who prowl Seattle both literally and figuratively looking for new kills like the lionesses they are?

"You're blushing," I say.

My remark is met by an even deeper shade of red, then she shrugs. "You caught me. I'm not accustomed to being caught. I'm all about control."

"Hmmm, I remember," I say and feel the blood rise in my face as well. "But we were trying to fix my problem before you floated away into your girlish past. Can we get back to 'me' now?"

My flip comment releases the tension in both of us and we laugh together.

"So," she asks, "can you think like a team player?"

"Doubt it. I've never been competitive. And what few sports I played, I sucked at. I made the tennis team but usually lost. And I ran the mile in track, but always managed to come in forth or fifth. Not much help then or now."

"This is not going to be easy. Somehow you have to convince Adele and Alayna to switch teams. They're clearly in this to help Sis get whatever she wants. I have a few ideas about what that might be, and, no offense, I doubt you really have a clue. But she may be misleading them the way Doc misled both of us. You might be able to turn the tables if you play it right."

"Yeah, well that's the problem. I'm no good at games. It worked on Doc, but I know him very well and he knows me, so our little subterfuge succeeded. But he would have figured it out sooner or later. These girls will see it coming a mile away."

"Maybe yes, maybe no. You have two advantages at the moment. Neither they nor Sis know you suspect them to be friends, yes?"

I nod but before I can speak, Gretch continues, "So they won't see it coming until you confront them. You want to do what Sis wants you to do; you just don't want to sleep with either of them. So, don't. Tell them the simple truth: you are in love with someone and even though she wants you to date other women and you are playing as best you can by her rules, you can't bring yourself to sleep with anyone else."

"But if Sis has asked them to sleep with me, and I won't, and then they tell her I won't, Sis will be angry, no?"

"Well, that's where it gets tricky. It may be that Sis

really does want you to sleep with other women. If so, you'll have to convince her teammates to play on your side. It's possible that simply telling the truth will turn them. There is nothing most women would honor more than a guy who says he won't sleep with them because he's in love with their best friend.

"But in order to make it work, they'll have to lie to Sis and tell you the truth: that they are all old friends and Sis has engaged them both in this charade. And Sis has to believe you are sleeping with at least one of them. My choice would be Alayna for obvious reasons, but you should choose the most believable, whichever that is. They could help you decide. And pretending to sleep with both is an option, but it might be more difficult to maintain the fiction.

"But if they decide not to come clean with you, it may still work. They will know your reasoning and Sis will still push them to sleep with you, but they may decide to lie to her anyway. It really depends on what they think of her ruse and how endearing they find your confession to be.

"But everything I've said so far depends on your assumption that Sis really does want you to sleep around. It may not be true. It may be a test either to see where you are in the divorce-dating transition or whether you are so in love with her you will refuse to do what she demands. Remember her reaction to Rebekah? She was an actual threat, not some bimbo from Teddies or Sis's controlled dates. Personally, I think her motivation may be a bit of both."

As I sit taking in everything Gretch is saying, I decide two things: first, she is way too good at this so it's no wonder she's such a successful lawyer, and second, I'm in over my head. I don't believe I can pull it off; I'm bound to blow it. It may be my only way out is to tell Adele and Alayna the whole truth, and nothing but the truth, including the whole lacrosse team scenario Gretch has put forward. If I'm honest about everything, I can't get caught in a lie. I'll go out with them, or at least one of them, and simply refuse to share details with Sis. That, I might get away with, but only if Adele and Alayna are willing to lie about what we do. Like any good lawyer, Gretch wants me to keep my options open by finessing the situation, but I'm more of an "all in or fold 'em" sort of gambler. I'll have to place my bet and take my chances.

~ ~ ~

On Monday morning, I call Alayna's cell and leave a message asking her out for a sail on Thursday afternoon. Before the end of the day, Alayna calls back and accepts, and I arrange for her to meet me at the marina a half hour ahead of the time I agree to with Adele. I plan to have Alayna already settled in with a beer before I head up the dock to let Adele through the gate.

This first part goes as planned. The weather is nice for a change after the past five days of rain and wind. Alayna arrives on time and settles in to ponder what I mean when I tell her, "I have a *little* surprise for you." I see Adele's car pull in, so I'm able to meet her before she can look down the dock by chance and catch sight of Alayna.

The second part goes well too, or as far as I can tell at any rate. The two girls are taken by surprise and are unable to cover it up.

"I believe you both know each other."

They exchange looks but neither responds nor does anything except shrug, as if to say, "The jig is up."

"You also know Sis, right?" Again, no obvious response.

"So, which one of you was captain of the lacrosse team?"

My gambit is completely successful. They respond in unison, "How did…?"

I'm tempted to say something cute like, "I heard it through the grapevine," but think better of it. If these two are half as sharp as Sis, I'll be outgunned as soon as the surprise wears off.

I climb aboard, leaving Adele on the dock then motion for her to follow and take a seat when she does. Then I proceed to explain much in the same way I described my problem to Gretch, beginning at the same place, "I need some advice."

The girls listen quietly, nodding or shaking their heads here and there and occasionally adding or subtracting from my assumptions.

When I'm done, there is a moment of silence then Adele says to Alayna, "She lied to us," then turning to me, "She said she wanted to make sure you wouldn't cheat on her."

"By asking me to sleep with other women? That doesn't make any sense."

"In Sis's warped little world it makes perfect sense," Alayna answers. "She's been burned before and she's set her share of fires, as well."

My confused look causes Adele to continue Alayna's thought. "Sis has had just one long relationship. That was in high school. She was the star of the girl's lacrosse team; Vince was the captain of the boy's team. But it was a match made somewhere other than heaven, as she liked to tell people. Truth is she was wilder than Vince and got caught flirting one too many times. So he turned the tables and started up with one of the cheerleaders. Sis could never see it was just his way of saving face and teaching her a lesson. After Vince, it was one guy after another, none longer than a few months, until her junior year at UW. She fell for this really nice guy but couldn't bring herself to trust him. Eventually, she drove him away with jealousy. After that it was back to one guy after the other, all with the same doubts and result."

"Then she gave up and started her "love 'em and leave 'em" Match.com pursuit of permanent unhappiness," Alayna adds. "But now there's you. It's like she wants to change but can't let herself. Maybe she's afraid to trust and thinks if she tests you she'll figure it out, or maybe she really wants you to be just like her, fucked up, so you can be fucked up together."

At this point I'm staring at my feet. I don't really know what to tell them but hear Gretch's voice in my head: "Tell them the truth." That's easy for her to say, but I really don't know the truth. In some ways I love Sis. And I'm not some dumb kid. I know how to love. I was happily married for twenty-three years before Carole left. She took a lot of me with her, but she didn't take my heart. I know what I want, sometimes at least, but I don't know what Sis wants, and, apparently, neither do Adele or Alayna.

"So how do we find out?"

"Find out what?" Adele asks. "What Sis wants or what you want?"

Both girls are looking intently at me and waiting.

"I think I could love her. I think that's what I want. But I know I haven't completely gotten over being in love with my wife. We're not even officially divorced yet; won't be final for two months. That's going to be my Christmas present from her." Then I pause to think a moment.

"Look, I know I'd be happy if Sis would just drop the rule about both of us dating and bedding others. I…I just want to be with her right now."

"She's not," Alayna says. And when she sees the confused look on my face, she clarifies, "She's not sleeping with anyone but you. The nights she tells you she's with some other guy, she's been at my apartment or with Chris. I'm between boyfriends and Chris never takes one on, so one of us always has a place for her to crash."

"I hate being lied to," I say. "But I'm not sure she's lied so much as misled. She just let me fill in the blanks. From me she demands details but refuses to share any of hers, so I suppose she just left it to my imagination."

"She's manipulative."

Adele nods in agreement. "Very. But she's a good friend too. And for what it's worth, she's spent a lot of effort to set this all up. I can assure you she hasn't ever invested this much before. Alayna's right. It's been love 'em and leave 'em every time…until now."

"And the obvious reason she's recruited the two of us," Alayna adds, "is that she doesn't really want you to find someone else. And neither does she. That was always true in the past. Now Sis thinks she knows what she wants, but she's conflicted. She doesn't know whether to trust either her own emotions or yours. And, as you admit, you're not likely to be over your wife yet. Sis knows that too."

What they say makes a lot of sense and I decide to accept it, but it doesn't get me any nearer a decision about what to do. Can we really continue the charade, with Adele and Alayna switching to my side, or will Sis figure it out and have the whole thing blow up in my face? I decide to ask their opinion. They've known her far longer than I have. What I get in return for my question are shrugs and sighs. They say they want to help, but each is afraid she will give the wrong advice.

"It's a toss up," Alayna says. "Two months ago I could have told you the answer, but today your guess is as good as mine. There's something different about Sis now, and that something is tied up in your relationship with her."

I turn to Adele, who has been silent but understands she needs to answer. "What she said. We'll help you as best we can. Right?"

Alayna nods vigorously, but I can see both helplessness and hopelessness written across their expressions. They're on my team, but the other side has a big lead, and time is running out.

~ ~ ~

When I get home, I pause at my door and take a deep breath. I'm losing my nerve. I don't know how to begin to say what I need to say. I decide to take the easy way out: humor. If I say I've just come from a date with both, maybe Sis will be amused. As I stand mulling over my first words, the door opens. She must have heard the elevator bell.

"What happened?"

Her expression makes me realize how I must look, like I just lost my best friend. I'm taking this way too seriously, I think, and launch into a lighthearted description of my afternoon, feigning as much humor as I can. She listens but doesn't smile. And when I repeat Alayna's "love 'em and leave 'em" description of her, she turns and walks away into her room.

I try her door, but it's locked. Then I ask, "Can we talk?" But there is no reply, just the sound of doors and drawers opening and closing.

When she finally comes out, two suitcases accompany her.

"Why?"

"This isn't going to work," she says sadly then reaches up and strokes my cheek. "You are too lovable and I'm not loveable enough."

"Don't you think that's for me to decide?"

"No, I stopped letting guys make my decisions for me a long time ago. I'm not going to change."

"But I'm not asking you to."

"Yes, you are. You just don't know that you are. And you're not ready yet. You still need to put Carole in the past and try out the future with some Alaynas, Adeles, Beths, and even a Rebekah or two. I'm just in the way."

"That's not fair. I've only been doing what you asked me to do."

"You're right. It's not fair. But it should have taught you something about yourself, except it hasn't seemed to. Like I said, I'm in the way."

"Taught me what? That I love you?"

"You don't, you know. Maybe a little, but not

enough to stand up to me. Think about it. You've been dating my friends, and even though I put them in your path and insisted you go out with them, you've played along and enjoyed it. Adele isn't much of an actress, but Alayna would have maneuvered you into her bed in no time if she put her mind to it. Look how little it took with Beth. Or with my mother, for Christ's sake. And the only reason you didn't sleep with Ms. Very Hot is that she wasn't ready. You get a few points for being a gentleman but none for restraint."

I stand mute, hands in pockets, and take what she dishes out. I'm hoping pity will soften her tirade but she continues unabated.

"And then you turn my friends against me. That's what I mean by too lovable. You can't help yourself. You're pliable and affectionate and open to suggestion, regardless of who does the suggesting. But it's not your fault. It's just who you are, and most women, hell, just about any woman, would fall for that in a heartbeat. Alayna already has. Look, I know you want me to stay. And, believe me, I want to stay, but I can't. It would be wrong. If I stay you'll never find out who you are. You'll love me because I'm here, the same way you loved Carole. I need it to be more and so do you."

I'm left speechless but can feel the tears rolling down my cheeks. Sis reaches up and wipes them away then kisses me goodbye and leaves, closing the door gently behind her with a promise to return for the rest of her things tomorrow while I'm at work. I make no further attempt to stop her and realize it's because I know she's right. I don't want her to be right, and I don't think she's right for the reasons she's given, but I can see my future lies elsewhere, at least for now.

~ ~ ~

In the days ahead, days spent alone with my thoughts, I will come to understand that Sis has been a catalyst. Her youthful body and enthusiasm, and even her demands for my extra-relationship concupiscence, have freed me of my ties to Carole, ties that have prevented me from taking any new relationship seriously, even my relationship with Sis. But right now, all I feel is the pain of an ending. Curiously, the pain seems worse than when Carole left, and this realization brings me back to where I started, thinking I was in love with Sis after all. But as the days pass, I understand it is not true. Yes, I miss her desperately, her quick wit, her touch, her sensuous kisses. Yes, her set of keys found the next day lying on my kitchen counter evoked pain. But no, I am not in love with her. I think I was in love with the idea of being in love with her. But, as she said, I was too easily distracted, like a kid in a candy shop, bouncing from one woman to another with little attachment and even less remorse for doing so. But isn't that exactly what she wanted me to do? Isn't that what she herself did? No, not when she was with me, though I didn't know it at the time. And my own wants and desires are not of her making anyway. I will need to discover them on my own.

Intermezzo

Four days later, on Tuesday evening, Alayna calls. I let the machine pick up as I've been doing each time Doc has tried to touch base. He has heard from Sis via Chris that we split up and he wants to console me, but I'm just not ready. Doc always has some ulterior motive and I don't feel like playing twenty questions with him.

I close my eyes and listen as her voice seduces, "Andrew? Andrew, it's me, Alayna. You're probably there, aren't you? I understand that you don't want to talk so just listen. Sis told me she left. I'm so sorry. I know it must hurt. But it's what she does, I'm afraid. Look, it might be good for you to talk to someone, and when you're ready I'd like it if that someone was me. I'm a good listener. So call me. I'm free most weekday nights, and I want to be there for you. Partly, I feel responsible for helping Sis create this mess, but partly…well, I like you, and I can't stand the thought of you being hurt and alone. Call me. Okay?"

I can hear Alayna breathing on the other end of the now silent line. She holds the connection open for a long ten seconds then asks one more time, "Andrew?" Another few moments pass and the machine clicks off. Do I really need someone to talk to? Maybe, but I can sense my resistance to the idea. Yes, I'm hurting. Yes, she could probably make some of that hurt disappear, especially if I'm reading her unspoken intention correctly, but what I really want is for Sis to call. I don't expect that to happen since she's made it clear I need to work through my divorce and its aftermath on my own, but I can still hope.

On Friday just before midnight, Alayna calls again. I surface from sleep and can hear restaurant background chatter and music as she tries a different tack. Her car has broken down and she could use a lift home. She's tried everyone else and she doesn't have her purse with her so she can't call a cab. She promises this isn't some lame trick and she won't expect me to talk to her unless I want to.

"Please pick up, Andrew. I know you're there. Aren't you? Pleeaasse…"

As I reach for the phone, I think what a sap I am to fall for this. Maybe Sis is right. Maybe I'm just too lovable. Alayna offers to meet me on the corner of First Avenue and Pike Street, just outside the Pike Place Market. I tell her to get someone to wait with her for safety's sake and say I'll be there as soon as I can. As promised, she's standing on the corner when I arrive twenty minutes later. Her trapeze artist outfit, which is covered only by a short jacket, makes her look like a streetwalker for the fatally kinky, so it's a good thing she found someone to wait with her.

Alayna's apartment is located just off Alki beach in West Seattle, a short drive in silence; neither of us speaks. When I pull up in front, she hesitates, looking from me to the building and back to me, as if trying to decide what to do next. She leans over and kisses me. There's as much question in her kiss as there is in her look when she pulls away. Then she nods, opens the door, and gets out. She fumbles in her jacket pocket for her keys as she walks toward the entry. I wait until she unlocks the outside security door and turns to wave and mime the use of a phone. "Call me," she's asking. I flash my lights to indicate I understand then drive away.

The week passes with no further contact from Alayna or Doc. No word from Sis either. It's peaceful, I think, to be on my own. The initial hurt from Sis's departure has fallen away, replaced by some internal quietude. By the weekend, our rainy weather pattern has fallen away as well, and though it is not replaced by a return of sunny days, the clouds part now and then, providing sun breaks, shafts of intense light opening and closing randomly, teasing us into believing tomorrow will bring back clear skies. But November is fast approaching, and I know the sun will abandon us soon and the rains will return.

I decide to take advantage of the dry weekend to button up *Repose* for the winter. I head for the marina on Saturday morning and drag down one of the dock carts in which to offload gear. The first task is to remove my sails: main, genoa, and staysail. That takes two hours. I stuff them into their corresponding sail bags, load them into the cart, and trundle the lot up to my car. Then I return to the boat with the cart for a second load: bedding, towels, miscellaneous clothing, paper charts, cruising guides, portable electronics, and anything else that will suffer from being left behind. On the last trip, I load the remaining odds and ends and stand up all seat and berth cushions so air can circulate around them. Mildew is a big problem in the long, clammy winter months of the Pacific Northwest. I also set out two driers: fan-driven, low-wattage electric heaters that will suffice to keep *Repose* mildew-free below decks over the six months she'll sit unused before spring sailing season begins. I'll return tomorrow to close all seacocks, winterize water tanks, fuel tanks, and holding tanks, and to do a final inspection. After this, I'll check once every few weeks to make sure all is well and the batteries are still on trickle charge.

Driving away from the marina, I experience ennui brought on by fall's end. The feeling is intensified by my other recent losses, first Carole then Sis. There is little I can do about either. I stop in at the Blue Star for a late afternoon lunch, or maybe it's an early dinner, expecting the presence of other diners to cause a sense of being part of life again, but it has the opposite effect, making me feel my loss more acutely. By the time I get back to my empty condo, I'm downright depressed, and the three beers I consume don't help. That's when I decide to give Alayna a call. Her voicemail answers, "Not here right now. Press one for business or two for pleasure." I pause before hitting "two," not quite understanding what sort of answering service this is. Then I hear her voice again, "Guess I'm out right now. Please leave a message. I'll get back to you later." Her tone is light and cheerful and brings a faint smile to my face. When I hear the beep, I begin to hang up but then say softly, "It's Andrew. You must be off to work already. Call me when you get home. Any time is fine. I'll be up."

One minute later, my phone rings.

"Hey! Want company?"

There is a long pause, during which I remain silent. I do want company, I think, but I have the uneasy feeling I'm making a mistake.

"Andrew? Are you okay?" Her tone is so sweet and receptive.

"Yes," I say, and mean to answer both questions at once. Yes, I'm okay, and yes, I want company.

"I'm on my way."

Before I can respond, the connection breaks.

~ ~ ~

When I wake on Sunday morning, the uneasiness from last night has evaporated. Alayna snores softly beside me, a mouth breather. I turn my head to watch her nearly flat chest rise and fall slowly, her small dark nipples still erect. I lift the covers to take her in, and even in sleep her muscles are tightly outlined and pushing against the thin layer of skin. Alayna has no appreciable body fat. The sexual athleticism I had expected, given her physical condition and given Sis's suggestion about what she could do with her flexibility, was all but absent in Alayna's lovemaking. Curiously, she preferred that I do all the work. She exercised no control. Instead, she lay submissively, allowing me to take her where I wanted and luxuriating in the slow build up and long release. There was one exception only. As I approached my own climax, she began to contract and relax vaginal muscles I didn't even know existed, pulsing from tight grip to free fall with each heartbeat. The sensation was exquisite. The memory makes me shudder. My movement causes Alayna to turn over in her sleep and drape an arm on my chest and a leg across my upper thighs. She nuzzles into my neck, her warm, moist breath comforting, lulling me back toward drowsiness. This is the part I love most, I think, a woman's warm body held against mine in surfeit and the implicit understanding that each day will begin the same way, entwined.

As this thought settles and I begin to drift, I make a mental connection and am suddenly brought wide-awake again. This is what I miss. This is what Carole took away when she left. Call it what you will: closeness, warmth, companionship, or even intimacy. The sense that she, whoever she is, is always there; there when I kiss her goodnight, there when I roll over in my sleep to hold her, there when I wake like this in the morning and watch her breathe. And in the daytime, there in my thoughts when I pause in whatever I'm doing and turn in my mind toward her. This is what I need, what I have to find again. I can feel a smile spreading over my face, a smile of satisfaction at having solved a puzzle. Then the smile fades as I realize this is only half the equation, and a moment later it disappears altogether when I come to the understanding that each of the women I have slept with over the past few months, Gretch, Margaret, Sis, Beth, and Alayna, and even Rebekah, who I have not slept with, have evoked this same feeling, this same sense of well-being that Carole stole from me. The trapdoor opens at my feet, yawning wide, obvious now: this incipient serial monogamy has no end. Doc hasn't found it, that's for certain, and I know now that it doesn't exist. The whole idea in serial monogamy is treating each ending as a new beginning. It is circular, a cycle I must find a way to break.

~ ~ ~

When she wakes, I tell Alayna I have to go to the office, a lie whose purpose is only to avoid having to spend the day together. I need to think. I make an effort to be affectionate and promise to call her soon, but I can see in her eyes she's not buying it. I imagine she thinks this is a brush-off, but she puts on a happy face and kisses me goodbye as if she believes she'll hear from me again. Once I shower and catch breakfast at the Blue Star, I head for the marina. I take a few minutes to complete the remaining winterization tasks then grab some life cushions and settle in on the foredeck, leaning against the mast and staring off into space.

The hours pass. I review my "girls," as I have come to think of them, and my relationship to each. I add Adele, Christine, and even my pint-sized cowgirl, Billie, to the list. I leave Carole off intentionally. She's history, though I accept I may have to face her someday, even if I cannot imagine how it might happen.

Beth and Billie and Gretch are the easiest to dismiss as sexual encounters of varying kinds and nothing more, though I put Gretch in a somewhat different category and will continue to think of her as a friend as well. Christine and Margaret are mismatched bookends to a plot that has run its course, but I must admit in some ways I envy the errant father/husband. He has what I do not: a loving woman who, despite their history, still wants to spend her life with him. Adele and Alayna count, even if I only met them as a result of Sis's machinations. Each is sweet and charming in her own way. I'd even call Alayna hot, though part of the reason I would is to irritate Sis. But neither Adele nor Alayna is really what I'm looking for. However, this supposes I know what I'm looking for, and it's obvious to me that I don't.

That leaves just Rebekah and Sis as models for some future relationship, the former who is not ready to commit or even begin, and the latter who may never be ready. But that's okay, they're only models at this moment, and for the purposes of this discussion, internal and transitional though it may be. I'm done with making snap decisions, except for the one I'm making right now: to cease pursuing any sort of relationship for the next two months until my divorce is final. It feels good to get that out of the way, even though I know it means living alone and going without sex. Probably be good for me, character building even. And I've had a taste of it already this past week; it won't be completely new.

Getting back to Rebekah and Sis; which would really be the better model, a woman close to my age who has had whatever family she wants already, a woman who shares some of the history I have lived, including marriage and divorce, or a younger woman who has never married, who wants children, and who has grown up with different cultural rules and expectations? The former sounds more comfortable, like a well-worn pair of docksiders. Extending the footwear metaphor, the latter would be a pair of stilettos, sharp and pointed, the kind that punches holes. I'm the one who will end up being walked on, so I need to decide which will suit me best.

Gretch immediately comes to mind and, when I call her, she agrees to meet at Ray's later. There must have been something unsettled in my voice, because when she walks in, worry is etched in her expression. I grin and shrug.

"So, more girlfriend advice?"

I nod. The hostess tries to swallow her laugh but fails miserably. We're halfway to our table before she finally stifles it. She redeems herself by putting a hand on my shoulder, saying, "Good luck," and accompanying that remark with a sweet smile.

"Thanks, I'll need it." I smile back.

I review my situation as best I can, congratulating Gretch wryly for correctly surmising the plot Sis had hatched. Gretch listens, only interjecting a question now and then for clarification of some detail or other. When I finish, she looks away out the window. It's still early but the sun has long since set. By the solstice it will be dark before 5:00 p.m. each day and not really light again until 8:00 a.m. the next morning. Winters here are a time for hunkering down to stay warm and dry. When she turns back to look at me, she's frowning.

"I don't think I like this girl."

I say nothing, but I know she can read the sadness in my look. Words aren't necessary.

"Andrew, she's too complicated for you. Someone or something has damaged her and I don't think you're strong enough to deal with the repair. In some ways, she's like me. In some ways, she's not. But I've learned to find my own balance. I don't think Sis has. And I can see from your face she has the capacity to make you miserable."

Again I say nothing, but nod in agreement.

"You have to let her go. Otherwise, you're in for years of getting back together only to break up again. I think Sis could weather that, maybe even enjoy the breakup/makeup aspect of it. You will not. You are adept at bending, but you have no tolerance for pain. You'll break."

I stare at my hands and drum my fingers on the table. Then I look out at the nightscape. A container vessel is passing, green starboard running light and white masthead beacon gleaming. The superstructure is lit from deck-mounted spotlights. It is the only thing moving either north or south. Beyond it, four miles away, house lights shimmer on Bainbridge Island. Are there couples out there sitting down over a meal to discuss their future, as I am considering mine right now? I want to deny what Gretch is saying, but it seems like sound advice. Sis is complicated. I can't change that.

"What should I have said to her?"

"When? Before or after she said she was leaving?"

"It makes a difference?"

"Of course. If you could have maintained the fiction you were dating her friends, she might have stayed. I think she would have left sooner or later anyway, but she would have hung in longer to see what happened."

"What could I have said to stop her from leaving? Would anything have worked?"

Gretch begins to answer, but stops. She is considering carefully.

"Look, I would have said and done different things, but that's me. You don't think the same way. If I told you what to say, it wouldn't matter because it's too late, and even if it wasn't too late, there would be a next time and a next time and a next time. You can only say what you feel. If that doesn't work then it doesn't work."

"I still don't understand why she would just leave with no discussion. It's as if she planned it all along."

Now Gretch pauses. Is she reconsidering or just

trying to find the words to let me down easily?

"You may be right. Maybe it's still part of a plan. If so, you fell for it. If Alayna was meant to wheedle her way into your bed, she succeeded, didn't she?"

"That's just too implausible. Alayna really seemed sincere, and both she and Adele were angry at being used as pawns in Sis's game. They couldn't all be that good at acting, could they?"

"Okay, maybe not. Maybe Sis has set up Alayna too. Maybe Alayna really does want to pursue a relationship with you and Sis is watching to see what happens. It plays right into her game naturally. No effort on her part necessary."

"It doesn't matter, does it? There's nothing I can do except refuse to play, and even that's playing in a way. Any advice?"

"Yes. Do nothing. You said you were considering a hiatus in dating until your divorce is final. Stick to it. If anyone asks, just say you want to put your divorce behind then you plan to give Match.com another try. But don't tell anyone unless they ask. That way you are no longer 'playing the game.' Word will eventually filter back to Sis through Doc or Alayna. And, speaking of Alayna, no more backsliding. Stick to celibacy for now."

I accept her summation with a nod, and we move on to other subjects, chatting aimlessly, first over cocktails, then dinner and a bottle of wine, then coffee. It strikes me what a good friend Gretch has become, and how much I appreciate her counsel. When the check comes, she opens it to assess the damage. I'm about to object, but before I can say anything, Gretch hands me the bill and glances at her wristwatch. "Not even close to my hourly rate."

"As a lawyer or lover?"

"Either."

When we walk out, I give the hostess a thumbs-up and she winks at me conspiratorially. We wait outside Ray's while the valet retrieves Gretch's BMW. She hugs me and plants a maternal kiss on my cheek then whispers in my ear a promise to come spend the night if I get desperate. I laugh and tell her I suspect I can go two months without sex. I'm not really sure about that, but it proves to be true. By mid-December, I've passed the test. I've also been tested several times by Doc, Larry, and Curly, and twice by Alayna; each time I insist I am content to go from day to day as I have been. I do share a meal with the boys a few times and join them for the occasional poker night, but since it doesn't seem to satisfy them, after a while they stop asking.

~ ~ ~

On December 17th, Gretch calls. My divorce has been granted and she can either ask Carole's lawyer to send my copy or I can pick it up at his office. Since that's just a few blocks from my condo, I drop by. When I arrive, he is standing in the office foyer chatting with Carole. I stop in my tracks and look at the two of them just a few paces away. She looks old, tired, and worn down, or maybe she just seems that way because I've been dating women half her age. My perspective is warped. But no, she really does look unwell.

Neither she nor her lawyer has noticed me. I could just leave and come back another time. But as I consider this option, Carole turns and looks right at me, her hand coming up to her mouth in surprise. Her lawyer turns too, but since he wouldn't know me from Adam, his expression doesn't change. I shrug, cross the short distance to the office door, open it, and introduce myself.

"Oh," he says, "I wasn't expecting you."

"My lawyer told me I could drop by to get my copy of the papers." I turn to Carole. "That's why you're here, right?"

Here's a new thing, I think; Carole is speechless. That never happened before. Her lawyer seems befuddled as well, but he spins on his heel and walks away, leaving the two of us standing there. I presume he's going for my copies of all the court stuff.

"You look well," Carole says after the awkwardness gets to her.

"I am. How about you?"

"I'm all right."

We both turn our heads to see where the lawyer has gone, but there's no sign of him.

"How's work?" she asks to break the silence again.

"Slow as usual. It will pick up after the boat show."

She nods. "When's that again?"

It amazes me she doesn't know. I've been going to the Seattle Boat Show for years now as a salesman and have attended for a decade before.

"End of January, like always," I reply mildly, trying to keep the irritation out of my voice.

"Oh, right. I should remember, shouldn't I?"

"No. Well, maybe, but it's not important."

She seems to accept my claim without questioning further.

"How's the real estate business?"

She looks up quickly, as if to gauge my intent, but

seeing none there, answers, "Not good. Nothing is selling. Do you never watch the news?"

"You know I don't. What's happening?" I ask, ignoring her critical tone.

"The stock market is down and the housing market has tanked, temporarily at least. Buyers are expecting prices to come down and sellers are waiting it out. Our sales are off nearly thirty percent."

"It'll come back. It always does."

"I suppose so. But I hope something happens soon to get either the sellers or buyers to stop waffling."

Animation and color have come back into her face as she explains. Carole lives for this, I think. Glad I don't. It does explain why boat sales have been particularly slow. Doesn't bode well for the boat show either, not that I really care, but Brian will.

I know I should resist the urge, but cannot. "How's Tony?"

"Gone. That's why I'm here. We dissolved our partnership. The paperwork is a nightmare."

"Sorry." She's caught me off-guard. I consider asking what happened but think better of it.

"You can say I told you so if you want. Turns out living with someone who's just like me is harder than living with someone who's nothing like me."

I chuckle. "Life is funny."

"Not lately, it isn't."

"Oh, come on. You'll bounce back."

"I think I've lost my bounce," she says with a wan smile to meet my lighter grin.

At this point, the lawyer reappears. He looks nervous. Probably worrying about what we've had to say to each other. He hands me an overstuffed folder with copies of all the documents and I shake his hand. Then I reach for Carole's, but she steps toward me and gives me a hug instead. I hug her back as well as I can with one arm, since the other is cradling the very papers that have obviated any future embraces. The irony is not lost on me.

As I walk away, she says, "Call me sometime."

I hear my answer as if someone else had said it. "I will."

Closure

Will I call her? Dumb question, of course I will. Seems I can never say no to a woman. Not sure why that's true, but I think it's so deeply ingrained that even if I could figure out why, there would be nothing I could do to change.

I manage to postpone the inevitable for six days. Call it nervousness or anxiety or fear of starting something I may not want to finish, or even misplaced loyalty to Sis. But, eventually, watching couples fighting their way through the pre-Christmas crush to buy the last present, or clinking glasses of wine in celebration of yet another year together, reminds me I'm alone, and I don't like the feeling.

Carole's cell rolls to voicemail when I call. I'm relieved and allow myself a wry satisfaction, knowing for Carole nothing has changed, it's always about business. I know very well the quick rollover probably means she's talking to someone and has decided not to put her client on hold just to answer my call. I leave a short message admitting it sucks to be alone during the holidays and wondering if she feels the same. Then I suggest, "How about a drink at Ray's? Won't cost you anything but a little time." Then, realizing this will sound like a dig at both her obsession with Folly and her financial loss from our divorce settlement, I backpedal, "Don't take it the wrong way, I just mean it's not a big commitment or anything." I pause, think to myself, "Shit, that sounds bad, too," and try another correction. "I'm not saying commitment was a problem. Hell, I don't know what I'm saying. I hate voicemail. Call me if you want to meet."

At 11:00 p.m. I turn off my cell phone. She's not going to call back. What did I expect anyway; we're divorced. I thought I had put all the mental masturbation behind me, but seeing her standing with her lawyer, and seeing the worn-out look, and hearing in her voice some vestige of regret, it's kicked in again. Even if there's nothing left of what we once felt, we did once feel it; letting go is not easy. I turn off my lights but toss and turn for hours, unable to shut down the computer between my ears. At 2:30 a.m., I'm just drifting off when I remember one of Carole's favorite telephone-tag ploys, and it brings me back wide awake again. I reach for my cell phone and turn it on, and as I suspected, it beeps its insistence: one new voicemail. She called only after she knew I'd have turned it off for the night. Another creature of habit.

Yes, I want my messages, I say in answer to the question wavering on the one-inch screen, and press the tiny green button.

Her voice, softened now after these months apart, answers.

"That was sweet, Andrew. Don't obsess about what I might think. Obsession is my department. How about Christmas Eve dinner, my treat? My new temp told me about a fun place. It's a surprise. I'll pick you up at 7:00 p.m.; no need to call back unless you can't make it. Dress up a little, okay?"

~ ~ ~

The next day I go shopping. Carole loves jewelry. I suppose that's true of all women, but she doesn't like anything gaudy or obviously expensive. Tasteful is the word she has often used. My success rate over the years improved but I seldom scored the perfect gift, so I'm nervous about doing this. In the first place, I don't even know if she'll accept one from me. I decide if I buy her something and she refuses, I'll still get credit for the thought. If she accepts, though, the gift has to be not so much as to mean anything. It's tricky.

I go back over the gifts I've given her in the past and remember one that stands out, a simple gold chain with a large droplet of honeyed amber that matched Carole's eyes. It hung low, nestled in her cleavage. I smile to myself. I remember remarking it was more of a gift for me than it was for her; I was the one who got to enjoy looking at it, and I particularly liked the setting. She often wore the necklace in summer when she had a nice tan going. She thought it looked best when her skin was darker than the amber.

Wonder if she still has it? Probably. Do women ever throw away jewelry? I have no idea, but I like to think Carole still has the necklace. I decide to look for matching dangly earrings. The search takes hours, each successive jeweler pointing me to another until I'm about to give up. Amber isn't popular they say, and most of the pieces I find are a deeper red color or not set as earrings. I'm told often what I want could be ordered but it would take a week or two. I don't have weeks, just hours, and not many of those. Frustrated and cranky, I finally ask if there isn't some sort of independent jeweler who actually makes jewelry instead of just selling what someone else has made. I get a cool look, but the clerk ducks into the backroom, and an elderly gentleman, who I presume is the owner, toddles out gamely and suggests I try a small business in the bowels under the Pike Place Market.

When I arrive, the storefront is empty, but bells tinkle as I open and close the door, drawing out a wizened fellow stooped with age. When I tell him what I'm looking for, he reaches into a wall cabinet behind the counter and withdraws a small selection of amber earrings and two large necklaces. The earrings are all the wrong color; cherry amber he calls them. One of the necklaces is precisely the shade of honey I'm looking for but I don't want a necklace. I ask if there's any chance he could remove two stones from the ends of it and fit them into one of the sets of earrings.

"Nooo," he answers with elaborate histrionics and in an accent that makes him sound Eastern European. "The set is perfectly matched and graduated. It is an antique. Very valuable. It would be a sin to break it up. Besides, it is a choker; the removal of those two stones would make the necklace far too tight on most women."

I know a sales pitch when I hear it but decide to play along. I explain that the stones are exactly the right color and clarity to match an existing necklace of modest financial, but great sentimental, value. He glances up over the top of his bifocals toward whatever god he looks to for guidance and repeats his claim that the necklace cannot be altered without bringing down the wrath of said god.

I then suggest a solution. I will buy both pieces. He will take the small end stones from the necklace and reattach the clasp. Then he will replace the cherry amber stones in the earrings. He can keep the extra stones. I have not yet asked the prices of either piece, and as I watch, I can see him turning over in his mind the two sales he is giving up if he doesn't agree. Finally, he comes to a decision.

"Do you have a daughter?"

Strange. I say no and ask why, but he waves off my question.

"Perhaps a favorite niece?"

My smile answers for me, even if it isn't really true. I imagine the necklace around Sis's throat and realize the reason he has asked: a young girl's neck would be smaller. Sis has a small neck, so my answer is in the spirit of the truth even if not to the letter.

"Very well. Two hundred for the earrings and two thousand for the necklace, no charge for my labor."

I know from looking at other pieces today that his demand is on the high side but what choice do I have?

"Deal, but I need it done this afternoon."

He snorts his disapproval, either because he really does think the necklace should not be altered, or because he thinks I should have bargained a little, or because he wants to close early for the holiday and I'm delaying that. In any event, he nods acceptance.

"Come back, two hours. No credit card. Cash only."

I drive around looking for an open branch of my bank, Wells Fargo, and get the cash. Then I grab a quick sandwich at Saigon Deli in the International District and head back to the Market. As promised, he's got the job done and has even provided nice jewelry boxes for both pieces. He seems to be over his displeasure and wishes me a good holiday. His parting comment, "Your girlfriend and your niece are lucky women," strikes me differently than he expects it will. My answer, "I doubt they'll see it that way, but it's worth a try," leaves him frowning and probably wondering what has happened to the world he once knew.

~ ~ ~

Three hours later, Carole arrives right on time and calls me from the car. I meet her street-side wearing a blue lightweight-wool suit, gray silk shirt with no tie, and penny loafers. Carole is dressed in black, as I knew she would be. She's sporting a short-sleeved, two-piece evening suit she has worn before. It seems either formal or informal depending on the setting. Her only jewelry is a pearl necklace and matching earrings. Her worn-out look from last week is gone, replaced by the self-assured composure she has always carried.

"You look nice," she says to break the tension as I climb in.

"So do you."

I'm unable to bring myself to admit she looks way better than just nice. I'm sure it's obvious that our comments are strained, and since we're both concerned with keeping this meeting on the light side, we make an effort to restrict our chatter to small talk as Carole maneuvers through traffic on the way to wherever she's taking us. Before long we're approaching the downtown area on First Avenue. She pulls into a parking lot just above the Pike Place Market. There are several good restaurants in the area, and since I've been to most of them, I wonder which she has chosen. What venue would rate being called a surprise?

Carole leads me through the Market, where I have been just two hours ago, and starts down the Hillclimb. I mentally review the restaurants accessed this way and only Trapezio would qualify. Naturally, I'm worried. Will Alayna be doing her act on Christmas Eve? If so, what will she think of seeing me out with another woman when I've insisted I'm not dating now? She won't make a scene, will she?

Once settled at our table, Carole looks around for her "surprise," but Alayna is nowhere to be seen. I check my watch. If I remember right, she'll begin her next set in twenty minutes at 8:00 p.m.

"What are you looking for?"

"You'll see. I told you, it's a surprise."

The waitress comes to take our drink order and returns with a bottle of Silver Oak cabernet, Carole's favorite. I ordered it from the very bottom of the red wine list where, at $90 a bottle, it belongs. It will be interesting to see who picks up the tab later. Carole said it was her treat, but maybe we should split the bill like a proper divorced couple.

Promptly at 8:00 p.m., Alayna makes a showing. She bows all around to the crowd and to Carole and me then mounts her trapeze. We're sitting at a table off to one side, so at least I won't have her gyrating over my head. Alayna had looked right at me but her expression showed no emotion, just her stage smile. Am I not recognizable dressed in a suit? I seldom wear one, so maybe that's it. Or maybe the spotlights were in her eyes. Or maybe she was looking at the entire audience, not individuals. Maybe, maybe, maybe. Maybe I'm over-thinking this.

Carole watches as Alayna stretches and insinuates

herself acrobatically into the dinner conversations, which fall off precipitously a few moments after she begins. I divide my attention between Carole and Alayna, charmed by Carole's entranced stare, and perplexed by Alayna's unfocused ignorance of my presence. I've just about decided Alayna really doesn't recognize me when she flips over, looks right at me, and winks. The gesture is fleeting but obvious, even to Carole, who now glances my way and grins widely. Why is this amusing? Shouldn't she be jealous or feign jealousy, or curiosity anyway?

My confused expression, looking from Carole to Alayna, who is just now dismounting, and back to Carole again, draws a laugh from her.

"My receptionist," she says.

My mind races through all the combinations and permutations that might have brought us to this moment. Does Carole know Alayna and I have slept together? That's my first thought, but it is quickly replaced with a more important question: can this possibly be a coincidence? And, if not, is this Alayna's doing or is Sis somehow involved?

Wait! Does Carole suspect any of this? No, she's just amusing herself by flaunting this young woman's body under, no, make that over, my nose. But why would she do that? To gauge my reaction?

By this time, Alayna has wandered off. To change into her other outfit, I suppose. I know my face is still registering what I hope Carole will read as surprise. Why is that? Why do I care what Carole thinks?

"Earth to Andrew, Earth to Andrew," I hear bleeding through. Carole is watching intently as I struggle back from wherever I have gone, but she's still smiling.

She must think Alayna has bewitched me. It's close enough to the truth and I decide to play it that way. "That was amazing."

"She's very flexible."

"Apparently. Thanks for the show."

Carole smiles appreciatively and wrinkles her Aussie nose.

I love it when she does that and I say so. The comment turns her smile from confident to wistful. Maybe there is no intention in her choice of Trapezio beyond the chance to see her receptionist perform and to enjoy my reaction. That's innocent enough.

"Would you like me to introduce you?"

"Why? You trying to fix me up?"

Carole shrugs an affirmation.

"But why?"

She sighs then confesses, "Doc called the other day. Said you were down in the dumps. That you needed to get out more and suggested I bring you here to meet Alayna. I'm not supposed to admit I'm in on the act...but I'm a terrible liar."

It takes me less than a minute to put the pieces together. Alayna isn't really Carole's receptionist; she's Doc's plant.

"You're supposed to call Doc later and report in, right?"

"Tomorrow. He's concerned about you, Andrew."

"Wrong. Doc's only thinking of himself and his twisted plot." How much should I tell her? Anything at all? Carole is waiting for me to continue so I oblige.

"Look, I know Doc is worried about me, but his reasons aren't exactly pure. It's a long story and you really don't want to know. The bottom line is I'm not dating anyone now. I told him I wouldn't until our divorce was final. And even now that it is, I know I'm not ready yet. I thought you were asking me out to…I don't know…start something."

"Oh, no, no. I'm not. Doc promised me you weren't still thinking about 'us'."

"He's right. I wasn't. But then when I saw you at your lawyer's office and you said Tony had left and then you said to call you sometime, I just started wondering…"

Her pained expression says it all. This was not some sort of rapprochement.

"Sorry," I say. "I just misread you. I guess that's par for the course, huh?"

Carole nods in agreement and looks downhearted.

"Cheer up. I'll adjust," I say then reach into my inner suit pocket and hand her my gift, carefully wrapped in holiday reds and greens. "Here. This is for you. Merry Christmas."

She sits quietly, staring at the tiny box topped by a bow that dwarfs it. I can't tell what she's thinking. After a few moments of silence, she opens it and holds the earrings up to the light.

"They're beautiful. Thank you."

"They're the color of your eyes."

"I know. I still have the necklace. You remembered."

"Some things you never forget."

We sit sipping our wine and looking around the room. Anywhere but in each other's eyes. There really isn't anything left to say. The waitress comes and takes our dinner order, then we return to silent observation.

At some point, Carole says, "Damn that Doc. I thought I could trust him."

"You never had it right, you know. Larry and Curly are the trustworthy ones, not Doc. He's always got his own agenda. Curly is crude and puerile, but he's faithful as an old dog. Larry is shrewd and cynical but loyal to a fault. Doc's the one you have to watch out for. But the truth is I love the old conniver."

As I say this I have turned to look into her eyes. She reaches across the table and takes my hand. "Are you going to be all right, Andrew?"

"Yeah, I'll be fine. I'd love to get Doc off my back, but I doubt it'll happen."

"Anything I can do to help?" She releases my hand.

"Everything I've tried so far has pretty much backfired. I'm not going to tell you the whole story, but Alayna is not new to me. I'm not sure what Doc hoped to gain by including you in this ruse. My best guess is he heard about Tony's departure and thought he'd see what happened if he threw the two of us together under Alayna's gyrating torso. From his point of view, the worst that could happen is just what did, nothing. But Doc's not the only player. And the question, now that I think of it, is do I like being played?"

"You're right. I don't want to know. I have enough of my own problems. But I owe you for listening to Doc instead of my own conscience. What do you want me to tell him?"

"Tell him...tell him the truth. That I thought you were asking me out on a date, that I bought you earrings, and that I was hurt to find out it was just part of his stupid, insensitive plan. And tell him I'm pissed at him."

"Okay. That seems reasonable."

She takes my hand again. "You don't really want me, Andrew. Let me go. Go find someone young like Alayna, someone who wants the children I never did. You'd like that, wouldn't you?"

"I don't know, Carole. I really don't know. I need time to figure it all out."

"Then take the time. And stop worrying so much."

Her words sound like an exit line, but I can't let go so easily. I need to know the answers to questions I have wanted to ask but have never found the guts to.

"Why?" I begin then pause to grope for a place to start.

"Why what?"

"Why didn't you want children?

"Oh, Andrew, I answered that long ago."

"No, you didn't. You just said you wanted to concentrate on getting the business up and running."

"Exactly."

"It's been "up and running" since we were thirty."

"That's not true…okay, okay, it's true from your perspective but not from mine." She holds her hand up to cut off any retort, sighs, looks away for a moment, then back into my eyes again.

"You have never been good at reading between the lines," she says. "How many times do you have to be put off before you realize what someone is really saying? It's not fair to blame me for not telling, when the real problem is you weren't listening."

I absorb Carole's words and digest their meaning. That's half my question answered. But why didn't I push? Did I think the occasional repetition of our original argument would change anything? I read somewhere years ago that the definition of insanity is doing the same thing over and over again and expecting a different result. Saying the same thing over and over again works that way too. Nothing changes.

But what about her claim that I should find a younger woman who wants children? If she knew I wanted kids and kept asking her to reconsider then doesn't the same criticism apply to her? Doesn't ignoring my question over and over and expecting me to stop wanting it constitute the same sort of insanity? I can feel color rising. Carole's always been able to spin me up with a few well-chosen words.

"So, you say I should find someone young, fertile, and willing, huh? Why, to make you feel less guilty? I'm a little old to be saddling up again, don't you think?"

Now she holds up both hands in surrender.

"I'm sorry. You're right. I know I'm just as guilty at not listening as you are. I knew you wanted kids and I knew I didn't. But you're wrong that it's too late. I know you meant it as a jab, but finding someone fertile might be just what you need to do. And you're older now. You'll make a better father."

"Even assuming you're right, why would a younger woman want a guy my age? What's the attraction? Why not someone her own age?"

She shrugs. "Lots of reasons," she says offhandedly then corrects herself. "No, only one reason: stability. Emotional, social, financial. A woman Alayna's age needs to know that the guy she's trusting to be there for her and for her children will have the staying power to meet that need. Twenty-something guys and even thirty-somethings are risky, at least the ones who aren't already spoken for. A guy your age has probably already gotten it all out of his system. And the prospect of having an attractive young woman who wants you is seductive, isn't it? I mean, look at Alayna. Can you honestly tell me you don't think she's pretty hot?"

I shrug and nod, but I'm not convinced. Still, I have ample evidence Carole is right, at least in the attraction department. The thirteen years that separate either Sis or Alayna from me does not seem to interfere with our enjoyment of each other. I definitely need more time to think about this and Carole's intercession with Doc may give me the break I want.

~ ~ ~

Carole drops me off at my front door with a kiss goodbye and a promise to help anyway she can. I tell her to call if she ever needs anything and stand there waving as she drives away. This is not the ending I expected to this evening but it feels right. I do have a life ahead, and even though I cannot yet say where it will lead, I understand a corner has been turned, a door closed.

Contrition

My other questions—Why did Carole start the affair, why did she keep it up so long without leaving, and why did she finally decide to leave?—go unasked and unanswered, un-confessed. I know they are all subsumed in the larger question: Why didn't Carole and I want the same things? I know the answer to that one. Change and chance. We all change over the years. Call it what you will: maturation, getting to know yourself, finding your niche. As the kids say, "Whatever." For some couples, change runs in tandem. For others, it diverges, sometimes just a little, sometimes in all but opposite directions. That's what I mean by chance. It's a crapshoot. As for the lack of confession on Carole's part, I really wasn't looking for one. Just a bit of contrition, and she gave me that. It's what I needed in order to forgive her. It's allowed me some degree of closure, though it's also true that doors never close completely.

~ ~ ~

Late on Christmas Day, Carole calls. "Merry Christmas," she says cheerily when I pick up. I parrot back her greeting and listen as she gives me a summary of her discussion with Doc. He chided her for admitting her complicity but accepted it was really his fault. My guess is the plan belonged to Sis; Doc was just the catalyst. I don't share that idea with Carole. Besides, he definitely deserves his share of the blame. She asks if there's anything else she can do, and I tell her, "No thanks, you've done enough," but say it jokingly. Still, she apologizes again for her part and hopes I'll be well. "You too," I say, and for a change, mean it.

As soon as she clicks off, I put on my angry face and call Doc. He answers with a hearty, "Merry Christmas."

Apparently he didn't check the caller ID to see who it was, because when I reply, "And a Merry Fucking Christmas to you too, asshole," there is shocked silence on his end of the connection, followed by a timid, "Deke?"

"No shit, Sherlock."

"Okay, I know you're pissed at me. *Mea culpa. Mea culpa.* We thought it might help..."

I cut him off with a, "We?"

More silence. I can almost see him wincing from his *faux pas*.

"Me and Sis," he admits after a moment. "We...no, not we...Sis. She thought you needed to get over Carole and the only way you would do that is if you confronted her or at least faced her and talked out whatever you needed to talk about. I just agreed to help."

"And you think that excuses you? You're just as much to blame as Sis. Didn't it occur to you devious twits that maybe Carole and I might want to do it on our own schedule? You lied to her on so many different levels I can't count them. I'm not letting Sis off the hook either, but you're supposed to be the one who has my best interests at heart. Sis is just looking after her own."

"Wait a minute. She masterminded this, not me. I was only helping. Why are you angrier at me than you are at her?"

"Jesus, Doc. You're dumber than I thought. Sis can still fuck my brains out. What have you got to offer?"

That shuts him up. All I can hear is breathing on the other end.

"Good point. What do you want me to do? I apologized to Carole, and I know I owe you for this. Hell, I owe you for more than you realize."

I laugh to myself, thinking I know way more than he suspects. But a frown quickly replaces the grin. What if I don't know everything?

No, the jig is up. The dance is over. Whatever tune left is for me to play, not them.

Before I sign off, Doc invites me for New Year's Eve at Connie's house. She's throwing a large party for a bunch of friends he hasn't met yet, and though he's looking forward to regaling them with some of his cosmetic surgery stories, he could use a friend of his own, even one who's still pissed at him.

"Suits me. I'll take Connie aside and tell her a few stories too."

He laughs, then realizing I may not be joking, asks, "You're not serious, are you?"

"Nah, I'll be good. Not that you deserve it."

~ ~ ~

On New Years, I head out early, as Doc has requested, so we can talk before the mob shows up. I circumnavigate Lake Union, driving along Westlake and pull into Connie's parking lot at 6:00 p.m. Connie's house floats. It's across Lake Union from my condo. If I had a good telescope I could probably look in her windows. The idea of watching her and Doc flits across my mind and causes me to wonder just how much detail can be seen from a half-mile away. It's not a serious thought, just one of those points of curiosity I have now and then at odd moments.

The stroll down the pier is pleasant. Houseboats and real boats are interspersed along its length and though it's all packed pretty tightly it doesn't feel claustrophobic. Across to the right is another pier populated the same way, boats and houseboats of assorted dimensions and value. At the end of the neighboring pier is a large home with a newer fifty-foot or so Hallberg Rassy ketch parked alongside. Pricey. Probably worth four times what mine is.

Like her next-door neighbor's, Connie's houseboat is attached to the end of the pier. It's huge, maybe thirty by fifty feet, two-and-a-half floors high, and surrounded on three sides by decks and water. Could be $2 million or more. I've been out of the real estate business too long to estimate properly, and prices around here have gone through the roof in the past seven years. Doc's money may be part of the attraction, but I'm guessing she has plenty of her own. Maybe I should sell my condo and buy one of these. I could park my boat just outside my door. But that would mean fighting the crowd at the locks every time I wanted to sail anywhere but on the lake.

When I get to her house, I notice she has no boat at all, save for the tandem kayak Doc bought her. She needs a daysailer. Doc is outside smoking one of his Macanudos, banished to the deck by non-smoking

Connie. He's used to that since I won't let him light up anywhere but my balcony, and even then, my neighbor above complains.

Doc doesn't turn as I approach and startles when I say, "About time Connie kicked your ass out."

He continues looking out at the water.

"Yeah. But this ass is freezing off. Pretty soon there won't be anything left to kick."

He's right about the cold. We've got a stalled front and dense Canadian air flowing down from the Frasier Valley. Doubt we saw thirty degrees today. I'll bet the docks get treacherous later as frost begins to coat. I can imagine Connie's inebriated guests slip-sliding away into the frigid water.

We stand side by side, silently watching the few hardy souls sailing out on the lake, running lights and masthead beacons shimmering in the rippled water.

"Are we okay?" he asks after a few minutes.

"Sure. But that doesn't mean I'm not pissed."

"She's trouble, Andrew. I've never met such a clever girl. Too clever for her own good, I think."

From Doc, this sounds like high praise, but I suspect he may also be thinking, "Too clever for you." I ask him if that's what he means, expecting an affirmative answer, but what I get is more balanced.

"You know, I'm not sure. I keep going back and forth. Some days I think you should run. Others, I can see the two of you together. It wouldn't be boring, that's for sure."

No, it wouldn't be boring. And I know what Doc means about going back and forth. That's just what I've been doing for the past two months.

"What would you do?" I ask.

That sets Doc laughing. He looks at me and just laughs harder. Finally, he gains enough control to answer. "Do you have any idea how ridiculous it is to ask a guy who's been married four times for advice about women and what to do with them? Have you lost your mind?"

"Probably, but you have to admit, you've got more experience than anyone I know."

Now we're both in hysterics, and apparently can be heard from inside, because Connie sticks her head out the door and asks what's so funny.

"Deke just asked me for advice about relationships."

"Are you crazy? I keep hoping he'll ask you." Then she disappears back into the house to continue the cleaning binge that's the actual reason for Doc's relegation to the deck.

Despite their claims to the contrary, Doc really does know women. After all, convincing four different ladies, five if you count Connie, and several more if you include the ones he didn't marry, to form any sort of long-term commitment has to mean something. It can't be just about money. I still want his opinion and ask again, coming at it from a different angle. "Do you think I'd make a good father?"

Doc doesn't answer. He puffs away, making inept attempts at smoke rings that look less like donuts and more like crullers. I suspect he's thinking about his own attempts at fatherhood. Most of his kids are estranged. He sees a daughter now and then who lives in Olympia, an hour's drive south, but otherwise has little or no contact that I'm aware of. Maybe it was the wrong question.

"Not sure I'm the best judge. But, yes, you'd make a good father, and you'd have the time to be one. Not like me, tied to my practice. You've always been more family man than type-A, ladder-climber. Your self-worth isn't all tied up in who you are. Nothing to prove." Doc pauses to flick the ashes off his cigar then adds, "Makes you a good friend too. If that girl had any sense, she'd stop messing with your head and take it a day at a time. But hell, Deke, what do you think? That's the real question."

Yes, that's the real question, isn't it? Maybe it all boils down to what I've got to lose. I suppose I could make a list. Let's see, there's my time. Not really all that valuable. There's my loneliness. Happy to get rid of it. Then there's my self-respect. Way overrated in my opinion. I guess the main thing I'm risking is avoidance of the pain she'll inflict each time she comes and goes if I let her back in. Does she want back in? If not, why go to the trouble of weaving all the cross-plots?

"Doc, do you think she loves me?"

"I think she's afraid she loves you," he answers quickly, so quickly it throws me off-balance.

"That sounds more like you. Always scared of commitment."

Doc shrugs off my gibe. "She's not afraid to commit to you, you idiot. She's afraid you'll leave her if she does. Sis lives by the steel rule: do unto others before they get a chance to do unto you. Her issues are with trust, not commitment."

Silence returns and we go back inside our respective heads. Sounds right, what he says, though not exactly right. But what do I do about it? Might be time to make my own plan. Trust, I know, is a thing that must be earned. For some, it is given easily. For others, it comes at a price. For those who have trusted only to be betrayed, the price was too high, the fall too painful. For them, to trust again seems foolish. And yet, without trust there is no true joy in life. You only get what you pay for. Trust is the currency.

~ ~ ~

At 7:00 p.m. the guests begin arriving and both Connie and Doc become absorbed in welcoming and cross-pollinating conversations. As in any gathering, the idea is to keep everyone occupied. I alone am left to my own devices. It gives me a unique opportunity to observe the two of them weaving this quasi-domestic web of celebration, a wish in one sustained loud voice for what we all hope will be a better year ahead.

Connie's floating residence is an upside-down house. The front door opens onto a foyer with a grand staircase leading up to the second level. The bedrooms are on the first floor. At the top of the stairway is a great room with vaulted ceiling and open rafters and beams. It encompasses a huge living space to the left with glass on three walls opening onto panoramic views of the lake and a gourmet kitchen with a walk-in pantry and a wet bar to the right. Also to the right are bathroom and sauna, each with its own shower. A cantilevered deck at the far end of the living space sports a spa big enough for twelve. If it was any larger, you could swim laps.

Connie and Doc flit back and forth between their guests and the kitchen, ferrying drinks and appetizers and pausing to join the conversations of each group.

Occasionally, Connie recomposes clusters to include others and, as the evening progresses, to extract a guest here and there in order to defuse tension or to gently suggest a slower drinking pace. As they cross paths, she and Doc exchange words, glances, casual touches, and, rare, fleeting kisses that provide a window for me into their relationship. This is what I want: the simple, companionable things that make up the heart of any joining of lives.

Once the party has been sufficiently lubricated, Doc begins his repertoire of surgical stories, his tit-illations, as he calls them, and shifts to performance mode. He is very entertaining. I've often thought he should do stand-up comedy. The separate clusters merge or lean toward him. I've heard them all, of course, and recognize the one he is just starting. The story begins in his interview room where a twenty-two-year-old girl, accompanied by her seventy-plus grandmother who has offered to pay the tab, is explaining her desire for an A-to-C cup transformation. Doc has her partly disrobe so he can see and feel what needs to be done and to take digital photos, which are entered into his computer software and projected back onto the wide-screen plasma monitor on the wall, revealing life-size before and after images.

Grandma, he tells us, sits quietly with her hands in her lap, listening and watching intently. Once the girl has re-buttoned and expressed her concurrence with Doc's recommendations, he turns to Grandma and asks if she'd like to see herself in his magic mirror. He's just teasing her, of course, but she reaches up and begins unbuttoning her blouse. For his audience, Doc now repeats the theatrics of looking and feeling, including an exaggerated lifting of Grandma's breasts from someplace down near the floor up to where they are supposed to be. "Oldest pair I ever held," he claims

Connie has heard this one before. She breaks away and heads toward my command post, the kitchen's center island, where I've been leaning on my forearms, watching the show. But as she turns, she tosses back a better punch line. "So far," she says. "So far."

The guests laugh appreciatively, and Doc smiles in a bemused way. He may have met his match, I think. To my surprise, Connie walks behind me and wraps her arms around my waist, spooning a firm hug. It is the intimate hug of a lover or lifelong friend.

"What do you think?" she whispers in my ear then straightens and leans next to me on the island countertop.

"About what?'

"Doc and me. Think we'll make it?"

They've been together over a year now, and though Doc still goes barhopping occasionally with the SSFC, more and more he is spending time only with Connie. I back away and give her the same once-over she'd expect from Doc. That's when I realize Connie is not as young as I thought. She might even be forty, though she looks like late twenties. The giveaways are tiny lines where they wouldn't be on a younger woman and cleavage that cannot be completely natural. It's too perfect. In fact, it's too perfect to be Doc's work. He refuses to give his girls balloon breasts. He insists they have to look like nature has been kind, not comical.

I answer, "Looks like you have all the right equipment for the job."

Connie laughs and says lightly, "Not so sure about

that. Doc doesn't care for his competitor's work."

"Are you going to let him?"

Connie understands my meaning. Will she allow Doc to drop her breasts a notch, taking them from their high-mounted, Dolly-esque D's to more natural-looking C's with just a hint of the pendulous.

"Depends. He has to decide whether he's the only guy who gets to touch them."

"Ah, there's the rub."

"Cute."

"Hmmm, I try to be."

As Doc's tale continues, Connie nestles closer and we face each other. Then she asks the question that's really on her mind.

"If I agree to be number five, do you think there'll be a number six?"

I ponder this as I hear Doc add the girl's mom to his equation. A new record, he claims, three generations of breast work, turning grandmother into mother, mother into daughter, and daughter into Wonder Woman. His audience applauds appreciatively and Doc bows to their adulation.

What should I tell her? It's not about numbers? There has to be a last, even if I don't know and never did know if it would be three, four, five, or whatever? Is Connie looking for an out or an in? I opt for a gambling analogy.

"Doc's like a roulette wheel in motion. You're the little ball spinning in the opposite direction, circling before dropping into place. He's slowing down and you know it. He can't keep up spinning forever. You want to believe you'll drop into place and that will be it. But you haven't placed your bet yet. You want to go all in but you're afraid you'll lose everything. So you wait, hoping before the ball clips that first slot you'll know whether to take the chance. But you also know if you wait too long, the croupier will stop taking bets.

"You want me to tell you if it's the right moment, if this is Doc's last spin, but the truth is I don't know. I could say, yes, go for it. I know he's tired of the game. Or I could say, no, he's only forty-two, plenty of spins left in him. But I'm not a disinterested party. I love the guy. I can see he's happy, and when I watch the two of you together, I wish I had the same thing. That only means I want you and Doc to stay together for now, and 'for now' is the operative clause. His happiness is what really matters to me."

I pause a moment and go back to her question to see if I've made a dent in answering it. That's when what she has already said hits me, "If I agree."

I ask, "Are telling me Doc asked you to marry him?"

Her wan smile answers more forcefully than anything Connie could have said at this moment.

"I didn't know," I say. "He hasn't said a word about it. I've been caught up in my own girlfriend problems and probably wasn't paying attention."

Connie pats the back of my hand. "Doc said as much. He's worried about you. For what it's worth, I think Sis is just where I am, circling the spinning wheel, afraid to place that bet. Doc thinks she can't quite bring herself to trust you. I think she can't trust herself not to hurt you. Maybe we're both right."

In the silence that follows, we turn away and gaze out across the room to where Doc is standing looking back at us. His expression is quizzical. He appears to be wondering, what are we talking about so intently? Whose relationship are we working on, theirs or mine? I put my arm around Connie's waist and hug her tightly. She melts into my embrace and kisses me on the cheek. We seem to be replying, better close the deal soon, Doc, or Connie will find a replacement. But he has closed the deal, hasn't he? He's popped the question, and if I'm any judge, there was a big diamond ring to go with it. Takes two to tango, though. And it takes two to make a contract.

~ ~ ~

The guests straggle out gingerly after the Space Needle fireworks have noisily heralded the New Year. They heed our advice to beware of the slippery pier; no one has to be fished out of the drink. We walk them to their cars to make sure they all make it then return to put Connie's house in some sort of order. She insists she can handle the cleanup on her own, but Doc and I politely ignore her. Glasses are loaded in the dishwasher, plates are stacked in the kitchen sink and covered with water to soak overnight, and tables and chairs are returned to their pre-party positions. Then Connie says goodnight, bestows hugs and kisses on Doc and me, and toddles off to bed. Doc and I repair to the deck for a cigar and a single malt scotch.

The late night quiet is broken here and there by celebratory hoots and hurrahs, but for the most part the lake has fallen silent. We are silent as well. We have things to say to each other but resist beginning. I'm not sure just what it is I should offer or ask, but I can feel it coming together in my head. It's time for a showdown with Sis. Maybe Doc is thinking the same thing about

Connie.

"What were you and Connie plotting behind my back?" Doc asks after a while. "Maybe mayhem?"

"Nothing so dramatic. She just wants to know your intentions are pure. When did you give her the ring?"

"You saw it?"

"Nope, but I'm imagining three flawless carats."

"I'm way too predictable. She told you she hasn't said yes, right?"

"Probably waiting for matching diamond studs."

"Could you be serious for a minute? She's had the ring since October. Keeps telling me she needs more time."

"And you? Do you need more time?"

"The ball's in her court. I'm just waiting for her to lob it back over the net."

I think about his tennis metaphor for a moment then reply in kind, "Maybe Connie needs to know she's hitting a winner: point, game, set, and match."

"Humph," is all the answer I get to my implied question: "Are you ready to stop playing?" I know it's more complicated than I'm suggesting, but maybe it isn't. Maybe Doc has always had it in him to let the ball just drop in. I go back to my own quandary and wonder how to ask Doc the same basic question about Sis: What do I do next?

We continue puffing on our cigars in silence for a long while before Doc flicks his into the lake and I follow suit. The two splashes seem like periods at the ends of our unfinished thoughts. Then I realize the advice I'm giving Doc applies to me as well. His gesture seems to agree.

It's late now, past 2:00 a.m. Doc wraps an arm

around me and walks me to my car. After I climb in, he suggests, "You know, Deke, I think Sis is waiting too. The difference is you haven't hit the ball. It's still on your side of the net. Give it a whack, why don't you."

Having come to the same decision just minutes ago, I say, "Might just do that. Want to help?"

"Sure."

"Think you can get Sis to meet for lunch some day next week, say Tuesday or Wednesday?"

"Easy. Where?"

I pause a moment to think what would be the most appropriate spot. My first thought is the Blue Star, where we went the morning after our first night together. I can still remember her phone innuendo with Christine. Then it hits me. I know just the place. "Think you can talk her into drinks instead of lunch? But late."

"Trust me. If I say I have something important to tell her about you, she'll be there, any time, any day."

My smile is one Doc hasn't seen before. Devious.

"Tuesday, 10:00 p.m., Teddies."

Confession

All that's left is my confession. I hope you'll accept it the way Andrew did. First, I must say clearly that the basic plan was mine all along. But whatever I have done, my intentions were good. You may disagree or think I'm lying, but I will still insist I was true to myself and to Andrew as well.

It begins where all confessions should start, at the beginning.

Doc had been lobbying Chris for months to hook up with him. Chris wasn't interested. And Chris had been lobbying me to help her find someone for Mom so she could even the score with our lame excuse for a father. You know, to rub his nose in it. I wasn't interested. But I was between boyfriends and Doc's description of his buddy, Deke, intrigued me. That is, until he told me Deke was just starting the divorce process. Mind you, I have no ethical problem hooking up with a guy who is separated, but I didn't want to be the one to "break him in," if you know what I mean. So I asked Doc whom he might suggest for that task. His face lit up like a jack o'lantern. I could almost see the wheels turning. Andrew was right when he surmised Doc had more than one plot going at a time. What he didn't know is Doc had help with both the conception and execution.

The plan was for Doc to convince Gretch to become

Diana for a night. That took some doing since Gretch was worried about the long-term consequences, but Doc talked her into it anyway. He's quite persuasive and about as persistent as a hungry mosquito. That satisfied my requirement to have Deke detached from Carole before I would hook up with him. Then I told Chris I'd help her get Mom laid if she gave in to Doc's fondest desire. Chris knew it would take both of us to wheedle, cajole, and bribe Mom into going to Teddies with us, so Chris agreed to the deal. I think Doc would have worn her down sooner or later anyway since she didn't put up more than token resistance to the idea, but we'll never know for sure.

All that was left was to get Deke and Mom to Teddies and inebriated enough to let it all happen. I figured if Doc could talk Gretch into her part, convincing Deke would be a no-brainer. That just left Chris and me to dress Mom up like a slut and make her do tequila Jell-O shots with us then have Chris make love to Deke on the dance floor while Mom watched. I think they call that priming the pump.

By the time Chris was done with her act, the only one of us who wasn't completely turned on was Chris herself. Mom and I were both crossing and re-crossing our legs, and I doubt either Doc or Deke could have done that comfortably. The little cowgirl who corralled Deke next must have thought he was sticking her up. As soon as she let him go, Mom was out of her chair. We didn't even have to push. And it was a hoot to watch the two of them locked together. Chris even shed a happy tear or two. When they headed for the backroom, Chris and I shared a high-five and Doc saluted from across the floor. When they walked out a half-hour later, we were cheering.

So it worked pretty well, though both Chris and I hoped she'd go back for seconds and thirds. Ah, well, best laid plans and all that, if you'll pardon my pun. As for Andrew's comment that I looked "like a deer caught in headlights," he mistook my bland expression. The fact is my plan worked, Chris the come-on, Mom the old switcheroo. I was pretty proud of myself but completely unsurprised. Chris was the one who doubted they'd just walk out and leave us there. Doc was fairly sure it would work but couldn't quite bring himself to expect success, so his little smile was for me.

What about sleeping with a guy who slept with your Mom, you ask? Isn't that creepy? A little, I guess, though, believe me, I have no regrets. That's when I stopped using his nickname. I knew Mom would sleep with Deke. When my turn came, I wanted it to be with Andrew. Let's call it a Greek tragedy thing and leave it at that. And how else would I know if they had actually done it? Do you think mothers never lie to you? Please! And even if it was creepy, it was naughty too. I never said I was a nice girl.

I remember feeling deceitful. I let Andrew believe the plan belonged to Doc and Chris. And I knew I was misleading him when I told him I was afraid he was falling in love with me. In a way, I was afraid, but I wanted it too, and that's a strange feeling for me. Casual sex means never having to say you're sorry, I suppose. Or maybe it means never having to say you care.

What did I fear? Being hurt again or being responsible for hurting someone else?

Both, I guess. If I could get Andrew to do this my

way, he'd learn for himself whatever it is that he wanted and needed. He'd have time to shake Carole loose and go out with enough women to be able to make a choice, and if I was right there to watch, I'd get to see how it all played out. If he really was in love with me, the others wouldn't matter. If not, neither of us would have committed so much that we couldn't just walk away.

Andrew was right though; it will never mean that much to me to mean that much to him. But that's the common story, isn't it? One of you loves the other more than you are loved in return, yes? How do you deal with that? Do you simply accept the love you are offered as enough, or do you keep looking for the one who will love you exactly as much, no more, no less? Can you ever find the perfect match? I doubt it, so which is better: to love too much, hold too closely, and risk driving away the one you love, or to love too little, hold at arm's length, and risk never having the very thing you want most of all, even if you have to admit you do want it?

There was one point when I almost lost control. Andrew was right, Ms. Very Hot Rebekah would probably have made a good partner for him, but I was not about to let him fantasize her into that position. And I know all about the hard-to-get act; her little ruse didn't fool me for a minute. She was just playing him. I suppose I could be wrong about that, but it seemed too convenient to get him all the way to the bedroom then back off. I kept expecting her to call to say she was ready.

Andrew was a good sport about Beth, wasn't he? She's Chris's friend from nursing school. I have a photo of Chris and me perched on Beth's shoulders, one to a side. Probably the only thing bigger than Beth is her poor bowlegged horse.

Back to Rebekah, I worried I was doing the wrong thing. Maybe she really was what Andrew needed. Or it could have been me, couldn't it? I mean, how could I tell? He did ask me to let him wait another two weeks, and I pushed back against that idea as hard as I could, or maybe a little too hard, but I caved in. I wanted him to be happy, it's just that I wanted to be the reason he was happy. Besides, Rebekah was probably too old to have kids, so Andrew was better off hanging with me anyway.

Then came the intermezzo: a brief respite between courses, a time to digest what had already been consumed and to have something lighter to ease said digestion. For me, though, it was a time of unaccustomed patience. I relinquished control. Andrew needed to get it out of his system, and I needed to let him. That's why I left and that's why I planted the seed in his mind about Alayna. But it didn't go to plan. Either Alayna wasn't doing her job or I misread Andrew. She said she tried seriously to engage Andrew's interest, but he insisted he was off women for the time being, whatever that meant. Doc was no help either. He claimed he tried to get Andrew back to Teddies but seemed to agree with Alayna's assessment that Andrew had become a monk.

Now what, I thought? Should I wait him out or make the first move? Alayna said I should give it more time. Give her more time, she meant. I really didn't trust her. I suppose I should have told Andrew the truth. Not sure what that would have been, though, and I'm no good at the truth anyway. But you already know that, don't you?

Then there was that last "Hail Mary pass": putting Carole and Alayna together. But it accomplished what I needed it to. It brought him closure. And it brought us together at the not-so-original scene of the crime, Teddies—

~ ~ ~

I feel his hand on my shoulder as the song begins, a song he has asked for. *Will You Still Love Me Tomorrow*, though with Carole King's voice, all sharp angles, cracks, and imperfections. Right somehow. When I turn to see him smiling down at me, I know it will be all right. It's a sappy song but true, an understanding that nothing is permanent.

And, after all, it's the only important question tonight, isn't it: Will we still love each other tomorrow? But the tingling of anticipation I feel for the rest of the night suggests I'll worry about tomorrow when it comes.

We slow dance, hold each other tightly, wanting nothing more for as long as the music lasts, yet it is his first touch and smile that remain in my mind. All else is consummation.

I never see Doc make his exit; my mind is elsewhere. Though I seem to remember hearing the coat check girl wish him a good night and hearing Doc assure her he is doing just that. When we return to the table, I am ready to leave. I want us to be alone. Then I think, this is Andrew's party, let him say what comes next. I make some comment to that effect, and he reaches into his sport jacket pocket and places a small jewelry box in front of me. "This comes next," he says.

There is no mistaking the contents of the box and I bite my lip. No, I'm not ready for this, I think. My smile vanishes as I search for something to say, but Andrew remains calm and confident. It's as if he knows I will give in, and I can feel myself almost there, almost ready to say, what the hell, why not. Then he says, "Open it."

I look at the closed box, so small but so significant, then I glance up into his eyes. What is there, what are you thinking? Do you really expect me to take this now?

And do I dare refuse?

"Open it," he says again.

So I do. Inside, in the place where a ring should be, is the key to Andrew's front door. I smile through teary eyes, knowing he understands, also knowing someday the box will hold the ring I was expecting. It will be there when I am ready.

~ ~ ~

My story ends here. This is my confession, the whole of it.

Tonight, as we ride the elevator to Andrew's, now our, home, my worry returns. What if I'm a zebra, unable to change my stripes? I put my key in the lock but turn around to search his eyes one last time.

"It will be okay," he says. "Just let it."

I close my eyes and nod then lift to kiss him. It will be okay. His words echo in my mind looking for an answering refrain. But I cannot bring myself to say it. Not now. Maybe someday, but not now.

A confession cannot end with a lie.

Made in the USA
Charleston, SC
29 November 2012